NO SANCTUARY

By the same author

Keep on Running
The Last Proud Rider

NO SANCTUARY

Ted Harriott

SECKER & WARBURG
LONDON

First published in England 1983 by
Martin Secker & Warburg Limited
54 Poland Street, London W1V 3DF

Copyright © Ted Harriott 1983

British Library Cataloguing in Publication Data

Harriott, Ted
 No sanctuary
 I. Title
 823'.914[F]   PR6058.A/

ISBN 0-436-19108-3

Photoset by Wilmaset, Birkenhead Merseyside
Printed in Great Britain

"When all the shooting was finished and all the dead were buried and the politicians took over, what had you got left? A lost cause."

—1920s' IRA leader.

For L.K. with thanks

CHAPTER I

July 1588

The great ship wallowed a few feet towards the watchers on the cliff top and was then carried off almost as far again by the backwash. She was a thing of awe to the watchers. They had never seen anything like her – a great painted butterfly from the sea. But the butterfly's wings were broken. The storms that had raged for days had smashed her masts, twisted her rigging into a giant's granny-knot and shredded her half-acre of sail.

Everyone from the village who could walk or hobble had come to watch what they knew were her last moments. They saw the officers – they had to be the big men, since they were dressed in court style – conferring anxiously. They could hear the orders being shouted, now that the wind had dropped. The seamen formed chains and began passing crates, boxes and bundles furiously from hand to hand – the cliff-top crowd stirred anxiously – to hurl them over the side. Below, the ports flew open and more of the ships's fittings, including the guns, where thrown out into the sea.

"What are they doing?" asked one of the cliff-top crowd.

"Lightening ship," answered a tall grey-haired man, without taking his far-seeing fisherman's eyes from the scene below. "They're hoping to float over the rocks and beach her."

"Any chance?" asked someone else – and it was hard to tell whether the note of anxiety was about the crew or the chances of the plunder being snatched from them.

"None. And if they've sailed that great thing all the way from some foreign land, they'll know it," said the tall man. "Looks as if their boats were carried away in the storm," he added. "There's no more they can do to save themselves than we can do to save them."

"And why can't you do something to save them?" asked the girl at his side. There was scorn in her voice and an angry glint in her blue eyes.

Like all the other women in the crowd she wore a variety of scraps of rough cloth as her dress, one draped over her head like a shawl. But she was taller than most, men or women, and strands of her flame-red hair drifted from under the shawl like a hint of sunset.

"Is it that you'd rather see the ship wrecked and them all drowned, so that there's no one to fight you over the pickings?" she demanded.

"Hush now, Bridie," said the leader, who was her father. "Just listen to that wind. I'd go for the boat but by the time I got it out it would be blowing hard enough to put me on the rocks with them."

As the wind began to strengthen, the crowd moved restlessly. Soon some began to slip away to the cove below, where the wreckage might be washed ashore. Clothes, medals, jewellery, even wood from the ship would be of use – and there might be gold. Eyes lit up at the thoughts they dare not voice. But not the blue eyes of Bridie. She couldn't take them away from the bright ship, though she thought she wouldn't be able to stand the agony of waiting for the scurrying men to die in the boiling water around the rocks. She stood and stared as the ship accelerated towards its doom.

"Aren't you coming down to the beach, Bridie?" called a ragged young man of her own age, who had stood as close to her as he dared during the tense wait. As the ship gained speed he fidgeted towards the cliff path and then back to her side, anxious about his share of the spoils.

"No, I am not. You go after your pickings. Don't worry that men are fighting for their lives down there."

"Come on, Bridie." He tried coaxing. "They're only foreigners."

"They're men just the same," she yelled. But her words were carried away beyond his hearing on the rising gale and the young man just shrugged before running down to the cove to claim his share.

It was dark, yet oddly light in the way of storms, when the

thing happened that Bridie on the cliff top and the crowd in the cove were waiting for. There was the unique crumpling sound of a wooden ship being rammed against rocks. There were some cries, if you had the ears and the imagination to hear them. Up on her look-out point Bridie saw the black specks of men's bodies plunging into the water. Some struck out strongly for the shore. Most disappeared at once. She watched, sick at heart, as one by one even the strong swimmers vanished. Still one kept going. She began to pray for him, for the impossible.

"Take anything, do anything to me, Holy Mother," she cried out aloud. "But let him live."

For a second or two she almost believed that her prayer would be answered.

Then a mighty wave rose behind him, followed him shoreward for another fraction of time, and, as he looked back frantically, crashed down on him. The water boiled, another wave lifted up on the spot—and there was no sign of the swimmer.

Bridie pulled her shawl close round her with a shudder and turned to go home. She didn't want to be there when the wreckage started to float ashore, to hear the cheering and see the fighting. Her father would have wanted her to help drag the prizes from the boiling surf. But she couldn't do it after what she had seen.

He was tired when he returned home and found her sleeping. But he was not angry. He understood. Next morning was different. He ordered and she obeyed. She and her father needed whatever she could find, for starvation was never more than a step away. She went, at his bidding, to a cove on the other side of the headland, where he believed the tides might have carried some of the ship's timbers. He returned to the near inlet.

One or two others with knowledge of the local waters were at the cove before Bridie. But their search seemed fruitless as they scanned the water's edge. Just piles of weed . . . and then there came the cry that was to change her life.

"Look, there's a body," shouted a man called McDiarmada.

Bridie ran with the others as he turned over a pile of waterlogged clothes. He grinned happily as he looked at the ornate jacket and imagined whatever else there might be in the pockets. But then a trickle of water came from the sailor's mouth. It was followed by a low moan.

"He's alive," gasped someone as McDiarmada dropped the body.

"Better finish him off then," growled McDiarmada. He reached for a spar he had picked up earlier.

"No," gasped Bridie, flinging herself forward and seizing his upraised arm. McDiarmada was strong. But Bridie fought him with the desperation of someone who was in danger of losing a miracle. Finally, wrenching the spar from him, she buffeted him aside. She turned on the others, eyes blazing and red hair streaming behind her like a great plume of flame. They cowered.

"Qué magnifico," muttered a feeble voice and she was just in time to see the sailor's eyes close again.

She hauled home her prize from the sea, the others following at a safe distance, mumbling and complaining. And when she got him inside her tiny home she knew instinctively what she had to do. First she built up the fire until it roared. Then she stripped off his clothes without flinching, though she had never seen a naked man before. She turned him on his face on the hearth and pressed with all her weight on his back. Water came from his mouth. When that stopped, she piled straw bedding on him. His body still felt cold to her touch. His eyes were open but he was shivering uncontrollably. She hesitated for the first time. Then, with a shake of her mane of hair, she threw aside her own rags, climbed into the straw and pulled the man's body to her.

There was nothing she could do about his broken leg. When her father returned hours later from a long search of the shore, he strapped the sailor's twisted limb to a straight stick. He watched with a frown as his daughter then propped up the stranger and fed him soup. It crossed his mind that it might have been better if he had not been saved. But from the look in her eye he knew better than to say so.

As the days went by the McDiarmada solution came to Bridie's father more and more often. He watched as the stranger's liquid brown eyes followed Bridie wherever she went, saw the smile that played on the man's lips. He stayed at home with them as much as possible. But he couldn't stay home on market day.

Bridie had also noticed the way the stranger watched her. She could almost feel those eyes on her as she heated the stew after her father had gone. And when she carried a steaming bowl to him, knelt beside him and held it out to him, she didn't need to know what he said in his strange language. Then, with a wide grin, he began to shiver theatrically. She tried to frown an annoyance she did not feel and shook her head vigorously. Her cheeks were burning. But she felt unable to move. Swiftly he sat up. His arms reached out to her . . .

When her father returned home she looked and acted demurely. And so did the lover with whom she was never able to converse. But whenever the old man left the house her sea gift seized her, threw her to the floor and tossed back her skirts. Or he would pursue her, hopping with the aid of a torn-off branch until, breathless, she allowed him to catch her. They made love in the garden, the barn, the larder and on the hearth. And it never felt like sin – until the day Bridie awoke sick and with a headache. She knew what was wrong. She realised that something else was wrong when she called and her black-haired Spanish lover did not answer. She had ignored the wistful looks of a man who dreamt of a far-off place. She had taken no notice when, with his leg mended, he started to wander off alone to gaze at the horizon. Now she knew he had gone for ever and would never look into the eyes of his son . . . and that she would never find a man like him again.

By her blithe disregard for the rules Bridie had made herself unmarriageable and her black-haired baby was born and would remain . . . a bastard. So were her five other children by as many fathers. But the Spaniard's baby was the eldest, the biggest and the blackest. Her prayer had been answered in full.

CHAPTER II

July 1963

"... And that was the origin of the Black Irishman," said O'Brien to his audience of village lads. "In every age since then the Black Irishman has reappeared – the wildest of the wild boys, the one the girls can't resist and the men have to follow. He's the killer of the English and the destroyer of everything he gets near, including himself. It's the mixture of the unmixable, you see, the Spanish fire and the Irish fury . . . And what do you want to say, Michael . . . ?" He ended his tale with a groan as a solemn black-haired blue-eyed boy drew his attention with urgent gestures. "For God's sake. D'you always have to say something?"

Michael was not to be put off. He knew he was right. He addressed himself earnestly to O'Brien, who at fifteen fancied himself as the story-teller and leader of the pack of younger boys. "It was just that I'd heard the Black Irishman was supposed to be the descendant of Finvarra, the King of the Fenians, who sometimes comes to ladies in their sleep and leaves them with a baby. Or . . ."

"Comes to ladies in their sleep . . . For God's sake, Michael! If old Finn came to any colleen she wouldn't stay asleep long and she'd know who'd had her." He grinned as he saw Michael's cheeks redden at the overt sexual reference he couldn't understand physically. But O'Brien was nettled. The little squirt was always arguing and spoiling his best stories.

'Perhaps you're one of the Black Irishmen, Michael," he jeered. "Maybe you're going to finish off what Michael Collins started and get the English out of our island forever." There was a roar of laughter and Michael rose to it with anger.

"Perhaps I am," he shouted and the gang laughed louder.

'More likely than you, O'Brien, with your lying tales and your dirty sex-talk."

The grin faded from O'Brien's face and he stood up. "Are you calling me a liar?" he asked menacingly, towering above the other boy. "If you are I'm going to have to beat you, for sure. No little bed-wetting genius is going to call me that."

There was a laugh from the other lads, a little more nervous this time. Most of them liked Michael, despite his cleverness, and O'Brien was a bully.

Michael stared up at O'Brien's grinning face. To him all the others had disappeared. There was only the gloating, taunting face. He could see the first hint of dark stubble on the upper lip, the red nose pointing at him like a challenge.

The mouth formed the words again: "Bed-wetter." And Michael punched with all his strength at that red nose. He saw O'Brien stagger back, the blood spurting . . . and the others reappeared. He heard his red-haired friend Sean gasp an anxious "Oh, Jesus" and saw O'Brien coming for him. "Run," yelled Sean. But he stood his ground. He was afraid but he would not run. He gritted his teeth and O'Brien's first punch drove into his cheek, splitting it. The second took him on the jaw and the world spun. He looked up dizzily at the older boy standing over him. "Had enough?" demanded his tormentor. For answer he hurled himself at O'Brien's legs, staggering him. He felt another blow and was sent sprawling again. Grimly he pulled himself up and O'Brien had time to look amazed before he hurled himself forward, arms whirling, and took another punch.

"For the love of Heaven, stay down, or he'll kill you," Michael heard Sean pleading, as if from a long way off. He crawled upright once more.

"All right, then. So I'm really going to have to hammer you," growled O'Brien. And he did so. Three more times Michael hit the ground and there was no sound from the others as he still tried to get to his feet. His eyes were puffed up, his jaw was numb and there was a dull ache in his ribs, but he could still see the face of the other boy . . . had to get to his feet . . . had to hit that grinning face.

O'Brien turned away. There was no more pleasure in it for

him. The lad was too small. There was nothing he could brag about later. Michael crawled weakly across the uneven ground towards him and he shook his head. "He's had his lesson," he said.

And Michael crawled on. His knuckles scraped on a rock and it moved under them. O'Brien bent to pick up his jacket. And Michael's hands closed round the stone . . . like those of a drowning sailor grasping a lifeline . . . He launched himself at the bending figure, with the rock clasped tight in one fist, swinging it, swinging it . . .

The others pulled him away and then backed off as he turned to face them. But he had no anger against them and they came to stand beside him and look down at the inert bully. Michael felt nothing . . . just tired. One of his friends whispered: "Is he dead?" Sean, the practical one, made a quick inspection of O'Brien's limp body and gave his verdict: "No, he's not dead. Just knocked out." He stood up and put an arm round his friend. "You'd better get off home now and get cleaned up. Your Mam will go barmy when she sees you."

They formed up like an escort party around Michael, eyeing him with something like awe. He felt comforted by their concern and didn't want to hear when one of them muttered: "Better look out. He'll be coming for you tomorrow."

They trooped into the village and there Michael sent them all on ahead while he stood by the memorial in the market square – "To the fallen sons of the revolution." The names were inscribed in Gaelic lettering down the two sides of the memorial. At the bottom on one side was the name Michael Sullivan and the date 1920 . . . Some time every day Michael Sullivan (1963) stopped there to look at his own name, clench his fists tight in his pockets and mutter: "He did not run away." He knew by heart the story of that other Michael Sullivan. "A big man and a brave one," they said. His grandfather had taken part in the ambush of an English Army supply column and afterwards, when his guerrilla group was pursued by Black and Tans, he made a stand to help them escape. He wasn't dead when the Tans got to him, just paralysed by a bullet in the spine. So they used him for small-arms practice.

After his private ceremony Michael trudged on alone. He

wondered if Sean's prediction would be true – if his mother would go barmy when she saw him. The chances were that she would not be at home when he got there and that he would be able to clean himself up before she got in. Since his father went away she had worked hard and long to keep them, washing and cleaning for other people.

His father had set out for Australia to take up a grant of land from the Australian Government. He would "send for them". Michael could remember clearly the day, just before his sixth birthday, when they had stood in the busy dockyard. His mother had grasped his hand as if to hold back her tears, as the man who had been his father strode up the ramp to the ship. He was another big smiling man. It was a picture-memory and the picture remained clear. Michael could not remember the trip to the docks or the return home . . . just that one vital snapshot. He received a card and a short note from his father on his next birthday. "I've got your present but I'll keep it until you can come and collect it yourself. It won't be long now. Things look good here. You'll enjoy the sunshine. It's a great place. Love, Dada."

That was the last they heard from him. His mother tried to find out something. But the Australian officials she spoke to in Dublin were kind, sympathetic – and totally unhelpful. She still waited with a strange sort of trust for the call that Michael had long ago realised would never come.

His father *had* run away . . .

"Hello there, Michael Sullivan," a taunting voice cut into his thoughts and, as he looked up, the tone changed. "What have you done to your face, boy?" It was Tina, the girl next door. She was a few months older than Michael, which was why she had first started teasing him by calling him "boy". Now it had become a habit and he didn't react to it anymore. She was also as tall – and as strong – as he. She had long straight legs, a willowy body, which she already used to signal her feelings and to taunt the stiff-backed lads, and hair the colour of an autumn cornfield. Michael, of course, never noticed any of these things. But today the battle was off. She hurried over to him and then reached gently with her finger-tips to the cut on his cheek.

"Who did this to you, Michael?" she whispered in genuine concern. "The pig. I'll kill him, I will." Her eyes blazed.

"It was just a fight," he said defensively.

"But who? It couldn't have been any of our boys. Not this." She held his arms gently, looking into the slits of his eyes, willing him to tell her.

He shrugged her hands off, lowering his head again. "It was an accident," he said.

"Accident . . ." she echoed the lie scornfully. But she knew he would never tell her. "Anyway . . . come on inside. We'll clean you up." She was leading him towards her home.

"It's all right," he protested, with a token show of resistance. But he was touched by Tina's concern and could feel the long-overdue tears welling up. And Mrs Foley, with five children of her own to look after, was fat, kind and capable. He surrendered and "nobody could really see the tears" as they cleaned up the mess on his face.

Tina and Mrs Foley did their best and when his mother got home he looked half presentable. When he refused to say more than that it was just an accident, she too let it go. She had learned the ways of her quiet, self-contained little boy and knew that he would never tell her what he didn't want her to know.

CHAPTER III

At school next day Michael found that his short-lived popularity and fame had not survived the night. In its place had grown awe. Some of the boys had been whispering together about the epic fight and had terrified each other with the madness of it. They would never have taken such a beating. They would have stayed down after the first punches and begged O'Brien's forgiveness.

They snatched nervous looks at Michael's battered, multi-coloured face when they thought he wasn't looking and made off out of his sight. All except Sean. Michael was his friend. He would always stand by him.

Michael didn't mind about the others and, though he was anxious about O'Brien, his main concern was the reaction of the "English Priest", the slight, twisted-mouthed Father who taught them and whose cutting sarcasm made them all hate him. Michael worked hard to please him. But nothing he did seemed enough to win him any praise.

Father Hodgson spotted Michael's colourful appearance as soon as he arrived in the classroom. "Stand up, Sullivan, if you can," he ordered. "Now, what have we here – a little brightness in those pasty cheeks? How did that happen? . . . No, don't explain. I don't want to hear about your savage perversions. Just come here. Take that chair by the blackboard and sit there with your back to the class – out of sight. I don't want to have to look at you and I don't want these other bog animals to be distracted by you – not that they'll be able to concentrate for more than a second or two anyway. That's right, just sit there and keep your mouth closed. I don't want to hear from savages today."

Red was added to the other colours in Michael's cheeks.

O'Brien had also seen, felt and been awed by Michael's fury. He did not try to seek his revenge. "You'd have to kill the little bastard to make him quit," he told a friend of his own age.

As Michael went home that evening, shaking off a crowd of smaller boys, who seemed only to want to trail behind him and stare, a mocking voice called from the garden of the house next door. "Fat-face, Chinee-eyes," it said, and Michael grinned with relief. Some things had not changed. But as a blonde head popped up over the wall he quickly turned the grin into a ferocious glare. He waved a tight-clenched fist and threatened: "D'you want a black eye too?"

"Like to see you try," taunted Tina. As he lurched towards her, she added: "But you have to catch me first." Then she was off like the wind with him panting after her. He didn't follow far. His limbs still ached from the beating. He watched her go, shouting after her: "Just you wait until I catch up with you then. I'll hammer you too."

He paused to collect his breath and then turned slowly to enter his own lonely home. For a moment he wished she hadn't gone – or even that it was yesterday all over again, so that he could feel cosseted by her concern. But his loneliness lasted only a moment. Suddenly she pounced from behind, pinning his arms and wrestling him to the ground. She held him there, sitting on his chest.

"Now who's the best fighter?" she crowed.

"Oh. Let me up. I hurt all over," he pleaded.

She looked thoughtfully at him, wondering if he were planning some treachery. Then she made up her mind. "Only if you give me a kiss," she said.

"Oh no," he groaned. "Why do you always want to be kissed?"

"Plenty would be glad of the chance," she pouted.

"Yes." He nodded sagely. "There's a lot in the blind school." He let out a yell as she bounced on him.

"OK, OK, I'll kiss you," he said – and she realised that he really must be in pain. She helped him to his feet and dusted him down.

"I'm sorry, Michael, I didn't mean to hurt you," she said

and meant it. He tried to look grumpy, gave it up and then leaned back against the wall pulling a face, closing his eyes and pursing his lips.

"For God's sake, Michael, what are you doing – imitating one of the gargoyles on the church roof, or something?"

"No, I'm just paying my ransom," he said.

"Ransom?"

He nodded, going gargoyle again and spluttering an incomprehensible explanation.

"What?" she demanded shrilly.

"The kiss," he grunted through contorted lips.

"Oh! That. It's all right. You don't have to. It was unfair anyway."

He looked at her, amazed. "You don't want a kiss?" Then: "But I promised to let you kiss me. You can't expect me to break my promise."

She smiled and took her prize, after first checking to see that no one was looking. When she released her victim she said: "Anyway, why I was really waiting for you was to ask if you'd care to come in for a bite of tea. Ma said to ask you. Uncle Gerald has come over and you like listening to his boring old stories."

It was true. And he was just about the only one who did listen to the old man. Uncle Gerald was nearly eighty, stunted and gnarled like an old bog oak, with two fangs of teeth, one either side at the top, and a faint fluff of white hair. He was obsessed with Ireland's history and legend. He would start talking, a faraway look would come into his eyes, and then he would ramble on about famous battles, larger-than-life Irish characters, great wrestling matches.

He would flow from one tale to the next, with barely a pause, sometimes lapsing into Gaelic, sometimes breaking into snatches of song. Though the Irish often lost the battles, it was only because of trickery, unfair odds or their great sense of honour. The English were nearly always the villains.

Uncle Gerald was on form this time. He started with the Battle of the Boyne; went back to Cromwell and the evictions; did a remarkable dive in time to Brian Boru and the Battle of Clontarf; moved forward to the eighteenth-century faction fights and then to his favourite tales of the giant strong men of old Ireland.

"That Donal from Kerry," he said. "Now there was a strong one. Famed throughout the land, he was. A great handsome fellow."

He told how Donal drove off a gang of cattle-thieves, armed only with a wattle, killing nine of them. When the strong man was in his middle years he heard that another great champion was travelling from Connacht for "a trial" with him. So Donal went to a pass in the mountains to await the challenger, found a flat stretch of ground and hailed him as he came in sight.

The stranger asked if he knew where the famous Donal lived, as he had come to wrestle him. Donal pointed westward, adding: "Ah, but he's a great strong man. Big as I am, he can knock me with one twist." Then, "It's a long way to go. Why don't you make trial with me first?"

They stripped off their jackets and set to, striving until near sunset — and finally Donal pinned his opponent. When they sat together later the loser asked, still puffing: "And you say Donal knocks you with the first twist?" "He does," said Donal. "Then there's no need for me to go any further," said the man from Connacht. When he had rested he strode off back home. And Donal breathed a sigh of relief, for he was not sure he could have bested the visitor a second time.

Finally (and this was the part Michael loved best), when Donal was very old he was approached by an Englishman, who challenged him to wrestle. "But I'm eighty," says Donal. "Come, it's only so that I can say I knocked the famous Donal," said the Englishman. So Donal accepted the challenge and in a flash bent the Englishman over his knee and broke his back.

"That showed the strength of him," said Gerald. He sang a little song in Gaelic and then told of a blacksmith from Cork.

"One evening, as he was about to close his smithy, a stranger rode up and ordered haughtily: 'Bring me a light for my pipe.'

"Angrily the smith struck sparks onto some tinder, tied it to the point of the anvil and carried it out to the man. 'There's your light,' said he and, with a great effort, lifted the anvil up high to the man.

"With a little smile, would you believe it, the fella took the anvil in one hand, held the light to his pipe and then handed it back to the smith. The smith said no more but went inside and shut the door.

"The smith always said that the stranger rode away from him up to the Slieve Daoine Sidhe, just to the south-east of here, and disappeared into the hollow at the top . . . Tuatha De Danann . . . maybe even Finvarra himself. It would have to be, of course."

Michael knew that the Tuatha De Danann were the legendary horsemen, who were supposed to have ruled Ireland before the Milesians defeated them in a series of great battles. After that they took refuge in the hollow hills, where they became the Daoine Sidhe, the fabulous dead riders led by Finvarra.

"Why would it have to be?" he asked.

The old man looked sideways at him with a sly grin, brought suddenly back to present time and his painful body by the question. He thought about it for a moment, as if wondering whether he should pass on all his knowledge. Then he said: "Sure and only the dead riders, the favoured of Finvarra, mostly colleens those, and changelings, can go into the hollow without harm." He began to hum gently now, some song about a colleen and Finvarra.

"And what if you went there and you weren't protected?" asked Michael.

"Consumption, Elf-stroke, which now they call fits or stroke, deformity – a humpback, a lame leg or popping-out eyes," the old man answered quickly.

"And what if someone went and they didn't come back crippled or ill?"

The old man's face creased into a chuckle, his dark eyebrows coming near to meeting in the middle. He looked like a leprechaun himself . . .

"Then everyone in Ireland – and especially the English – had better watch out . . ." He paused for what seemed like an age. "He will be the blessed and chosen of the Daoine Sidhe and ride as one of them to drive out Ireland's enemies. The only thing he need fear is himself and the friends he chooses. The only thing his friends have to fear is that, in following him, they may suffer disaster by getting too close. Those who pose as his friends and cross him will die . . . And the only thing that can stop his mission to destroy or drive out Ireland's enemies is that he might get too involved with the colleens or too sick at heart over the treachery and betrayals of the Irish."

Old Gerald gave Michael his slant-eyed look again and chuckled more deeply. "You see, the chosen of the Daoine Sidhe is the Black Irishman himself . . . Maybe, the way you look and all, you could be the one."

He reached out an arthritic, gnarled hand and ruffled the boy's hair, grinning broadly at his joke. Then he began to hum to himself, tapping his feet as he drifted off in time and space.

"Come now, Michael. Better eat your tea," said Mrs Foley. "Your mam will be back soon."

Michael did as he was told, ignoring Tina's attempts to draw his attention. Like Uncle Gerald, he had other things on his mind.

CHAPTER IV

Next day he told Sean and his less nervous cronies the story of the Slieve Daoine Sidhe. They listened – because most of them had seen the battle with O'Brien – but there was a lot of restless movement before he had finished. Fairies and magic were not popular among eleven-year-old boys, even in Ireland. Michael fixed the most restless of his audience with a hard stare and demanded: "What's wrong? Don't you believe the story then, Tom?"

Tom looked round anxiously and then took a chance. "It's just a load of old superstitious nonsense," he said defiantly. Then, as he caught a hint of agreement from the others: "Anyway, old Gerald Foley is daft, moonstruck. I reckon the leprechauns stole his brain. He makes up his tales as he goes along."

"D'you all think it's nonsense?" Michael demanded fiercely.

There were mutters of "Come on, Michael. It's only an old story."

"You all feel that?" he asked. They shifted uncertainly. But finally they all agreed.

"Right then," said Michael triumphantly. "I challenge you all to come up the mountain at the weekend. Then we'll see who believes what."

There was more muttering. Then Tom said: "Right, I'll do it. Not this weekend, there are too many things on. Make it the one after."

There were half a dozen other takers – including Sean, whom Michael expected to follow him anyway – and he it was who took the tension out of the confrontation.

"It's an expedition anyway," he said. "And no one much will

notice if we all come back looking like this." He hunched his back, swung his arms low and adopted a strange limping, hopping gait. They all followed suit, including Michael.

"Hey, lookit old Michael," yelled Sean as they marched around the school playground in contorted procession. "With his face he doesn't need to act."

Michael lurched after him in the odd new fashion, pulling even more fearsome faces.

"Hey, if he goes up to the hollow mountain, he'll probably come out looking normal," shouted a boy called Barry. Michael chased them wildly for a few moments. Some of the smaller children screamed and, suddenly, Michael noticed that he was the only one playing. He looked up to see the English Priest striding towards him.

"That will do, Sullivan," the man snarled, his thin lips twisting. "Though you're all damned little savages, I will not have *you* behaving like it. Go inside and get that awful face out of my sight. You're frightening the infants. You will take the seat I gave you yesterday and, until you look a little more like a human being, you will go in there as soon as you arrive at school and stay in there at breaks and free periods. You will also stay after school for ten minutes each night so that the rest of us can get away. Go now."

There was silence as Michael did as he was told and marched off to the classroom. He hated the English more than ever that day.

Though Sean – and sometimes one or two of the others – made a point of waiting for him each evening just out of sight of school, and Tina was unusually kind, Michael's ten-day sentence seemed to drag on forever. The isolation was almost complete. So he was bursting with energy when the day of the expedition arrived. It was a gloomy day, the rain falling steadily and the clouds hanging low.

"Surely you won't go in this?" asked his mother before she cut his sandwiches.

"Ah, and it's only a bit of old rain," protested Michael.

His mother knew there was no point in carrying on the conversation. He was determined.

It was a conversation he had several more times that morning. In the end only he, Sean, Liam Barry and Tom set out for the mountain. The only good thing about the weather, he told himself, was that it prevented Tina from insisting on going with them.

By the time they had cycled for an hour the grumbling had stopped. Everyone just squelched on in grim silence. It was uncomfortable and wet and you could only see a few hundred yards ahead.

Then, as they rounded a bend in the lane, Michael peered over the hedge and his heart gave a leap. There it was: the Slieve Daoine Sidhe, as Uncle Gerald called it. The clouds hung over the lower slopes like steaming nightshirts, fresh from the boiling tub. But suddenly, eerily, the top half of the mountain emerged clear and sharp above the mist. It looked almost as if the rocks were floating two hundred feet above ground.

"There it is," he shouted.

"It looks awful big," said Tom doubtfully, after a nervous survey.

"And we can't climb in the mist. You know it's dangerous," said Liam, picking up the note of anxiety.

"It's not very thick. Besides, it will probably lift by the time we get there," Michael told them. Whatever happened, he knew he had to get to the top and scramble into the hollow.

When they left their bikes he couldn't wait to get started. Tom and Liam found things to do and even began investigating their lunch packs. Sean, for once silent, prepared himself grimly to follow his leader.

"Come on, you two," urged Michael at last.

"Why don't you just go on with Sean?" said Tom. "Liam and me will catch you later. We just want a quick bite."

"I'm saving mine until later," said Michael, hoping to persuade them by his example. But they were clearly determined not to be hurried. He hesitated a moment and then called: "OK. We'll see you later. Come on, Sean."

As they started, Sean looked back at the others and suggested tentatively: "Perhaps we should wait for them? Keep together in the mist?"

"Come on," said Michael grimly and Sean surrendered. He hadn't enough energy to protest for a time after that. The ground began to rise steeply as they crossed a field and Michael feared that the mist was thickening rather than lifting. His breath began to come faster, his heart to pump. Ahead the going didn't appear any easier. He looked back at Sean, who was puffing doggedly in his wake. It was reassuring to see him breathing hard and looking strained too. If only it had been a brighter day it would all have seemed so much easier. It was as if he wasn't meant to climb the mountain. Perhaps the Daoine Sidhe had blown up this mist to deceive him. Were they out there somewhere, watching him struggling towards their resting place with lordly, disdainful smiles?

He remembered Uncle Gerald's story of the smith and the anvil, and pictured the smile on the face of the stranger as he lifted the anvil. Were they looking like that? He peered harder into the swirling cloud-shapes. Was that a rider on a great horse? Was that the sound of bridle and bit, out there among the rustling, dripping leaves of the pathside trees?

"Damn you, Finn," he grunted and Sean, who had almost caught up to him, asked: "What are you saying?"

"Oh . . . just . . . come on, Sean . . . It seems like hard work up here, today."

"Sure and it will be worse further up, Michael. God knows why we have to go today."

"Because, if we turn back now, we may never try again," said Michael enigmatically.

"Can't think why not," grumbled Sean.

"I can," said Michael. He had remembered the memorial in the village square and the name on the side – the one who didn't run away.

Then, with an assurance he didn't feel, he told Sean: "We'll soon get our second wind. Then it'll be better. We have to keep going anyway. Can't let those other two overtake us." He listened for a moment. Apart from his and Sean's heavy breathing there were no other sounds on the mountainside. And he felt a faint shiver that had nothing to do with the cold damp. They could have been anywhere – even in the dead heart of the mountain itself. He quickened his pace. It was awkward here, walking along the side of a steep incline. One leg was permanently bent and the other swung free. His bent knee and the ankle of the other leg began to ache. One of his boots was beginning to rub his heel. He darted nervous looks around, through the trees, behind and ahead. If his breathing was hard now it was not just because of the exertion.

"What do you keep looking for, Michael?" asked Sean in a voice that started as a hoarse croak and ended in a squeak.

"Just trying to check that we're going the right way," Michael lied gruffly.

After a few hundred more paces Sean called again anxiously: "Don't get too far ahead, Michael. I might lose you."

Michael stumbled over a boulder he had not seen and grunted. The mist was definitely thicker.

"Shouldn't we turn back?" asked Sean.

Michael rubbed his ankle and shook his head. "Better to go on. While we're going up we know we're heading in the right direction," he said.

He stumbled on, falling over rocks and slipping in deep mud patches between them.

"Shouldn't we stop until the mist lifts?" asked Sean in a voice that was barely more than a whimper. "We could eat our sandwiches."

"If we stop we'll just get colder and wetter," growled Michael.

They were clear of the trees and that meant they would soon be at the hard part, where they would have to climb and scramble up steep rocks.

Soon they were spread-eagled on those rocks, clawing their way up.

"Michael, I'm frightened," said Sean at last.

Michael looked back into his friend's pale upturned face. He didn't need to be told. He was frightened himself. Not now of nameless figures lurking in the mist. But of the mountain itself. The rocks were wet and, at each move, he felt his boots slide. His fingers were numb with the cold and he had no idea how much further they would have to go like this. But it was no use telling Sean that.

Instead he said, with a hint of irritation, as much at his own fears as at Sean's: "Well, we can't stop here. There isn't far to go now, anyway." He hoped he was right. Then, seeing his friend's pleading eyes, he added: "It's all right. You'll be OK if you just follow me."

And finally they reached a ridge. Michael scrambled onto a broad slope and lay panting for a second. Then he reached down and helped Sean. He looked up at last and through the mist he could see the summit a few yards further on. A short walk, a quick scramble and he would be looking down into the hollow. "Come on," he said to Sean. "It's just up there."

Sean looked up and groaned. "No . . . You go. I can't. I just want to sit and rest," he gasped.

Michael looked at him in amazement. "But it's just up there," he said. "We could test the old story together."

"I know where it is," muttered Sean, head down, angry with his tormentor. "I know where it is but I don't want to go there. This mountain has given me enough bother already. I'm frightened and I've had enough. D'you understand that, Michael Sullivan? You damn well do what you like, and get killed if you want. But I've had enough. I just want to rest and then try to get down from this terrible place." His anger was dissolving into tears and the last word ended in a swallowed sob.

Michael realised that there was no point in forcing him to go on. And at the same time he was glad. He remembered the way Uncle Gerald had looked when he asked what would happen if someone went into the hollow at the top of the mountain and came out unscathed. "Then everyone in Ireland—and especially the English—had better watch out," he had said.

To be special, Michael had to go alone. He wondered suddenly about the other two. He went back to the edge of the ridge and listened. He could hear nothing. He looked hard at Sean, who stared back at him from eyes red with fear, tears and exhaustion. Sean half rose on hands and knees, his fists clenching. He was willing to fight to avoid going any further, though he knew Michael could always beat him.

The black-haired boy suddenly lowered his gaze and allowed himself a half-smile. "All right, Sean," he said. "You don't have to go. I'll just stroll up there alone and have a look. Just watch me."

"I'll watch you, Michael," said Sean warily. "You're mad, you know that? And I'm mad to have come this far with you. We should have stayed down there with the others. They've got more sense."

Michael shrugged. He glanced up at the top again and hesitated. Suddenly it seemed further off—as if the Daoine Sidhe had quietly stretched the whole mountain while he was looking the other way.

"I'll be going then," he said.

"OK. And I'll be watching," said Sean dismissively.

"You'll be all right here?" asked Michael.

Sean nodded.

"Well, I'll be off now."

Sean looked away and reached for his sandwiches. Michael had to go on alone.

As he had seen, the first hundred yards were easy, though his legs felt shaky. Then there was that sharp rise, a hump of rock to heave himself over. The mist seemed suddenly to be stirring about him, eddying and moving. He looked back again. Sean was already just a dark bump against a barely discernible skyline.

He reached for the crack above his head and began to haul himself up—and the breeze whispered like the sound of a hushed watching throng. He breathed deeply and concentrated, kicking with his toes at the rocks. There was a faint rattle—displaced stones or a movement in the crowd? He reached up again and the sound of the crowd grew. It had to be the breeze. But at last he was on top. He looked back and the mist closed in smartly behind him. He could not see his friend below. He looked down into the crater. It was grey and unfriendly. He took a half-pace forward, the voices shrilled sharply and it was as if someone had grabbed his ankle to trip him. He tottered, arms flailing, and fell. He rolled over, bounced off a rock and sat up dizzily at the bottom of the crater, the voices cackling above him.

It was warmer and dryer here. He looked up again at the crater edge, only a few feet above. He could see the dark scar where he had displaced a large stone. The mist was swirling and clearing in the freshening breeze. He stood up gingerly and, suddenly, he felt like laughing and cheering. He had made it. He was unhurt.

Then he was aware of a muffled voice calling from a distance: "Michael, Michael." There was a hint of panic in it.

"OK," he yelled to Sean. "I'm O...K..." It was time to show himself.

He scrambled back to the crater rim and saw Sean, half-way up the slope below. He waved and he could see relief reflected in the other boy's stance. He slithered and trotted down to Sean and flung an arm round him.

"You see I've not turned into a hunchback," he yelled. "Now the English had better watch out."

"I'm sure they're already climbing into their boats," growled Sean, and Michael laughed with him. It was good to hear that he had recovered his sense of humour.

"And look how far you can see," Michael pointed excitedly. Everywhere the mist was disappearing.

"Sure and we'd better start down before it closes in again," said Sean, practically.

Michael insisted on eating his sandwiches. But soon they were on their way.

It was a lot easier going down. Though he was stiff, his wet trousers clinging to him like the cloth on a pudding, and his feet sore, Michael strode out briskly. Sean, catching his mood, scampered along close behind.

They found the others where they had left them.

"Look, I'm not turned into a hunchback," yelled Michael as soon as they were in shouting range.

"Did you go all the way up, then?' called Tom.

"Yes, we made it," said Michael, carefully covering up Sean's final surrender.

"And you went into the crater?" asked Liam slyly.

"He did," said Sean, his face reddening to match his hair. "I'd had enough by then. I let Ed Hillary here go on by himself and grab all the glory."

"Yes," nodded Liam and he walked carefully round Michael, inspecting him. "Yes," he said judicially, and began to move off towards the bicycles.

"What do you mean?" demanded Michael. "What's got into him?"

Liam grinned. "Don't say we didn't warn you. It's the curse of the mountain." He grabbed his bike and pedalled to a safe distance as Michael lunged after him. "I wonder how Tina's going to like kissing such a poor crooked thing," he jeered at his pursuer.

But the ride back soon turned into as grim a procession as the journey out in the rain. Sore feet and aching limbs made it an ordeal for Michael and Sean. The four parted silently in the village and soon each suffered a further ordeal at home as angry mothers stripped the muddy clothes from them and herded them to bed.

Next day, at school, Michael found that the climb, added to the battle with O'Brien, had made him a character with an oversize reputation – to be shunned by most but to be challenged by the daring.

The English Priest never missed an opportunity to continue his countrymen's hundreds of years of oppression of the Irish heroes.

CHAPTER V

That left Michael to complete the second part of Uncle Gerald's story and put the English to flight. But it took him three more years to discover the Fianna, the junior league of the IRA...

As he walked home from school late one evening after an extra class with the English Priest, Brendan O'Shea staggered out of Finnegan's Bar. O'Shea staggered, drunk or sober – though mostly drunk – because of the Civil War explosion that had left him with a stiff knee and a missing right hand. He put his good arm round Michael's shoulders to steady himself, and leant close. His breath was like the bottom of a poteen boiler.

"Are you off to the Fianna?" he asked thickly.

Michael shook his head.

"Why not?" demanded Brendan. "A fine big lad like you. Go on with you, up to Murphy's back barn and tell them I sent you."

He gave Michael a shove in the general direction of Murphy's, and nearly fell on his face. "Ach, this damn knee," he grumbled in explanation.

The Fianna. Michael was excited. It was what he needed. Tea was waiting. But this was much more important.

"Thanks, Brendan," he called as he turned towards Murphy's.

"Thanks? For what? Did I give you something, then?" muttered the puzzled veteran. He had already forgotten what he had said to the boy and he was momentarily disturbed by the idea of giving instead of receiving. He turned and stumbled back into Finnegan's. Perhaps he would be better able to work it out over a glass or two of the strong stuff—if some of the big spenders were still there...

Michael saw as he approached that there was a light on in the barn. Sounds of physical activity echoed inside and he hesitated. How would he be received? He wasn't sure if he would know anyone.

Michael stood for a long time, staring at the dark shape of the creaking building. He stood in the shadows, away from the flickering light from the windows, and looked at the bright lines of light where they seeped between the gaping boards. Suppose they wouldn't accept him? But if he didn't try to join them he might always remain outside the battle. It was like the hollow at the top of the mountain. He had come so far that there was no sense in turning back. He tapped timidly on the door. No answer. And he was glad they hadn't heard him. That was no way to face the unknown. He pushed hard against the creaking panels, flung the door wide and strode in. Half a dozen familiar heads turned briefly and then looked back to where two boys faced each other. One lunged at the other, who swayed away from the onslaught and hurled him to the floor.

"That's better, Brian," called the tall, powerfully-built man who was supervising their scuffle. He looked only then at the newcomer. "Well, come on in, lad. Don't stand there letting in the cold. Come and squat down here with the others and SHUT THE BLOODY DOOR." With a shock Michael recognised the harsh Ulster accent of Mr Driscoll, the owner of one of the two garages in the village. He did as he was told and sat with the others to learn the rudiments of unarmed combat. At the end of the session he was enrolled by Driscoll, sworn to absolute secrecy about all the doings of the group—and relieved of most of his pocket money.

Even then, little happened to bring the legend of the mountain any nearer to realisation. The Fianna under the direction of Driscoll seemed like nothing more than a military-style boys' club. It was more fun when he persuaded Sean to enrol but it still seemed a million miles away from his objectives. And as the first Civil Rights rumblings from the North began to herald the reawakening of the perennial Irish crusade to drive out the English, and the thunderous voice of

Ian Paisley started roaring revenge against "the Papists", Michael felt a stirring in his heart and noticed no response from the Fianna.

Only the English Priest seemed aware of what was going on when he quoted to Michael from Yeats:

> ". . . Patrick Pearse had said
> That in every generation
> Must Ireland's blood be shed."

"And usually to no end," the priest added.

At the Fianna, Michael demanded: "Why don't we do something now?"

"We wait for orders," was Driscoll's reply.

Then came Cathal Linane . . . and Michael began to understand.

It was a big event in the village. Linane, the man from the Central Council, was coming to talk to the Fianna.

Michael's mother had the tears of memory in her eyes as she watched her boy start out for the meeting. But she knew better than to say anything. Tina was outspoken in the way of modern young women – even in Eire.

"So you're going now to drive out the English," she called from her step as he passed. "You and Sean and poor old drunken Brendan. God help that Paisley when you get to him. For God's sake, Michael, that was all forty years ago. The war is over . . ."

"The war will never be over until the English have gone," he growled.

"And you're going to get rid of them?"

"I'm going to try," and, as she opened her mouth to make another retort, he shouted her down. "And what's it to you, girl? What do you know?"

He marched on without looking back. If he had he would have seen tears in her eyes too.

In the hall he felt the first stirrings of disappointment when Linane arrived. The "big man" was slight and short, with receding reddish hair and twisted thin lips that reminded him of those of the English Priest. He smiled faintly and politely through the introductions, his slender musician's hands folded on the table in front of him. And when he started speaking they had to lean forward to hear his soft voice. He began with some unconvincing flattery about the fine turn-out of brave boys and Michael groaned softly. But the note began to change.

"It's good to be brave and eager," said Linane. "There are other groups like yours, full of eager lads, all over the county . . . all over Ireland. You've been bred and filled with tales of the brave boys who got the English out in the bold days of the 'twenties; filled with tales of Michael Collins, and Padraig Pearse before him, and Wolfe Tone before that . . ." He paused and everyone hung on the pause.

"They were a crowd of stupid amateurs who let themselves be cheated at every turn . . ." The crowd gasped and some angry mutterings began, only to be stilled by a slight gesture of those expressive hands and the need to hear the next blasphemy.

"Stupid amateurs and dreamers, who put the cause of Ireland back nearly as far as they advanced it and fell for a pack of tinkers' promises that wouldn't have fooled a Boy Scout." He let the murmuring grow for a second and then went on quickly, hardly raising his voice higher than a contemptuous whisper: "Well, at least we ought to know now about Englishmen's promises. We ought to know now that you can't do a deal to get back what they have stolen. We ought to know now that the only deal we can do with them will be when we are in the position of power; when we run things here in our own country, unaided by the fine landowning copy-Englishmen who sit in the Dail; and when we have reduced Ulster to a heap of ashes to roast the fat arses of Captain Terence O'Neill, William Craig, Ian Paisley and the 'B' Specials.

"And I'll tell you something else, my brave and eager lads: we won't win the victory by being brave and eager in Roscommon, or Connemara or Cork or Kerry. And it's a damn sight harder to be brave and eager when you're a hundred and something miles from home, looking into the hard face of an RUC man or the eye of a British Tommy's rifle; or when your own country has put a price on your head for working for a banned organisation; or when your church has made it clear it doesn't approve the things you are doing. How would you like to be buried in unconsecrated ground, my lucky boys . . . ?

"This is going to be that sort of fight and, this time, I can promise any of you who stay in the fight that you won't have patriotic songs sung about you, or crosses in the market squares with your names on them. They won't tell of your courage and martyrdom for the cause. They'll tell instead of a murdering bunch of swine who played nearly as many dirty tricks as the English, who planned and schemed and cheated as well as the English. But they'll tell of a victory. It will be a victory won by treachery, by waiting on dark corners for the moment to strike, by hitting and running and bombing and maiming, by ambush and stealth. We won't stand up and wait for them to mow us down with their tanks and their super weapons. We'll fight them the way the Vietnamese have fought the Yanks. We'll fight them until they're sick of fighting for a cause they don't believe in any longer. We'll fight them until they say: 'What the hell are we fighting for, anyway? Let the Irish sort it out between themselves. It's not our war.' And they'll pack up and go away, and we'll have to start all over again – only then it will be our own people we'll be fighting . . ."

He paused at last, as if he were drawing deep breaths along with most of his audience. Michael gulped for air himself in the tense silence of the back bar at Finnegan's. But he had time to notice that Driscoll had his head buried in his hands as if in despair.

Michael's gaze was quickly drawn back to the cold blue eyes of the little man, to the nearly expressionless face and the twisted cynic's mouth. He didn't like much of what he heard. But this was the man he was going to follow into the struggle – not with a gay heart and a song on his lips – just with the promise of betrayal and possibly even death.

The quiet voice was droning on now with its message of no hope: "I expect some of you will be saying to yourselves: 'Well, if that's the sort of fight it's going to be, I don't want any part of it. I have school to finish, a job to go to, a good girl round the corner I'm going to marry . . .' I wouldn't blame anyone who said those things. And I wouldn't want anyone standing beside me in an ambush who was dreaming of the girl back home or worried about the crops lying untended or the mortgage unpaid.

"What I've just told you is the only bit of fairness and truth you're going to get in this war. If you're in, it has got to be like a Catholic marriage – till death us do part. But even those who join aren't going to enjoy it.

"And now I'll answer any questions, though I don't think there will be many. Then I'm going to have a cup of coffee and be on my way."

He sat down abruptly and Driscoll, visibly shaken, stood up. He didn't thank Cathal Linane for his speech or compliment him on it. All he said was a gruff: "Any questions?"

There was a brief staccato of challenges about the little man's denunciation of Pearse and Collins. He dismissed them with a shrug and the answer: "Look at the results and at who is ruling you now."

Then Michael was on his feet, almost as if he had been willed there. His question was simple. "How long do we have to wait? When do we start?"

The cold eyes stared at him curiously. And, though the reply was curt, it was not a dismissal. "We have to wait until we are ready and the time is right. Then the orders will come . . . and they will be obeyed." Linane waited for a second, still staring. He seemed surprised. "What is your name, lad?" he asked. Michael told him and he repeated it. "I'll remember that," he said.

The meeting broke up quickly. There were some scornful mutterings about the "big man" but most were too stunned to talk about what they had heard. His speech had been intentionally harsh.

Michael was as silent as the rest. But for reasons he could not explain he was not stunned. It was as if the harshness and the promise of a life of ascetic devotion to a cause were what he was seeking.

. . . And that night came the dream.

. . . He was running, stumbling as he went, along an unfamiliar, yet somehow familiar street. Stumbling because of the awful pains in his legs. He looked down at them and his trousers were red with his own blood. But he had to go on. He wanted to give up, collapse where he was and watch the blood form in a pool round him. The feeling was almost overwhelming. Relax, no need to run any more. And they'll catch you and take you to the hospital. A bed . . . comfort. He felt the big gun in his pocket. It was heavy. Perhaps if he just sat there beside the wall he could get the gun out. He tottered round a corner of the grim street and stumbled against the wall of one of the redbrick houses. The windows were boarded up. Blocked with corrugated-iron, some of them. He knew the reason, but he couldn't think of it now. No matter. This was a good place to wait. They'd have to come that way. Then he could fight it out with them . . . take a few of them with him. It wouldn't be running away. It would be like that other Michael Sullivan, whose name was on the stone memorial a long way away . . . in the place he had once called home.

There was a reason for running this way. He knew . . . he thought he knew . . . where he was going. There was a place. He started to picture it. Then he put it to the back of his mind. Not yet. He hadn't got there yet . . . His legs were hopeless things. They didn't seem to go the way he wanted. Numb now, they were . . . and heavy. He cannoned against a wall, bounced off, staggered a few steps into the middle of the deserted street and sat down. But he didn't want to sit down. Had to get up and go on.

He crawled along the centre of the silent street. Deserted? He wasn't sure. It was as if someone was there . . . a lot of people. But he couldn't see them. He seemed unable to see beyond the next row of cobbles. It was blurry and everything kept receding into the blur and then coming back into focus. They were there somewhere, all those people. He could hear them – or perhaps sense them. Behind the boarded windows, peeping through the cracks. If he could shake away the blur and turn quickly, he would catch one looking and then they'd have to help. He shook his head and turned quickly. But he didn't catch them. Perhaps if he crawled up to one of those doors and banged hard they would take him in and hide him . . . safe, safe. He crawled on, up over the mountain slopes of the kerb. And somewhere in the distance he heard the hunting call of a police car. Coming after him. It was echoed from another direction. How was it that every police car sounded different? They were closing in. He thudded on a door. He hauled himself upright with a supreme effort. His head swam. He banged again. "Come out, damn you," he called hoarsely. But there was no answer and he had known there wouldn't be. "Bloody cowards," he roared, in something more like his normal voice. And the silent street echoed his shout. And the police view halloo sounded nearer.

What was he doing, wasting time here? He knew where he had to go. He stumbled on, keeping to the wall. "The weaker go to the wall" ... He stumbled and slithered along it, keeping his balance with his hands and arms and shoulders, like a mountain climber on a difficult face... like a boy scrambling over the rocks on the Mountain of the Daoine Sidhe ... And there they were, just out of sight, chattering and laughing. He shook his head again and plunged forward. The hunters were only a few streets away too. But he hadn't far to go. If he could look up he could probably see it. He tottered, missing his handhold, and landed ludicrously on the ground again. There wasn't time to find another prop to haul himself upright. "God, what a mess to explain to that sneering bastard Linane. What an unholy mess." And there were the steps. Three steps to safety. And the mechanical hounds brayed in the next street. He dragged himself up the steps, with the sound of them spurring him on. He scratched at the door. "Like a bloody guilty dog," he thought.

But he couldn't arrive at this house on his knees. One more effort. He was upright... or nearly so. The door flew open and he staggered in. But it was Tina's face that swam in front of him. Tina's face, twisting with an unexpected mixture of emotions. Horror and fear and something else he couldn't put a name to. What was she trying to tell him? What? That dear face. He stumbled forward and she backed away. He stumbled and fell. It was all going black. There was just her voice in the blackness, almost a scream. "Michael, Michael. Why did you come?" And he was afraid and cold. But it wasn't Tina he feared, nor the police somewhere out there ... And then he was awake.

He sat up in his own bed in his own home, his pyjamas soaking with sweat, his heart thumping. Yet he was deathly cold. He stared around the room, getting his eyes into focus in the darkness, checking over the familiar things, reassuring himself. Everything was there. He was there. Tina, soft silly Tina, was next door. Just a daft old dream. But his heart took a long time to slow down, his breathing a long time to steady. And it was a dream he knew he would never forget.

CHAPTER VI

A mist of rain hung in the air and formed haloes round the glowing street lamps. "A fine soft day, as they say in Kerry," said the big man in a heavy overcoat, as he met a slighter figure on the doorstep of a neat Georgian house in Dublin.

The other man just glared out of pale blue eyes and muttered: "They say a lot of damn fool things in Kerry – but not many as foolish as those we're going to hear tonight."

The smaller man's nose was pinched with cold and there was no colour in his cheeks. As the two of them stepped inside he grumbled as he removed his shabby raincoat and scarf: "God knows why we keep on fighting over this sodden mess of a country. The climate's going to be the death of me."

The bigger man chuckled: "If you have your way, it's going to be the death of a few more too in the next year or so." He had a faint American accent.

"Year or so. You're an optimist, Jack," growled Linane. "The English have been here eight hundred years. They're not going to give up so easily. They never give up. They're like peasant farmers holding on to their bit of land. Besides, a few more tricks like the one we're here to talk about today and they'll be convinced there's nothing to beat. Whoever let a brawling clown like McHugh loose on an important mission?"

Linane was clearly in one of his grimmer moods and Jack Fallon sought to cheer him. "At least it will give them a laugh – might even make them underestimate us."

The pale blue eyes fixed his and stopped the inevitable chuckle. "Underestimate us . . . they couldn't. We're an Irish joke. They'll be inviting us to put on their next Royal Show at the Palladium."

Fallon laughed – he always laughed. But the constant joviality concealed a ferocious determination, which came close to matching Linane's. "Sure, we'll be the IRA Follies and we'll put you in the front row of the chorus."

Linane's thin lips twisted close to a smile at last and Fallon, encouraged, went on: "That's right. With your skinny legs in tights – and a pocket full of the jelly – you'd bring the house down."

"We'd better go in, we're late," the little man urged, anxious now that his grimness shouldn't be dissipated by Fallon's good humour.

Though, at this stage, they were allies in most of the disputes that rocked their organisation, they were different animals. So different that Linane wondered often about his friend – about his loyalty and determination and, most of all, about his courage.

As soon as they were seated and greeted the chairman began. He was trying, without much success, to look solemn.

"For those of you who haven't heard, Ed McHugh was taken as he drove off the ferry at Fishguard. They got the van and the stuff as well."

Linane glowered as someone called: "Tell them how he was taken, Gerald." He bit his lips and stayed quiet as the chairman told the story.

McHugh, a burly red-faced man with a brawler's nose and twisted ears, had driven onto the ferry at Rosslare with no difficulty. He had then gone up to the lounge, met a few friends and shared a drink . . . or three or four. When he drove off the ferry at Fishguard and into the big shed for clearance, he had taken enough to expose the sensitive nerve-ends of his temper. He had smiled benignly at the Customs man who stepped up to the van window and asked for identification. He produced his new passport.

"It's a pretty picture you'll be looking at in there," he cracked.

The Customs man looked at him, intent and unsmiling, and then glanced at the document. "Not if it's of you . . ." He paused and a wily grin appeared. He looked up into McHugh's eyes. "My, it does make you look pretty . . . *Edwin*." He stressed the name. McHugh's smile began to fade. Edwin was his first name and the reason for many of the scars.

The Customs man noted the change in McHugh's expression. He grinned at the big man knowingly. "And where might you be going . . . *Edwin?*" He asked.

"Birmingham," said McHugh, gritting his teeth to fight back his rage.

"And what are you going to do in Birmingham . . . *Edwin?*" asked the man.

McHugh's voice rose a little. "I'm going to see my aunt." He was keeping to the rehearsed script, but he was reaching for the door-handle.

"And what's Auntie's name . . . *Edwin?* Is it . . . *Edwina*, by . . ."

He didn't finish his question. With a roar McHugh flung the door wide, catching his tormentor in the midriff with its edge. Then with a mighty swing of his ham-fist he knocked the man to the floor in a spatter of blood.

As a dozen other officers ran towards him, he leapt back into the van, slammed it into gear, rammed his big foot on the accelerator and wrestled the vehicle out of the queue. He raced for the shed door, scattering the men who tried to block his way. And then he was out on the narrow roadway leading from the docks. He threw back his shaggy head in a mighty laugh of triumph – and drove straight into the back of an unlit lorry. As he scrambled clear of the wrecked van half a dozen of the pursuers were on him. He fought with fury and joy, using all the tricks he had learned in the Dublin back-street bars. But finally, with four men clinging to his massive shoulders and a couple more to his legs, he was dragged to the ground, handcuffed and overpowered.

"Three policemen and the Customs officer were taken to hospital," the chairman added. There were rebel yells, and shouts of "good old Ed".

But the thin voice of Linane cut through the laughter: "That piece of lunacy has cost us £5,000 and alerted every policeman and detective in Britain. What the hell can you fools find to laugh about? My God, if this movement is even to begin to be taken seriously we've got to stop sending clowns to do our work.

They're laughing at us now. Every newspaper in Britain is going to tell the latest 'Paddy' joke. I don't think it's funny."

The laughter was stilled and it was a subdued committee that went on to discuss the next move. They had planned to start building up caches of arms and explosives in the big cities of England, in preparation for the next stage of their war. Though they resented Linane for the way he had made them feel stupid, they all realised that McHugh's moment of madness had set back that plan – if not stopped it totally.

The feeling gained ground that they should concentrate on the build-up in the North. First the street fighting, raising the pressure on the Northern Irish authorities until they started making Civil Rights concessions to the Catholics; pushing them on further, to the inevitable British answer of sending troops and starting up internment camps for suspects . . . They went on and on with their plans. But after his initial outburst Linane sat quietly, head lowered, making them uneasy with his silent disapproval.

Finally, the chairman turned to him with a sigh. "What have you to say, Cathal?" he asked.

At last Linane looked up. His blue eyes settled on each in turn and his lips twisted to reinforce their message of scorn. They waited and finally the cold voice rasped out its cold douche of a message.

"Surrender . . . that's what I say. Give up now. You're never going to win anything . . ."

"For God's sake, Linane, what are you saying?" gasped the chairman.

"What I'm saying is that if you drop every plan at the first setback you'll never win anything. You might just as well stop it now."

There was a chorus of protest and he held up one thin hand to silence them.

He waited a long time, as if he were thinking. Then: "In the old days, when a man bought a horse he used to put a lump of turf on its back. If he didn't bad luck followed."

He waited again and someone muttered: "Now we're getting phishogues to fight a war with . . ."

Linane located the man and favoured him with a cold grin.

"Sure now, Denis, and there's nothing wrong with the phishogues." He said it in a mock-nasal Connemara sing-song. Then, abruptly: "McHugh is our Irish whimsy, our phishogue horse." They grinned at that. "And now we must put the lump of turf on his back."

"Perhaps you'll explain," suggested the chairman gently.

"He's lost me," said the man called Denis.

Linane tilted his head back and looked at the ceiling for an instant. Then he lowered it again, with a sigh and a small smile.

He explained: "Now the Brits, though they'll stay alert for a few days, will reckon that we'll be hit hard by losing a big shipment of jelly. They'll be underestimating us still. They know how much the stuff costs us and they'll reckon that we can't afford to lose much more. They'll also believe that, since we've been so cosy and quiet all these ten years and more, the fight has gone out of us . . ." He stilled the protests with an irritated twist of his head and lips.

"They won't expect us to try it again after our much-publicised first failure. They'll figure we'll have too much on our hands, trying to take over the protests in the North."

"So . . ." prompted the chairman.

"So, we'll put our lump of turf on the back of the horse," he repeated. "We'll follow it up with another run – in the next couple of days."

Delegates started to object but he talked them down.

"There's enough stuff for a couple of small loads. Most important are the sample timers and fuses. We'll get them through. We have to, or our cosy colleagues over in England may begin to get nervous. We have to, because this time we have to be ready a few months ahead for each step we intend to take. And one of the later stages in the plan is that, when the Brits have sent in their troops and taken over the running of Ulster, we will have to start them thinking about getting out again. If they get a few bombs on their own doorsteps they'll start thinking. Because, unlike us, they really have gone soft."

"OK, Cathal," interjected Fallon. "But how do you propose to get the next load through? Who's going to be your lump of turf?" He laughed and some of the others joined in.

Linane sighed. "Always the joker, Jack . . . So we send a lad . . ."

There was a gasp and a muttering. He closed his eyes expressively and raised both thin hands in mock despair.

"We send a lad, a bright lad I've had spotted for a little time now. A good-looking country boy with a mind as sharp as a needle, with a fine fury in him about the English – they killed his grandfather or something. A lad who'll do as he's told, will go where he's told and who'll be a big man in The Movement. God knows we need some young blood and some young heroes."

"And may we know who this boy is?" asked the chairman.

"You'll know when you need to know," snapped Linane – and they didn't like him for the implications behind the remark.

"So we're to rely on your judgment alone in this?" asked one of them.

Linane's voice was a mere whisper as he replied: "Why not? I didn't choose McHugh."

A few hours earlier, Michael had stood in the teeming rain at a country crossroads with Uncle Gerald and Tina, watching as big, country farmers haggled, retreated for a few moments behind the rows of parked vans, carts and lorries, came back and argued some more.

It was like bedlam – strung out over a mile either side of the crossroads. Everywhere there were horses and farmers and dogs. The men grew redder and redder in the face, more and more unsteady on their legs, the arguments grew louder, the dogs barked excitedly, vans drew up, horses were loaded and unloaded, vans drew away jerkily. The breaks for strolls behind the vans became more frequent. Horses broke loose and trotted off, dogs ran after them, men swore.

It was a horse-fair, miles from anywhere, unadvertised, the word being passed from farm to farm with the occasional unnecessary admonition: "And bring a keg of that good stuff you've been storing in the barn."

Somehow it all seemed to sort itself out and, as the light began fading, some of the farmers drove off with their new purchases – or with wads of crumpled notes in their pockets – to finish the day in snug little bars nearer home.

Uncle Gerald was hopping about like a frog, chatting to this one, greeting that long-lost crony, wandering off behind the vans, at the invitation of this old friend or that new one, to try a drop of the stuff.

They were just making up their minds to leave when a farmer, indistinguishable in smell and stagger and red face from any of the others, grasped Michael tightly by the arm and thrust a knife towards him.

"Hey, lad," he slurred. "Would yez cut me a piece of the turf and put it on me pony's back?"

Michael looked questioningly at Gerald, who nodded his old head shrewdly. "It's for luck," he said.

So Michael strolled into the field beside the road, hacked out a slab of peat from the diggings and put it on the horse's back.

CHAPTER VII

Michael was late out of school . . . and seething. An extra hour with the English Priest again. Enough to try the patience of a saint, let alone a lively teenage boy. It was still, as it had always been, the English Priest who was the enemy, who pursued him with his sarcasm, drove him on with the spur of his scorn. Over the years little had changed. Except that now the little man did not use detention as a weapon. Tonight they had been doing extra Latin reading.

"If you want to get a scholarship, we will have to do the work. There's a need for a few boys with brains and ability at Trinity if they're ever going to lift this stinking country out of the bogs of ignorance," he had said. "If I'm willing to give the time to drum some facts into the thick skulls of the Irish, some of you are going to drop your people's centuries-old habit of idleness and work with me. Out of the bunch of lumpish peasants I've got here as pupils, you, Sullivan, are the nearest approach to one with a mind, and I'm damned if I'm going to let it go to waste."

That was the nearest approach to a compliment anyone could ever remember from the little priest. It didn't excite Michael with admiration for the man, though it fed his growing conceit of his own brilliance. But Michael wasn't even sure he wanted to go to Trinity College, Dublin, in a few more years, to study even longer and probably end up as another teacher-priest. His ideas of where his future lay were as confused as those of most young lads with intelligence but no family position and tradition to map it out for them. There were vague notions of something in the mode of the old heroes. In the North, it seemed, "The hour had come but not the man." It was all happening too early for him. He was not ready to take his place among the heroes. He was too young and nobody would take any notice of him . . .

"Michael," a stranger stepped from the shadows, a burly man, with a slight American accent.

The boy was startled out of his dreams. "What? . . . Who?" His fists clenched.

"I'm sorry if I gave you a shock, your honour," said the man with a chuckle and a mock tug at his forelock. "'Tis only that I have a message for you and it's been a cold wet wait. What the hell have you been doing in there . . . ? Never mind, don't explain . . . Let's go to Driscoll's garage."

He led the way and Michael followed, seething with questions. Inside the dimly lit garage the man spoke briefly to Driscoll, and then led Michael to the back office.

"My name's Fallon," he said. "Linane asked me to come. Here's a note from him."

Michael took it eagerly. He read: "The time is right for you. Fallon will explain. Do not fail me, Linane."

He looked up at Fallon, astonished. The big man was grinning.

"Doesn't waste any words, does he? Anyway, what he wants is for you to go to England for The Movement, carrying a few things to some of our friends over there who still remember they are Irishmen. In a way it's a simple messenger job. You'll go to Dublin with me, pick up your tickets and a case which you will take on the ferry from Dun Laoghaire to Holyhead. I'll tell you more later, when I'm sure you're ready and willing . . ."

Michael was nodding eagerly throughout the short explanation, though he wasn't sure he had taken in a word of it. "Of course I'll go," he said. "But what . . . ?"

The big man laughed aloud. "Now just hold on a minute. There are a few things we have to check out first, and you can save all your questions until you've answered a few of mine." It was an order, though it was delivered with the smile Michael was to come to know well. He shut up and waited.

"First," said Fallon, "I want you to realise one or two things. If we send you on this mission we will give you a cover-story and you will not break that cover to anyone." He saw the boy's brow furrow and explained: "What I mean is that the story we tell to cover your absence is the one you will tell to everyone – your best friend and the girls you cuddle included." He stilled the protest of innocence he knew was coming. "No bragging, no parade of heroics, no impressing the colleens so that you can get inside their knickers – just the boring ordinary tale we tell you. Nothing to do with The Movement, nothing to do with delivering messages. The Movement is illegal here – more so north of the border and in England. If you breathe a word here it will be round the town in a matter of minutes, in the Garda reports in a few days. People will be arrested inside a week, here and in England."

Fallon shook his head as the boy began to protest. "Don't think I'm blowing it all up to impress you, lad, it's true. There are enough big-mouthed fools on our side already, without me coming all this way to recruit another. The discipline has to be absolute. So, if you're in, remember this – I'll not say it again – there's no talking or dropping hints or letting things slip. You do as you are told and keep your orders to yourself. If you betray us, the penalty is death. If you fail and the Brits get you, you'll wish you were dead. Now . . ." he paused significantly, "Are you in?"

"Yes," said Michael, without hesitating.

The man looked at him with narrowed eyes, as if he were trying to read his mind or spot some sign of fear. "You know what you're saying?"

Michael nodded.

"OK. Now, we have to see your mother – and that's not going to be as easy. I'll just have another word with Driscoll."

Michael strolled to the door of the garage to wait and looked out to the mountains. The last of the light was outlining them in silver. Perhaps, he thought, in a rush of mock-romantic heroism, this will be the last time I ever see them.

But Fallon left him little time for mooning over the scenery. The big man bustled from Driscoll's office, wiping his mouth with his hand, and led Michael homeward. This time he was not smiling.

The mother might be hard to deal with. And that, Fallon knew, was why he had been sent on this errand by Linane. Just about the only thing in the world he had seen bother his cold friend was a tearful woman.

It wasn't that he responded emotionally to them – as far as Fallon knew, Linane responded emotionally to nothing. It was solely that he was unable to fit them into his picture; was unable to understand responses that were not dictated by logic; and, Fallon suspected, was afraid to admit the attraction of their alien emotionalism.

Fallon, the professional charmer and good humour man, was facing a task that made him feel far from charming or funny. He was to snatch an only child from its mammy's apron-strings to send it on a mission which had defeated a hairy, brawling Dublin tough. Still, maybe the boy had a clue or two to offer.

"What do you think your ma will have to say, Michael?" he asked.

The boy looked puzzled. He didn't know. Though he knew what he feared.

"Let's put it this way," went on Fallon. "We can be sure she won't be pleased. But will she try to stop you if you are really determined?"

"No, I don't think so. She never has made a fuss when I've really made up my mind to do something."

"But you're not sure, eh? Will she take money – a little sweetener?"

"No, I don't think so." Michael frowned. He had never before been asked by one adult to assess the possible reactions of another. Like most boys he sailed through life with a blithe and blind unawareness of what went on in adult minds. He did roughly as he was told and reacted instinctively to the unwritten laws of what you could and couldn't do. He had, of course, broken the rules. But he had always tried to be fair by his lights. This whole business of analysis and rehearsal of a situation was something he had never considered. It was part of the grown-up world and he was just on the borders of that strange country. He tried hard to think out the steps ahead.

"No, I don't think it would make a lot of difference," he said. "Though she's always short of cash, I don't think it matters much to her."

He thought again, and Fallon let him wrestle with the

problem. "Let the boy use his brain," he told himself. "And anything he comes up with might be useful."

"But . . ." said Michael, "I think she knew my grandfather when she was a little girl. She liked him, as far as I can tell, and was very sad when he was killed by the Tans. It might be a good idea to mention him when you talk to her – just drop his name into the conversation. It's the same as mine."

Fallon nodded and smiled, genuinely pleased. "Anything else I should mention?" he asked. "What about your father? What happened to him?"

Michael's lips tightened. He lowered his head and shrugged.

"C'mon, Michael. Think, boy. I know it's painful. But you want to go on this mission, don't you? Do I mention him or not?"

Michael shuffled some more and looked even more unhappy. But he answered at last: "No, I don't think so. He's never mentioned around the place. I've never heard her speak of him. He left when I was tiny and we only heard from him once."

Fallon seized on the information. "Are there any other men?" As he saw Michael's eyes blaze he added quickly: "You know what I mean. Are there any fellows who visit, bring gifts and generally hang around in the hope that she might look their way in her loneliness?"

Tight-lipped, Michael shook his head. He felt the angry responses just below the surface, but told himself that Fallon was probing for a good cause. It could take him one step nearer his dream of freeing Ireland. If only he had felt he could trust Fallon more. But there was something about the easy smile and calm assurance that put him off – and always would.

"No," he said at last. "I'm sure she has never even looked at another man since my father left."

Fallon nodded. Even allowing for the romantic and chivalrous natures of teenage boys in such circumstances, it seemed pretty convincing. He asked more questions until he had a picture of a lonely mother locked into a strange, cool relationship with a teenage boy whose head was full of heroic notions. The mother was that rare thing, a one-man woman. She still carried to her cold bed a memory of her laughing Irish lad who had loved her and left her – not because he intended to leave, but because it became too complicated and needed too concentrated an effort for him to bring them together again. She couldn't really cope without that man. She needed him for the humour and colour in her life. So without him she could only manage the material things, and had little time for the real emotional needs of her son.

Fallon was glad Linane hadn't blundered into this swamp of heavy emotions with his logic. But maybe that was why the little man had sent him. Maybe he actually understood that there were gaps in his understanding. Fallon scratched his head. They were at Michael's home.

As they walked through the narrow space between the houses, a tall slender girl flitted out of the shadows, where she had been waiting for Michael.

"You're very late," she began. Then she spotted Fallon and saw Michael's angry signals at the same time. Tina stood confused and irresolute. Fallon's warm smile made her ignore the go-away gestures of her friend.

"Hallo," said Fallon with a twinkle in his eye and the silent wish that he was twenty years younger. "Were you wanting to talk to Michael? Maybe you can wait a few minutes until he's taken me into the house. I have to speak with his mother. Then he'll be able to come out to you."

Michael began to protest but Fallon said, with mock amazement: "Now, Michael, don't you know better than to keep a colleen waiting, especially when she's as pretty as this one? Just introduce me to your mother and then take your girl walking."

Fallon led Michael round the corner of the house and clear of the girl's gaze before adding: "It's best that I talk to your mother alone anyway. Introduce me to her and tell her the truth about me. But don't tell the girl anything. Just say that I'm a friend of your uncle in England and I've come to see your mother to arrange a trip. OK?"

Michael carried out the first part of his instructions perfectly, introducing Fallon to his mother, explaining that he had been kept on at school for extra studies, and that this man had been waiting for him as he left.

A quick look into Fallon's jovial open face temporarily

reassured Mrs Sullivan about him. He offered his hand in a businesslike man-to-man way. Then he nodded to Michael.

"Why don't you go along for that walk while I have a word with your mother?" He turned to her: "Now, if we could just step into the house, I promise I won't take up too much more of your time."

Michael left, reluctantly, as the adults went to decide his future. He would have liked to have insisted on taking part in the discussion. But Fallon's suggestion sounded very much like an order and he had already been told about The Movement's attitude towards disobedience. He was irritated, but the irritation vanished as soon as he saw Tina waiting anxiously, bursting with questions. His mind was spinning. He wanted time to work out his story before she started probing.

"You look pretty tonight," he said and drew her into his arms, smothering the flurry of questions with his mouth. She resisted him for only a moment.

CHAPTER VIII

When he released Tina, Michael had almost forgotten why he started kissing her in the first place. They had kissed a lot, mostly at her insistence, before they reached their prim teens. They had drawn closer over the years since. But they had been more like siblings than lovers. Now, after his first desperate move to still Tina's questions, Michael was amazed by the wild rush of passion he felt.

Tina tried to sound indignant. "What d'you think you're doing, you great fool?" she demanded. But he thought he could see a look in her eyes that belied her tone.

"This," he said and kissed her again.

She struggled free after a moment. "No, Michael! Wait! Someone will see us. We'd better go for that walk. Please."

But she didn't disengage her hand from his and she didn't move away when, after a few paces, he slipped his arm round her waist. They walked quickly away from the street lights and the houses to find reassuring darkness in the shadow of the church. And there Michael soon forgot Fallon's warnings about careless talk. First he kissed Tina again, amazed at how easy it was. Then his hands moved fast, exploring and confirming some of the things he had read in seclusion and sniggered about later with the other boys. She tensed and struggled briefly as his fingers located her breasts. But he held her mouth with his and pressed her back against the church wall gently with his arms. The kiss went on as they edged into the deep shadow of a buttress. He freed one hand from under her blouse. For a moment he let it rest lightly on her hips. Then suddenly he reached under her skirt. There was a half-second's pause before she pushed him away from her with a fierce thrust of her hips and twisted free of his grip.

She tried to sound angry. "Michael, have you gone mad?" she hissed. "What's wrong with you?" Then, softening: "Don't you know how to be nice to a girl?"

She took a step as if to walk away. "We'd better go home if you don't know how to behave." Another step . . .

He had recoiled from the first flare of her anger. But he reached out and stopped her with a touch on her arm. He'd never realised before how soft were her arms. "Please," he said – and surely he could trust her, of all people – "Please, it's just that I'm going to England on a mission."

She stopped . . . still as a stoat's prey. He sensed her dismay over his message and chuckled inwardly. He had made the momentous discovery of one of the oldest male tricks – "I go to face peril and danger from the awful foe. Let me go to my death happy in the certainty of your love."

"What mission?" she asked. "Tell me, what mission?" She was standing close to him, her breathing quick and shallow.

He took her back into his arms. "I had to promise to tell no one," he said piously, kissing her tight lips until they softened.

She drew her head back. "Michael, you can tell me," she pleaded.

He slipped one hand back under her blouse. "You must say nothing. Tell no one. Not even drop a hint. Not even to the priest." She nodded hard at each demand and he delighted in the ripple of movement he felt with his finger-tips. "Promise," he ordered.

"Oh Michael, of course I won't tell anyone. I love you," she whispered.

He moved an inch or so away from her. "I can't tell you so much myself. I've just got my orders tonight. That man I was with is a Commandant in The Movement. I have to go to England with an urgent message to make our people over there join in the fight."

"But you'll come back, won't you?" she asked. Already she was considering the news suspiciously, wondering if he was just trying to trick her.

"I hope so . . . eventually. Just last week the Brits took a man who was carrying the same message and I hear they're still torturing him."

"But why do they want you to go?" She asked the question he had been asking himself. "You're only a boy."

"That's why. Because I'm young they think I'll get through unnoticed, where a man or a known member of The Movement might not."

"And that's why that man is talking to your mother?"

He nodded just before pulling her close and kissing her again to stifle any more questions. She struggled briefly, anxious to ask more, but then surrendered to his insistence. He eased his hand under her skirt again and there was only a momentary clenching of thigh muscles in resistance.

She sighed and moaned softly into the cushion of his lips as he sought more and more advantage. And she could not deny him.

The wind sighed softly around the gutters and old stones of the church. There were tiny movements among the gravestones as the small night creatures relaxed. An owl blinked in the tall trees, its bright eyes watching the movements, its tufted ears twitching at the soft rustling sounds, distinguishing between those made by the creatures it hunted and those made by the humans grappling in the shadow of the building. Its head jerked forward urgently. Its eyes opened wider. It hung, tense, for an awful moment. Then it plunged, the air parting with a plop as it dropped.

There were two tiny screams, one only slightly louder than the other: two tiny deaths in the darkness of the churchyard. The owl returned to its branch. It balanced on one leg, then reached down speculatively with its fierce bill, lifting it again, bloodstained, to the night sky.

Michael held Tina close to his chest and felt her shake with sobs. He lifted his head and let out a shuddering sigh . . .

In the cottage which had been his home for all his life, another woman nodded her head and then sobbed another sort of woman's tears – over the loss of her son, going to war against the English. Her tears were an echo of countless others down the centuries of the perennial war.

Fallon made a fresh pot of tea and comforted her as well as he could. As he waited for the kettle to boil he wondered again about the morality of what he was doing. But there was no room for doubt. If you began to doubt the validity of what you were doing you stopped doing it. "Thus conscience doth make cowards of us all," he muttered to himself. Then in a jump he found himself thinking of another quote from the same play – and what did Shakespeare know of Ireland and Linane that made him so accurate? – "Yond Cassius has a lean and hungry look; He thinks too much: such men are dangerous." Doubts about the validity of the cause; about Linane, the burgeoning leader; about all the killing and awfulness to come – had no place in the heart and mind of a man who had been given a leading role. He sighed. It had all happened too late for him. He had grown soft and sybaritic in the years of waiting – the phoney peace. He heard the hoot of an owl. "Yesterday the bird of night did sit, Even at noon-day, upon the market-place, Hooting and shrieking," he muttered.

"It's a bloody old owl you are, this night," Fallon told himself. "It's all these tears. Never could stand a woman weeping." And with a flash of anger: "Why in hell can't Linane do his own dirty work for a change? And what is that boy doing?" His place was here with his mother now, not off with the colleens. A short walk, he had said. And if Michael came back, he, Fallon, could go away and leave the weeping and no longer be troubled by conscience. He shrugged. "You must be getting old if you don't know what he's doing and if you think that, in his place, you wouldn't be doing the same."

The kettle boiled and he finished making the tea. The activity drove away the grim mood and he was smiling again when he carried the cups back to Mrs Sullivan. She had stopped crying and had composed herself, he saw. A good woman. A waste it was, for her to be atrophied in perpetual mourning – for a man who would never return and, now, for a boy who was about to fly the coop. Covertly Fallon looked at her legs and wondered if on some better day he might find a reason to come back this way. But he knew he never would.

"I wonder where Michael has got to?" she asked.

"He's probably gazing at the sky and forgetting what time it is," said Fallon. "Youth's a great time for dreaming."

The mother sighed and Fallon feared that she might start crying again. She didn't.

Instead she said: "And there's never enough time for them to do their dreaming, is there, Mr Fallon? You and your like make sure of that. There's always another war for the lads to fight on behalf of old men who can't fight for themselves. Is there never to be any peace in Ireland?"

Fallon was startled. He had thought he had won. Was she already regretting her agreement to let Michael go?

"Sure, it's only a message he'll be carrying," he said. "He'll be back soon enough . . ."

"He will not," she cut in sharply. "I'll be saying goodbye to him for good in the morning and you know it as well as I. But don't worry. I'll not go back on my agreement. It would be cruel to the boy and he's bound to go sooner or later. But don't expect me to like you for being the one to bring the call. Don't expect it. Now, why don't you go and leave me with my thoughts? I'll tell him when he comes in that you'll be collecting him in the morning."

Fallon thought of protesting, of suggesting he should stay for a little while . . . No. He collected his coat. It had to be Driscoll's place. He looked into the hard eyes of the woman. She wouldn't forgive him. There was no room for him here. Pity, he told himself as he went to the door. He let himself out with a gruff goodnight.

Michael's escape from a trap of tears was not so easy. He had thought he would be able to retire quickly to his bed to wallow in the remembered delights. The tears would soon go and then he would be able to go too, he told himself – and kept telling himself.

But when Tina's tears of mourning for her lost innocence dried up they were replaced by others – first of fear for herself (would she become pregnant?), then for Michael (would he be taken or killed by the British?), then for herself again (Michael would be killed and she would be left with his baby); and then came the tears of anger – at the Brits, at Fallon, at The Movement, at Michael.

Michael found himself comforting her; then defending

himself as she beat on his chest with her fists; then trying to explain why he had to go; and, finally, shouting back at her in fury.

The owl moved off with a hoot of derision after finishing his first meal of the night. The small animals of the churchyard had gone to ground with all that noise of humans. He had to find a new place to hunt.

Michael turned away from the gentle girl he had transformed into a harridan, intending to sweep off into the night like the owl. But he had gone only a few steps when her imploring wail called him back.

"Michael. Help me," she pleaded.

He was at her side in two strides, anxious and caring. Had he injured her with his brutal lust? "What is it? What is it, my darling?" he whispered.

"I can't find me pants," she moaned. And he bellowed with laughter, as much from relief as at the craziness of the situation.

"I don't know what you're laughing about," she said sharply. "They're me second-best ones . . ."

Then she was laughing too . . . and clinging to him and kissing him . . . and whispering that she loved him . . . and he felt the tenderness sweep over him . . . and he whispered that he loved her . . . and he meant it.

They talked a lot of nonsense about marriage and babies, when the war was over, and how she'd wait for him forever if need be, and he'd never look at another girl. All of it was punctuated by kisses. Somewhere in a new hunting-ground, not too far away, the owl hooted again. Tina went home much later without her second-best panties.

CHAPTER IX

As Michael walked home from the churchyard with Tina he still delighted secretly in his first conquest. He also gloried in a complex mixture of new ideas and emotions. They came out as a sort of awe. The sensation of the actual love-making was lost forever.

But he hadn't much time to dwell on it that night. When they came in sight of home other anxieties took over: his about his mother's decision, which he had been taking for granted; hers about her guilt and whether what she had done had left some mark, clearly visible to her parents and everyone else who looked closely. Her parents would certainly know if they saw her now, red-eyed and minus her second-best knickers. She began plotting ways of getting into the house undetected. She said goodnight to Michael with a quick anxious peck of a kiss and a whispered "See you in the morning".

She escaped easily to the darkness of her room and undressed as silently as she could in a corner, hoping not to disturb her three younger brothers. She did not succeed in that.

Brian called out in a sleepy voice: "And where have you been, then? Is it off kissing and cuddling with that Michael Sullivan that you were?"

"Hush, be quiet," she hissed. "You'll wake the others."

He giggled: he was at a spotty age and was excited by the sneaky glimpses he got of his elder sister's body and her love-life. The only thing that held him in check was that she packed a powerful punch.

"Hey, sis," he called again: "are you going to marry him?"

Until a few weeks ago that remark would have led to a scuffle and a cuffed ear. Tonight she didn't respond normally at all.

She slid quietly into her own bed, stretched lazily and said: "Maybe I am, Brian my boy. Maybe I just am."

He puzzled over it in a tired way for a moment, then drifted off to sleep with the problem unresolved. Sleep came less easily to Tina. She didn't feel guilty about what had happened – she had always known that Michael would eventually become her lover and she felt less physical discomfort than she had expected. But Michael was going off to danger and she could be pregnant already. She wasn't even sure that she would mind if she was carrying his baby so soon. But there was the chance that he would be taken by the English and that she would not see him again for years. Alternatively, if he got away with this trip, he might be drawn into the coming struggle and face even more danger. After what seemed hours, Tina offered up a silent prayer to St Thérèse, her favourite figure in the church, outside which she had so recently committed a sin. She wasn't sure what to pray for. "I'll leave it to you to sort out what's best," she told her mental picture of the serenely smiling saint. And with her problem left with a wiser head she slept finally, unaware of her new lover's struggle to find peace in his bed only a few feet from hers.

Michael had left one weeping female to find himself trying to deal with another. His mother's tears, as she flung his clothes furiously into a case, were even more harrowing than those of his girl. Everything was happening too fast for him to be able to sort it out. He had been chosen to go on an important mission and he had made love to a girl – he was back to gloating triumph about that. After all these years of waiting, both things had happened at once, and he could not deal with the unexpected revelation of his mother's weakness as well. Where he should have put an arm round her and reassured her, he felt only embarrassment and impatience. Only when he got to bed did he regret that he had not been able to give her more evidence of his caring.

Though sleep had been elusive for both of them, Michael and Tina were awake early. The dramas of the night before had left no visible mark. Soon, despite his mother's reproachful looks, Michael was hopping from foot to foot by the window.

"I'll pick him up early," Fallon had said.

"For God's sake, Michael, you're making me nervous," said his mother at last. "Why don't you go and say goodbye to Tina and her mother? He'll not go without you."

Tina was at the door as soon as she heard Michael's footsteps on the path. She flung it open and if her mother hadn't been close behind her would have thrown herself into his arms. Michael wanted to hold her. The scruffy long-legged torment from next door had blossomed in a few hours, in his eyes, into a rare and beautiful woman. But he had to shake hands with Mrs Foley first, then joke with Tina inanely and pretend not to notice her tears. His mother's tears were another matter. The last thing he wanted was to be seen hugging a tearful mother as his new commander drove up to collect him.

And then he was off to Dublin with Fallon. The hours in the car were to be his last peaceful ones for a long time. In the city they drove to a crumbling Georgian house in a decaying street. Fallon took his case from him and gave him a new one. It looked large but Michael found he could barely get his few clothes in it when he transferred them. It was heavy. Fallon gave him no chance to ask questions, quickly describing to him what he had to do.

"You are to catch the 8.45 ferry from Dun Laoghaire tonight. A fellow will drive you to the terminal. Board the ferry but don't let anyone look at your case. Keep it close to you all the time. You will arrive in Holyhead at midnight, and get the one o'clock train for Euston. You will travel first class and will get into an empty compartment in the first section you come to at the station. You will be wearing the tie and jacket laid out on your bed upstairs – doesn't matter about the rest of your clothes. Your tickets are all in the jacket. In your compartment, you will put your case on the luggage rack opposite where you sit. Then you will go to sleep – or try. At some time during the night someone will come into your compartment and will put a leather case on the rack next to yours. When he gets out he will take your case and leave his own. You will ignore this and show no sign that you have noticed the change. The case that will be left will be very similar to yours, so there will be little danger of anyone else noticing the change. You will stay on the train to London where you will go to this address . . ." He handed Michael a piece of paper. "They're our people but they'll be a bit nervous about you staying with them. You will have to keep out of their way. Stay with them until you are contacted and then come back. On no account must you let the British Customs see your case as you travel over. On the way back it won't matter."

Fallon stopped abruptly. Michael waited, expecting further directions. None came.

"But how will I get past the British Customs?" he asked finally. That was the difficult part and they were telling him nothing about it.

"And the Irish Customs," added Fallon. "They're collaborating with the Brits."

"Yes, but how do I get through?"

"Ah now, that will be up to you," grinned the big man. "You'll have to see when you get there. But on no account must they look too closely at the case."

That was it. No further guidance. No details about how to beat the eagle-eyed professional watchers in Dun Laoghaire and Holyhead. Michael felt his heart beating faster already. He pressed Fallon for more advice but clearly his instructor had no intention of giving any. The big man led him towards the stairs. As they went up to the room where the change of clothes was laid out Fallon added: "Oh, one more thing . . ." Michael listened eagerly and then sighed as his leader told him: "On no account depart from the cover-story you have already been given. You are paying a visit to your relatives in London, who have news of your father and who have not seen you since you were a toddler. You'll tell that to anyone who asks."

Michael began to change his clothes and Fallon left with the final instruction that he must be ready and waiting downstairs when the driver arrived.

It seemed like a long wait for the boy. It was hard to settle down to read and he looked often at the clock. For the first few hours the seconds dragged, then the hands seemed to speed up until at last they galloped past the time he should have left to be sure of catching the ferry.

He began to wonder if this was some sort of weird initiative test devised by Linane to check his suitability to go on missions. He looked at the telephone and wondered whether he should use it to call a taxi. But he couldn't afford the fare. He wasn't even sure where to tell them to call for him. He supposed he could step out to the next corner to find the street name. But while he was away the driver who was supposed to take him to the ferry might arrive. If it was an initiative test he had obviously failed. And what sort of organisation was it that would send a boy with a vital package in a suitcase with a false bottom, on a route he had never travelled before, with no instructions as to how he should beat a group of smart professionals at a game they knew well? "Bloody amateurs," Michael muttered to himself, echoing Linane's comments about Michael Collins and the other Irish heroes. Then came an idea that he found hard to shake off. "They want me to fail," he told himself. "The pigs want me to fail. Well, I'll damn well show them."

He heard the screech of brakes at the door and had his case in his hand and was reaching for the doorknob before the bell rang. "You're here at last," he snarled at the startled driver, who recoiled as he flung the door open. "Let's get going – and you'd better get me there in time."

The man opened his mouth to protest, but Michael was already past him and striding down the path to the car. "Come on," he called back over his shoulder, "unless you want me to drive myself."

The driver grinned as he hurried after the angry lad, who had already thrown his case into the back of the car and was settling into the passenger seat.

He told Michael: "Don't worry. We'll get there with a minute and a half to spare. I could do it on roller skates in the time."

Michael had noted the name of a hire-firm on the dashboard of the car. "Not so amateur," he thought, "if they're using a hire-car." Then, with more anger: "So they're expecting me to be caught and don't want to risk the car being traced. Well, maybe I'll show them a thing or two yet."

Aloud he growled at the driver: "Come on. Come on."

The driver gave him a glare, thrust the car into gear and raced away from the kerb. "Is it teaching me my job you'll be?" he asked. "I said I'd get you there and so I will. I was only held up a minute or so on my last job." He swung the wheel professionally and they slid round a corner, leaving a black streak of rubber on the road surface. Inside a minute Mountjoy Prison was flashing past in a grim blur. They stormed through the city centre in a whirl of white faces – shouting at them from kerbs and pedestrian crossings, or peering at them from stalled and braked cars.

The Liffey with its quays and walks rushed past; there was a whirlpool of narrow streets and near alleys as the driver skidded and slid through a series of his favourite short cuts, and then they were out and roaring along the Bray road.

"Are you all right then, my young pup?" chuckled the driver, looking across at Michael, who sat braced and with gritted teeth. "Do you still doubt that we'll make it? Must say I had a doubt or two myself, back there."

"And we still have to get to Dun Laoghaire," Michael reminded him firmly.

"We'll get there. We'll get there," yelled the driver and turned his irritation onto his driving, concentrating grimly and silently.

They got there – just. It was after 8.35 when they raced up to the dock and the car skidded to a halt. Michael was out and running before they stopped moving.

"Thanks, and I'll see you," he called to the driver.

The driver waved and then, as he sat waiting for his stomach to catch up with him and his pulse-rate to drop, he muttered to himself: "Not if I see you first, you won't. And God damn Fallon for telling me I had to get here at the last blast of the ferry horn."

Michael was running, urged on by ticket-checkers and officials.

"You've cut it fine, son," growled one. There was no time for anyone to notice the case he was carrying, let alone look into it. And there was no time for Michael to cringe away from the knot of plain-clothes police on the quayside.

He was past them, on the boat and on his way to England.

And as he slumped into a seat in the characterless, sparsely filled lounge of the ferry, near the line of duty-free shops, he realised that this was exactly as Fallon had planned it. The taxi had been sent deliberately late – though perhaps it had been later than Fallon intended – so that there would be no time for watchful eyes at the dock to look over the country boy, wonder about the fancy new case and pass on their suspicions to the Brits at Holyhead. He looked round quickly and slid it down to the floor between his legs. He thought about scuffling it around and kicking it across the room a few times to make it look older. But there were other passengers and the thing's false bottom was big enough to contain almost anything – even explosives or detonators.

Fallon had carefully worked out how to get him aboard the ferry. But what about the other end? He couldn't believe that would be as simple.

He remembered reading somewhere – or maybe Uncle Gerald had told him – "the Brits might look simple and sound honest but, behind their po-faces and expressionless eyes, they're thinking up schemes a-dozen-a-minute and every jovial laugh means they're half-way to robbing you again." The bit about the jovial laugh reminded him of Fallon. Why had his leader refused to offer any advice about how to get past the Brits, and why hadn't he mentioned his plans for getting him onto the ferry?

"Maybe he wants me to fail," thought Michael. Again he felt the rush of anger. "Well, maybe I'll work out a way to beat them all." Included in the last collective noun were Fallon, the British, Linane and every other imagined enemy – especially the English Priest.

He peered across the water as the ferry moved away from the dock and the up-and-down movement made his stomach lurch. Sea-sickness. He hadn't thought of that . . . But he mustn't be sick. He must use all the time he had to work out a way to escape the attentions of the British Customs and police. He tried to break down the problem the way the English Priest had told him to deal with algebraic equations. "Don't stare blankly at a whole mass of figures," the man had said. "Take it a step at a time, look at each part separately and decide how you are going to reassemble it to help you reach a solution." So he'd use English methods to solve his problem.

The boat gave another lurch and his principal problem slid between his ankles and clattered to the floor. The case. It was too shiny and new . . . too obvious. If only there was some way to make it less obtrusive.

The boat was pitching and wallowing regularly now. A group of long-distance drivers arrived at the duty-free counter and began an urgent and loud discussion about the merits of the goods on offer. One had already bought a cigarette-lighter from the shop two doors along.

"That's the best buy on the boat," he was insisting, as he passed it to the others for their inspection.

"But I thought you didn't smoke," said one of his pals. "What d'you want that for, Pat?"

"I'll give it to someone," said Pat and the rest guffawed.

"Who's that, then?" asked another. "The blonde in Bexley or the redhead in Brussels?"

"I hope it works," said the first questioner with a snigger. "I reckon you can't beat a bottle of booze to warm them up."

"I'll take the booze as well," crowed Pat. "Besides, no one's going to notice a lighter in me pocket when I go through Customs."

The boat gave a specially deep roll and plunge, sending them staggering, and Michael wished they'd go away before he disgraced himself.

"You feeling all right, boy?" asked one of the men, who had tottered near him at the last roll of the boat. Michael looked up with an effort and nodded. The man grinned. "Better get yourself something to eat," he suggested with a wink at his mates. "Better to have something to be sick on . . . How about a nice greasy bacon sandwich . . ." He guffawed.

"Come on and leave the poor lad, Tom," called one of the others. "He can be sick on his own without your help . . ."

"He doesn't need any bacon – or fat slimy pork – to make him heave," roared another.

Michael grabbed his case, pushed between them and ran to the lavatories. He was there a long time.

"And what a dismal way to fail on your first mission," he told himself. "Damn Fallon and Linane," he groaned aloud. He could imagine their reactions if they could see him now—a thunderous laugh from one and a sneer from the other. "And especially damn the case and the fool carrying it," he muttered.

CHAPTER X

Michael was nearly right about Fallon and Linane. Fallon *was* laughing about his Dun Laoghaire trick as he spoke to his colleague in their usual meeting place, a room over a bar not many strides away from O'Connell Street. He explained how he had kept the boy in the dark and in a mad rush so that he would arrive just in time to race onto the ferry.

"And what about the other end, Jack?" asked Linane. "Did you fill him in about what to expect there?"

"No," confessed Fallon, still full of his ruse.

"Then what in hell's name were you thinking about? . . . I know you worked out a way to get him onto the bloody boat — that didn't need much thought, for God's sake. But couldn't you give him one clue about how to get off again? The boy has never been to England. I doubt if he has ever been more than a few miles outside his village."

Linane watched his friend closely as he spoke. "You learn more from one twitch of an eyelid than from a thousand words," he reminded himself. He saw only the contrite appeal of a lapdog there. Fallon, he knew, was no one's lapdog. Perhaps it was the contrite appeal of a consummate actor.

"Look, Cathal," Fallon began apologetically, "I thought the idea was to fling him in at the deep end. There's little danger — a mere lad like that — if he doesn't panic. Now is there?"

"You're asking me, Jack?" said Linane conversationally. "But you're also flinging in at the deep end detonators and circuit-gear worth hundreds." He kept his voice deliberately casual, holding himself back now for the telling blow, watching. "How were they packed?"

"Oh, you know, a false-bottom case," replied Fallon,

apparently lulled, beginning to believe Linane was being mollified. "It seemed the best thing – simple, unobtrusive, you know."

"Sure, I expect you're right, Jack. Was it one of the new ones we had made up?"

"Yes, that's right. Nice smart case, nice smart boy. No bother." Fallon allowed himself a smile.

"Sure, Jack . . . And you didn't give him a placard saying 'IRA messenger' as well, did you? You didn't know that we've been sending boys with messages since the 'twenties and that the British know it as well as we? You didn't think that a country boy from Ireland with a shiny expensive new case might be noticed, did you? It didn't occur to you that the British might have seen a false-bottomed case before?"

Fallon recoiled, appalled, and Linane couldn't tell whether it was because of the sudden revelation of his stupidity or because of the sudden revelation that he, Linane, was suspicious.

"But Cathal . . ." he began.

"But Cathal nothing. It was unbelievably stupid to send a boy out as unprepared as that and as obvious as that." He half turned away in disgust. "God, Fallon, where was your brain?"

"OK, Cathal," and Fallon wasn't smiling now. "And whose bloody idea was it to send a country boy to do a man's job? Who sold us the scheme because a boy might get through where one of our regulars might not? Whose idea was that, then, if the Brits know all about sending boys as messengers?"

"Mine," said Linane icily, stopping the bluster and creating an actor's pause, dramatic and unbearably sustained. Then, as Fallon prepared to break the dragging silence again, Linane fixed him with his stare. "Mine," he said, louder. "But I didn't expect someone to deliberately make the lad stand out like a neon sign, ready for the newest boy in the Special Branch to spot and score another victory for the British over the dumb Irish." He waved Fallon down. "There was a chance that a bright boy, carefully instructed about what he was to expect, might slip through, even though they are watching for the next trick . . ."

Then his mood changed abruptly – or at least it appeared to. "Still," he said, a ghost of a smile flickering across his thin lips, "he is a bright lad. He might surprise us all. The British might still believe we have shot our bolt with the van and the idiot McHugh. They haven't had much time to hear from the informants on our side . . ." He was watching Fallon carefully as he spoke. ". . . I'm sorry, Jack. It was a trial run and that boy carries a lot of my hopes. Maybe I'm just a bit too anxious about him. I'm sorry I snapped your head off."

He might have added: "And I've kept you too busy these last few days and sent you off to the country as my messenger boy to keep you out of the way of your contacts. So they won't know he's coming as they did the van."

Fallon smiled and shrugged. "It's all right, Cathal," he said. "I know how you feel . . ." And he wished to God he did. ". . . I took to the lad myself. Anyway, I must be going. I've had a long day."

Linane smiled at him, apparently genuinely contrite. "Oh, come on, Jack, you'll have a drink with me. I owe you that. And there are one or two other things I need to discuss with you while you're here."

He put an arm round the big man's shoulder and drew him back to the fireside. There was no way Fallon could refuse – and, anyway, he wondered what the hell his partner was up to now. He seldom apologised or made friendly gestures.

Some fifty-five miles away from the bar in Dublin, the object of all the heat and suspicion decisively flushed the lavatory where he had spent most of his journey. His legs felt like foam-rubber and his hands trembled. But his head was clear. He had won the first and most important victory in his battle against the English . . . a victory over himself. Now, he told himself, I have to keep my eyes open and my mind working. There's no more time for sickness. He staggered out into the lounge – and the case felt as if it were packed with lead. The duty-free shops were closing. The lorry crews had long since left them with their piles of contraband. The more anxious of the passengers were beginning to make their ways towards the exits, fussing and shepherding their shiny English cases . . . cases as shiny and new as his own. He leaned against a bulkhead and watched them. What did they put in all those cases? It couldn't just be clothes. It was as if they went on holiday with everything they owned. Strange people, the English. He could see the well-bred suspicion in their discontented faces. Maybe they thought there was nowhere to wash things in Ireland.

"You Irish keep so many pigs you manage to look and smell like them most of the time," the English Priest had said once, when someone arrived for school after falling headlong into a puddle. But maybe the Brits just thought no one was as clean as they. He believed they took dozens of cases everywhere.

And so, of course, did the Americans, he told himself. But THEY did it to prove how much of everything they'd got. He watched as a perspiring woman struggled towards the exit near him, pushing her way past people, using her load of cases like a battering-ram. She had three large bags and a couple of hat boxes. Was she English or American? She was fat and her clothes looked expensive. But she was pushing. She couldn't be English. They pretended to stand back and look down their aristocratic noses at people who barged – except that they seemed, from the history he had read, to be always at the front of the queue for anything they wanted.

The plump woman battled on and suddenly ran full tilt into a tall Englishman. For a second they both staggered. Then one of the hat boxes rolled across the floor towards Michael. It was like a revelation. He bent to stop it and heard the woman bellow, "Goddammit," in the unmistakably aggrieved wail of a spoilt travelling Yankee. He picked it up, quickly closed the lid and then carried it over to the woman as she glowered at the tall man. Michael could understand her anger because he had seen the not-so-accidental movement of an elbow which precipitated the calamity. But for once he had to head off trouble for an Englishman.

"Excuse me, ma'am," he said quickly. "Can I help you with the bags? You seem to be struggling."

"You're damn right, son," the woman told him, not taking her eyes off her adversary. "And some people round here aren't being too helpful."

Michael gathered up most of her cases. He felt strong and fit again, now that he had a plan. His shiny new case fitted in well with hers. He moved her quickly out of earshot of the tall man, who had begun drawling to his equally elegant wife about people who expected the world to stop and step aside for them simply because they were making the return journey across the Atlantic. It wasn't part of Michael's plan to get involved in an international incident now. He quickly began questioning the woman about her visit to Ireland.

He agreed with her about how beautiful it was in Kerry, though he'd never been there, and about the rain. "But it wouldn't be an emerald isle without the rain," he said. "And the mountains – enough to make a man weep with their beauty... and Connemara... and Achill Island... and Donegal. There's plenty to weep about in Ireland," he told her, "and maybe that's what the rain is, God's tears for the oppressed."

He'd heard a man stagger from Finnegan's bar one night in poetic mood and call it that. He'd liked the expression enough to remember it, and the woman liked it enough to forget her quarrel, though not all her grievances.

Henry (that was her husband Michael guessed) had "gotten" himself called to his firm's London office half-way through their Irish tour. He had left her to struggle on her own with all the bags.

"Ah, but think now, how much he's missed. The things you've seen that he hasn't," put in Michael, at the same time wondering at himself. He'd never said more than a few words to a stranger before in his life, and yet he could hear himself smoothly keeping the woman talking.

He kept her chatting as they walked to the dock. He got her to describe her family background (her great grandfather was from Ireland); led her to tell him about where she lived in America; her home; her neighbours; her politics; the Kennedys. He hardly registered that at last he had set foot in Britain – even if it was on a Welsh island. He didn't have time to worry about his case and the contents. Inside the Customs shed she took over, bustling them past the sleepy officials and through the immigration formalities, his time-bomb of a bag neatly sandwiched between hers. He was barely noticed in the tow of the confident, constantly chattering woman. It was almost painless. Once an official stepped out of the shadows and seemed to look at him penetratingly, only to be repulsed by her firm, "He's with me."

She went on chatting as they waited to board the train. But by now Michael's flow of talk had dried up. His knees began to tremble with relief. It was nearly all over. He couldn't hear what she was saying any more. He could hardly believe it had been so easy. He shot glance after glance over his shoulder. Surely they'd realise. There would be the thud of running feet behind them, voices shouting . . .

"Let's get in here," said the woman loudly, obviously repeating herself for at least the third time and looking at him oddly. The cases suddenly weighed tons. He didn't know how much longer he could cope with them. Gratefully he shepherded her aboard and hurried her into a compartment. He wanted to escape from her now, to tell her to shut up. He wanted to be on his own. He stowed her cases. He was perspiring. He had to get away. He made a rush for the door but she caught his arm. She was grinning broadly now. "Haven't you forgotten something, sonny?" she asked. He wondered if he would have to punch and kick her into silence.

"What?" he demanded fiercely. But she didn't recoil – just grinned more broadly.

"Don't you want to take your own case – or has it got a bomb in it?"

He felt stupid. But he grabbed it quickly from the rack, where he had put it with hers. He made for the door again. But again she stopped him.

This time he couldn't trust himself to speak. He just glared, at the same time weighing her up, seeing her for the first time. She was plump, but from the weight of her hand on his arm he realised she was strong. If she started to yell now, he was finished. He'd have to run and leave the damn case to the English. And where could he run to? He wouldn't get much help from his side if he failed . . .

"I just want to say thank you . . ." she told him, smiling knowingly. "And . . . here . . . You'd better take this. I'm sure you could do with a bit of spare cash." She handed him a crumpled note and he still couldn't speak. He just grunted his gratitude and fled.

He didn't go far. He was already in the nearest first-class carriage to the barrier and there weren't many passengers. He stepped into a compartment, put the black case on the rack and sat down on the seat opposite. He was glad to be sitting. His arms and shoulders ached and he felt great alternate tremors of relief and fear. He tried to close his eyes, to breathe deeply and relax. But he couldn't look away from the black case with the false-bottom. There was another worry. The train was still in the station and the woman must certainly be suspicious now. He listened for her loud American voice.

"If she calls out or moves . . ." he threatened mentally . . . "and then what will you do?" he mocked himself. "Run, with or without the case, and get caught?" He looked at it, hating it. "Or sit tight and be caught or . . ." and here was a sensible thought at last . . . "toss it out of the window onto the track." He looked round. In two strides he could be at the window across the corridor and get rid of it. He settled back in his seat, easier in his mind again, now that he had a plan. But he still listened hard. He could hear a couple talking, a compartment or two away, in muted English voices, the words indistinguishable. And someone on the other side of the partition was rummaging through cases – the American woman probably. He wondered what she could be looking for . . . a gun? Perhaps she would appear in the doorway, hold him at gunpoint, snatch the case and then turn him over to the police. He almost laughed aloud at the image of the plump matron with her blue-grey hair pointing a gun and wheezing asthmatically through a James Bond act. But suppose someone else came and stole the case? He watched it fixedly – as if it would climb off the rack by itself and float away into the waiting hands of a stranger.

Even when the train started unexpectedly, with a jolt, he barely flicked a glance at the platform to confirm that they were moving. He drew a newspaper from his pocket but he couldn't concentrate on the words as his eyes kept drifting up to the rack opposite and to that shiny black case. Finally he folded the paper and put it back into his pocket, slumping in his seat, crossing his legs, but never shifting his eyes from his burden. At first it stayed still. Then it began to swell and undulate in time with the rhythm of the train. It started to blur. The shiny locks began to grow. He blinked and for a moment the case resumed its normal size and shape. But, after a few seconds more, it began its odd activities again. His eyes ached with the staring. Slowly they closed. He forced them open again with a yawn. Perhaps he should really relax for a few minutes, rest his eyes . . .

At first the bag figured in his dream. He was running with it . . . despite the pain in his legs . . . staggering along a mean street of redbrick houses with boarded-up windows and chalked slogans on nearly every square foot of brick. The pain in his legs grew. He ran on, fell, picked himself up and ran again. The case was gone. But the sounds of the police cars behind reminded him that there was no time to stop and go back for it. There was blood on his trousers. His legs were numb. But he had to go on. Not far to go. Lean on the walls of these deserted houses, pray that someone will come out and give a hand. Not far to go. There it was, the house he was looking for. Stagger, stumble, fall, crawl up the steps. Haul yourself up by the letter-box. Thump on the door. The police close now. And there was the familiar pretty face, but it was not welcoming. It was warning, screaming. He was falling . . . and the door closed.

He sat up sweating, grasping for the relief of wakefulness. The compartment door HAD closed. There was still a feeling of movement about it. Footsteps were retreating along the corridor. He leapt to his feet and wrenched the door open again. Too late, the corridor was empty. He thought of running after the intruder. But why? He looked anxiously at the rack. The black case was there. Nothing had changed. He sat back in his seat and stretched. He had fallen asleep. He had failed. The case could have been stolen. He looked up at it again, seeking reassurance from its black shininess. But was there something different? Was it as shiny? There was a mark surely on one of the locks that hadn't been there before – the sticky mark left by a price tag. The handle looked different. More stained and warped by the sweat of palms. He sat forward. Then he stood, reached up for his case – his Atlas burden.

But it was not so much of a burden now, he discovered as he lifted it. It felt different in his hands. He took it to his seat. Close up, he was more certain. He ran his hands across the new/older case. He liked it. It was better. He sighed and relaxed for a moment with it across his knees. Then he eased the locks open. The clothes inside were new – and they floated loose in the extra space of this bag. There was a note on top. Michael reached for it and flipped it open.

It was brief. "Well done and thanks," it said. "Wait at the house in London until you are contacted."

He shut the case, slipped the note into his pocket and closed his eyes again. He could sleep peacefully now . . .

CHAPTER XI

It was the door that woke him again. As he struggled out of the confused world of his dreams, where Tina and Linane were in league and laughing at him, he looked into the weary face of a railway porter.

"Ain't you getting out, son? This is as far as you go. Train's been in an hour now."

"Euston?" he asked fatuously.

"Was when I came on – about ten hours ago. An' I hope it ain't moved since, I wanna get the bus 'ome to breakfast."

Michael gazed in amazement at the man. He was ugly, with a growth of grizzled stubble and a grimy wrinkled neck. He wore a greasy, open-neck shirt under a battered British Rail cap. Michael wasn't sure what the man was saying. It was an accent he had never heard before and he could hardly believe this was an Englishman. He certainly didn't fit into any of his mental images of the English.

Michael picked up his case from the floor and scrambled out. He quickly located the station clock. It was 7.40. Yet, in the grim, grey, early morning, London was already beginning to wake up. The first workers were plodding on unwilling feet towards their factories, yawning capaciously. Michael shivered.

"What you want's a nice cuppa tea to wake you up," said the porter. "Buffet's open or if you want real tea you can go out that way," he gestured, "across Eversholt Street to Tony's Caff. E'll do you a nice bacon sanwidge."

Michael grunted his thanks and went the way he had been directed, drank hot, strong tea and ate a thick bacon sandwich. He groped in his pockets and produced the address, "London

NW6". He looked round at the other men in the "caff". They were all shabbily dressed, all slumped wearily over their mugs of tea. Two men sitting at a table near the counter stabbed their fingers at an already grimy newspaper as they discussed the races.

Michael caught the eye of the man behind the counter, a grubby dark man with a greasy, off-white apron knotted round his skinny waist.

"You wan' something else?" the man asked. He sounded Italian.

Michael hesitated. Then he showed the man the address. "I'm wondering how to get there," he said.

"NW6? What's that?" the man grumbled. "Anyone think I was a travel bureau, not the owner of a caff."

"NW6, that's Kilburn innit, 'Arry?" asked one of the two racing buffs of his mate.

"Yeah, that's it," said 'Arry, nodding sagely. "Go Victoria line dahn to Oxford Circus, then change onto the Bakerloo to Kilburn."

"Wouldn' 'e be better orf walkin dahn the end to Euston Square an' goin' to Baker Street?"

"Could do that," interjected another man at the next table. "But I'd get a number 14 bus outside the station an' change at . . ."

Michael looked and felt bewildered as they debated the advantages of the different routes and the Italian café owner leant on the counter, watching them with a grin.

Finally, they seemed to agree and the second punter appointed himself spokesman. He gave Michael careful and detailed directions, with much finger-pointing and hand-waving. He made him repeat it all and then repeated it himself, correcting Michael's mistakes.

As Michael left the place, with its welcoming smell of bacon and tea, he looked back. The man behind the counter was morosely drying cups; the punters were back studying form; the rest were slumped over their mugs of tea. It was as if they had all fallen back into a state of suspended animation until the next stranger walked in seeking directions.

Michael walked towards the bustle of Euston Road, where

the rush-hour traffic was building up. The smell of exhaust fumes was overpowering. He found himself quickening his step to keep up with the hurrying people. Click, click, click, went the heels of the scurrying girls, who made up a fair proportion of the crowd now. He was amazed at the variety of their clothes. Skirts ranged from thigh-high – and he averted his eyes from them – to ankle-length, from grubby to neat and severe. There were trousers, overcoats, raincoats, long hair, short. And the colours – of the people as well as their clothes.

He was even more astonished when he boarded a packed underground train and was squashed against a partition by a plump blonde girl. She was avidly describing to a friend the events of last night and wriggling her buttocks against Michael's legs with every jolt of the train. She, like the men in the "caff" and almost everyone he had heard since he had been in London, spoke in the same lazy, ugly accent with its dropped aitches and lost word-ends.

"'Ere, I said, I dunno what you're lookin for dahn there, but you can git your 'and out of it," she said. "But I couldn't do nuffing, I 'ad me ice-cream in one 'and and me bag in the uvver."

He felt enveloped in flesh, crushed and beaten by people, suffocated by the smell of under-arms and cheap perfume. The day he had left upstairs had been cold and grey. Here in the permabright it was steamily hot.

He looked round anxiously and caught the eye of an elderly woman, who looked away hastily, her mouth narrowing quickly so that the lips furrowed white with disapproval. That was how he felt about the grubby, ugly English at that moment.

But the train was decelerating beside another crowded platform. There was a mass move towards the door and Michael went with it. They had reached Baker Street.

A few more claustrophobic minutes and he had reached Kilburn, another grim area, part building-site, part fading Victorian property long past its prime. The High Road was a gaudy jumble of shops with too many colours and too many signs. A slight breeze stirred up unexpected sandstorms that caught the eyes and wrapped grubby newspapers round the ankles.

After another stop and another direction debate he stood on

the steps of the house he was bound for. Like all the rest it had seen better days, the paintwork was peeling and the woodwork rotting. He pressed the bottom button of a long row and heard a bell ring somewhere deep in the house.

The clamour of the bell was followed by silence. Nothing moved in the house. Michael peered along the row. It looked as if they were all divided into small flats. Yet each seemed as deserted as the next. Not a curtain moved. No face appeared at a window. And in their look of abandonment the houses were like a visual echo of his dream. He shuddered, and leant on the bell again.

This time a window above him shot open and an angry voice called: "Can't you wait a minute? Is there a fire or something?" The accent was familiar and he felt an immediate response of joy.

"There's no fire," he said cheerily. "But I'm from the Garda about the still you're operating in the back yard."

"Is it daft you are, boy?" called the woman, barely changing her tone. "If I had the poteen boiling I wouldn't be answering any door-bells. I'll come down."

The woman who answered the door to him was small and wiry, with a tight little frown of a face.

"Moira Duggan," she said. Then she thrust her head forward to peer at him. "What is it they're sending us now, the kindergarten? Are we going to war with the Brits with an army in short pants?" As he stammered over an angry response she rattled on: "Well, you'd better come in, anyway. God alone knows what Duggan thinks he's up to, but he's told me we're keeping you for the week."

She showed him his room, repeated to him his orders about keeping quiet and out of the way, warned him about "that Mary Duggan" – her niece, who also lived in the house – and then scuttled away.

Later he met Duggan, a big, raw-boned, taciturn man, who spent his days as foreman of a construction crew, staring down at the backs of others as they dug holes in the roads. Mary, the scarlet woman he had been warned about, took him tea next morning in bed, teased and tormented him briefly and then went off "to feed the starving English" – she worked as a waitress. She made the morning visits a regular excuse to flirt with him. And he found them a welcome relief from the screaming boredom of being "locked in quarantine", as he described his isolation to her. Mary, nearly thirty, her looks fading and her body becoming plump, welcomed his stay as a way of relieving her boredom too. But, her breezy visits apart, Michael waited anxiously for the call to return home, knowing that there would be nothing he would regret leaving in London, a city he had found miserably inhospitable.

CHAPTER XII

And then it was Sunday . . . and Monday . . . and Tuesday . . . and Wednesday. All the same. A blur of reading, dozing and waiting anxiously for Mary's next visit.

And then it was Thursday. The morning flurry of the household woke him as usual and he looked out onto another grey day. But this day *was* different. He realised it as soon as Mary arrived with his tea. She looked cleaner and fresher than usual and there was an air of repressed gaiety about her. She thrust the cup into his hand and stood back, hands on hips.

"Drink that, lazy," she ordered, "and then hurry up. You can't lie here all day."

"And why not?" he asked.

"You're taking me out, is what. You've been creeping around like a hermit all week and it upsets me . . ."

"But what about your job?"

"The starving English can do without me today. I do get a day off now and then from rushing about to serve at me tables. It's a nice day and I've neglected you."

Michael looked out of the window. The day looked no better than any of the others he had spent in London. But there was no arguing with Mary. He began to respond to her joy.

"OK. Where am I taking you?" he asked.

"We'll start off with the zoo – you can see your family there. Then we'll go to a film and maybe end up with a little drink and a cuddle. Come on. The day'll be over before I get you moving," she urged.

They went to the zoo – a short bus ride from the end of the road. They travelled along the Regent's Canal on a pleasure boat, her head on his shoulder and his arm round her as if they were young lovers. They cuddled enthusiastically in the cinema and she took him to a pub afterwards.

She stood close to him at the bar as he ordered the drinks. He had never ordered drinks in a bar before. He felt strong and manly and Mary seemed like a pretty young girl. He took her hand and looked down into her eyes . . .

"Heard the one about the Irishman who went down in a submarine? . . ." said a loud voice just behind him. "Took his parachute in case they crashed."

Michael turned sharply. Three men stood close to him at the bar. They were in their late twenties and flashily dressed. As he turned the laughter became louder. The teller of the joke, taller and broader by inches than Michael, fixed him with a stare and went on loudly: "There was this ventriloquist, see. He was telling all these Irish jokes and a *big thick Mick* stood up in the audience and yelled, 'If you don't cut out all these insults to the Irish I'll come up there and smash your head in.' The ventriloquist started to apologise and the *big thick Mick* said, 'You shut up. It's the little fella on your knee I'm talking to.'"

He didn't once take his eyes off Michael, who returned his stare. The others hooted. And, still keeping his eyes on Michael, the man began again: "There was this *big thick Mick* . . ."

"Cut it out," snapped Michael. Mary was pulling at his arm, the landlord was hurrying across. The story-teller stopped and a look of mock-surprise appeared on his face.

"There a ventriloquist in 'ere? I thought I heard someone speak. Didn't you, 'Arry?"

Harry looked round as if searching for something. "I don't see nothing, Jim. Nothing you'd expect to be able to talk."

"Come on, Michael," hissed Mary.

"Oh . . . I see," said Jim. "It's the Irish washerwoman. She's the ventriloquist. She's got this little wooden doll on her knee."

He reached for his pint and sipped speculatively. "You heard the one about the thick Irish kid and the old tart?" he began.

"Listen," bellowed Michael. "You heard what I said. Cut that stuff out or I'll . . ."

"You'll what, son," said Jim, putting down his pint and advancing a pace. "You'll what . . . run to your mum there. Go on home to Ireland before I smack your bottom . . ."

Michael leapt forward, Mary grabbed him and the landlord smashed a huge club on the counter between Michael and his tormentor. "Stop that!" he roared.

"You and you," he gestured at Michael and Mary, "Out! . . . I'll have none of your Irish brawling in this pub. Out!"

Michael stood his ground for a second, hesitating. It was all so unfair. "But he . . ." he began to protest.

"I'm not interested. Out! I said." The landlord pointed towards the door with the club. His hands tightened on it.

"Come on, Michael," pleaded Mary again. "He'll call the police."

"Better do like the man says," said the comedian called Jim. "You might get in trouble."

Michael was outnumbered. They were all against him, it seemed. He dropped his head and started to turn away.

"That's right, sonny," his tormentor put in again. "Mummy'll look after you."

Michael turned again, fists flying. One hand caught the man Jim in the face. The other landed in the bulge above his belt, doubling him over. But they were the only punches Michael was able to throw. Jim's two cronies seized the boy, twisting his arms behind him. Jim straightened up slowly.

"I told you to get out," said the landlord to Michael.

"All right, Bert," said Jim grimly. "We'll look after him. Don't you worry. I think someone needs serving over there." He nodded dismissively and picked up his pint again, with a glint in his eyes.

"Look, I don't want any trouble in . . ."

"There won't be. We'll just get him out and take him for a little walk to cool him down, won't we, lads?" He grinned at the others. "And just for starters . . ." he tipped his pint over Michael's head.

The landlord turned away. But Mary intervened now. "Look, he's only a boy," she pleaded.

"Just keep out of this, missus," said Jim wearily. "If he's a boy he ought to learn a bit more respect for his elders. Don't they teach you nothing in Ireland? We're just going to have to punish him for you. Come on, let's get him outside."

Michael was struggling helplessly in the hands of the other two.

"Look, I'll buy you a round," said Mary.

Jim thrust her aside and led the way to the door. "Why don't you stay here?" he told Mary. "Come and collect him in five minutes. I think he's going to have a little accident."

"Mother of God," she moaned and she appeared to accept his instructions as the door slammed between her and the punishment party.

It was dark in the pub yard but the group of men dragged Michael into an even darker alley. "That was idiotic. How could it have happened?" thought Michael. It had been such a good day. His orders had been to stay inside the Duggans' home and keep out of any trouble. And what was it all about? Just some silly jokes in a pub. And now he was going to be beaten up. He slumped in the arms of the two who were holding him, gritted his teeth and stared at the pub wall. He was facing a stone buttress. It would do as a memorial, he thought grimly. Then he frowned. A memorial, like the one in the town square back home, with the name Michael Sullivan and the date 1920. *He* hadn't run away. Michael tensed against the two men holding him.

"Now, son," said Jim. "I want you to say you're sorry." He drove a fist into Michael's stomach. Michael buckled. He felt the tears coming to his eyes. "Sorry," Jim repeated and drew his fist back to add the punctuation. But, before he could do so, there was a flurry behind him, the sound of smashing glass and Jim slumped to the floor. It was Mary. She had emerged from the side entrance and stopped the party with a powerful blow from a bottle.

As Jim fell, Michael gave a mighty heave and swung the man holding his right arm against the buttress. He turned as the man's grip was broken and swung his fist at Harry, who had been holding the other side.

But Harry blocked the punch and countered with one of his own that sent Michael staggering. Jim was slowly picking himself off the ground. The man Michael had flung against the buttress was straightening up. "Run, Michael," yelled Mary and started off. But that other Michael Sullivan had never run.

Michael hesitated. "Come on," she called anxiously, as Harry swung again, rattling his teeth. The man by the wall weighed in with a swift kick that caught his knees and brought him down . . . and a police-car klaxon sounded like the Harp of Tara, miraculously close.

"Shit," swore Jim. He stepped forward and smashed a punch into Michael's face as he struggled to his knees. "Let's get out of here. It's the cops."

The three men made off and Michael swayed, blood oozing from his mouth.

"Michael, are you all right?" wailed Mary.

"What's going on here?" demanded a voice from the entrance to the alley.

"It's all right, officer," she answered. "We're OK."

Two burly shapes appeared in the dim light.

"It was just a little accident," said Mary again. She was trying too hard.

"Looks like it," said one policeman, nodding to where Michael was propping himself against the wall. The second walked up closer and shone his torch in Michael's face. Then he wrinkled his nose and stepped back a pace.

"Stinks like a brewery," he growled. He swung the torch towards Mary. "You do this?" he asked. She shook her head and he went on: "Didn't think so, or I'd have put you in for fifteen rounds with our 'Enery, for the British title." He shone the torch up and down her body and with heavy gallantry added: "Not that I'd put you down as a heavyweight, love. More like a feather, wouldn't you say, Dave?"

Mary swayed her hips provocatively. Maybe there was a way out of this bother. "Sure and I'd be like a feather in your arms," she said. "Though some would say I'm well-enough built." She smoothed her jumper close in to her waist and thrust out her chest.

"Yeah, love," said Dave, with a sigh. "You're a bit of all right. But what happened to the lad? We . . ." and he stared significantly at his partner as he spoke, "were called out to an affray. The landlord reported trouble . . . a couple of drunken Irish fighting in his yard. What have you to say?"

"She'll tell us she saw a crowd of fellas scrapping as she tried to leave the pub," cut in the second policeman with a grin and a wink. "Fists were flying all round her and she got pushed about and frightened. We arrived just in time and the mob made off, leaving her hysterical. We offered to drive her to the hospital. But, on the way there, she changed her mind, so we took her home instead. Took us quite a time to calm her down, though. Got it, Dave?"

"Yeah, I see," said Dave. "But what about him?" He nodded to where Michael was standing stiffly by the wall.

"I don't see anything. He's half-way back to Co. Kilburn now with the rest of the mob, leaving us to look after this frightened little lady." The second policeman put an arm protectively round Mary's waist.

Mary leaned against the protective arm and signalled with her head for Michael to go.

The policeman called Dave chuckled appreciatively. "Yeah. We'll give you a hand to the car, miss. Little ride'll calm us all down a treat." He reached out and took Mary's arm. "Just put your arm over my shoulder, love. I'll give you a hand up."

Mary gave a little jump and a squeak as he moved closer.

Michael watched, numb and horrified. He knew what she was trying to do for him. But he couldn't expect . . . not that. He pushed himself away from the wall. No Irishman, and especially not the Black Irishman, could ask a girl to protect him. "No, Mary," he called desperately. "I won't let you do it." To the policemen he shouted: "Leave her alone. It's me you want."

The second policeman removed his arm from Mary's waist and stepped a pace clear. "You hear anything, Dave?" he asked. "I thought we said they all scarpered . . ." He gave Michael a hard-eyed glare. "Do it, son, before we change our . . ." He didn't finish as the boy lunged despairingly at him.

It was the only way, thought Michael, as the man side-stepped his attaack, caught his flailing right arm and brought him down on the concrete with a thud.

"Thick as pig-shit," he heard the man mutter. "They never learn, do they, Dave?"

The two policemen were staring down at him as if he were some strange specimen. One of them grabbed the short hair on his temple and hauled him to his feet by it. The other caught his arms behind him. They began hustling him towards their car at the entrance to the alley. "Resisting arrest, obstructing the police in the execution of their duty, drunk and disorderly, causing an affray," intoned one.

Michael caught a glimpse of Mary, standing helpless in the alley, tears in her eyes.

"Go on home, love," said Dave. "We'll see you another night."

CHAPTER XIII

Michael groaned and tried to sit up. His head spun and every part of him seemed to ache. He waited and tried again, more slowly. The grey, dawn sky misted as the tears came to his eyes with the effort. The pain was worst around his ribs. He guessed the crust around his mouth and nose was blood. He waited until everything stopped spinning. Had to get up. The grass was wet and muddy. He reached for the railings of the park where they had taken him. He got to his knees and stopped, trembling as if with fever. He waited there a long time.

"Christ, what happened to you?" asked a voice close behind him.

Michael peered round slowly – and wanted to cry as he saw a peaked cap with a man underneath it. "No more. Please, no more," he gasped.

"'Ere, let me give you a hand, mate." The man moved closer and Michael flinched.

"It's all right, mate. Just want to help," said the man reassuringly. He put an arm round Michael and eased him to his feet. "OK, mate. Just lean on me. Christ, who did this to you?"

Muttering reassuring words, as if he were talking to a restive horse, the park attendant edged Michael foot by foot across the square to a wooden hut, supported him against the wall while he found the keys, and then helped him onto a bench.

"Just sit there and I'll make you a cuppa tea. Then I'll call the cops."

"No, no," Michael gasped, and something about the urgency of his appeal got through to the man.

"OK, OK. No police. No ambulance? OK." He busied

himself starting the kettle going on the gas-ring. He found an old blanket and put it round Michael, propping him up and making him comfortable. "Got to do something with you," he muttered, half to himself. "Can't have the residents finding you here like this. They like their square kept tidy."

The man chatted away while he made the tea. He pushed a steaming mug into Michael's hand. "You all right? You can hold that? There's a fella." Michael was grateful.

"I got it," said the man at last. "I'll call a cab." And, as Michael straightened up in suspicious alarm, "All right, all right. I know. No cops. No ambulance. Just trust me. Where do you live?"

Michael told him and the man hurried away, leaving him to sip the tea and enjoy the comfort of the warmth of the cup. He started to nod. But the man was back.

"Cab's coming. Soon have you home. Clean you up a bit before he gets here..."

The man helped Michael to the gate of the little locked square and into the cab. He pressed a pound into the taxi driver's hand and told him where to go. Then, with a last anxious look through the window, he was off to worry about the litter and the state of the grass.

And I didn't even get his name so that I could send him a thank you, thought Michael in an instant of regret, which was quickly overtaken by the feeling of relief that he was going home. Home! Even that strange silent house in Kilburn was inviting this morning.

But the house wasn't so silent when Michael reached it and was helped along the path by the cabbie. As he fumbled with his key the door flew open and Mary hurtled out to grab him and gabble her relief. Moira was close behind her, nagging about him not keeping out of trouble the way he had been told. Even the taciturn Duggan hovered in the background, rumbling his anxieties in the form of questions.

"Did they charge you? Have you to go to court?"

Michael shook his head painfully and Mary headed off any more queries by grabbing him round the waist and helping him into his room. "Stop it, will you," she shrilled at Duggan and Moira. "Can't you see what they've done to him? Let's just get him to bed so he can rest, the poor wee lad."

She managed well enough by herself, and the other two retreated as she began undressing him. When she got to his trousers he showed some reluctance and the old Mary reasserted herself.

"Come on, now. I've seen bigger things than that between two slices of bread," she said. Despite the pain he chuckled as he tried to work out the significance of the remark.

She bathed his cuts and bruises, tucked him in bed and reassured him when he woke from a sleep troubled by the dream. In the evening, rested and already feeling better, he played cards with her and listened to her gossip about the family, and how she was saving up to go back home and start a restaurant. But as the evening wore on he began to feel dizzy and stiff again. Anxiously, she lifted him to her while she straightened the pillows and he closed his eyes with a sigh as he felt his head press into her full breasts. When she went to lower him he held on to her tightly. She smiled as she cradled him to her and settled down on the bed beside him.

There were no dreams as he slept this time, vaguely conscious of the womanly form close to him, feeling warm and safe, clasped close to her. In a little while she slept too. She was asleep when he woke. He could hear her breathing softly beside him. He reached for her. She looked almost beautiful, her soft brown hair spread on the pillow. He struggled upright, leant over and kissed her. She moaned softly awake, protested mildly. "Michael, you can't. You're hurt. You . . ." He silenced her with his mouth and when next he released her lips she whispered: "Hold me, Michael. I'm cold."

CHAPTER XIV

It was the Black Irishman who woke in the morning as the weight of a warm plump body made the bed creak once more and a pair of moist lips pressed on his. Mary Duggan had to go away "to feed the starving English", leaving him to gloat over his triumphs. "The wildest of the wild boys," O'Brien had said all those years ago, when he told a group of village lads about the legend. And in a little more than a week, Michael told himself gleefully, he had scored a victory over the Brits by getting past the Customs at Holyhead, where other members of The Movement had failed; he had sacrificed himself against overwhelming odds to protect a woman; and had ended with another triumph, a fitting reward after his other achievements. There would never be another morning quite like it for him, though he wouldn't have believed it at the time.

He had also learned first contempt and then hatred for the English – he had taken the first step on an endless downward spiral.

A faint scratching at the door about an hour after Mary left began to bring him back to reality. Moira poked her head round the door and, with an anxious twitch, tossed a small brown envelope onto the nearest chair. "It's for you," she whispered.

It was a telegram, and he felt a twinge of anxiety as soon as he saw it, even though he realised immediately what it must be. "Return immediately, mother needs you," was the message. It was the sentence he and Fallon had agreed before he left Dublin. It meant that he was to report as soon as possible. Going back – and what would his mother have said about his triumphs? What would Tina have said? But he hadn't long to waste on guilt. "Immediately," the telegram said, and would the Black Irishman, that furious fighter and swashbuckling conqueror of women's hearts, have wasted time on remorse after one of his conquests? Michael packed hurriedly. He thought about leaving a note for Mary. But, after chewing a pen and staring at a blank sheet of paper for some minutes, he found he couldn't resolve the problem of what to say to her.

It would have seemed odd, after all, to write: "Recalled to Dublin, Love, Michael." It was also doubtful whether he should put anything on paper about his orders. And he couldn't say: "Thanks for everything." He could imagine her sharp-tongued fury if he did.

The trip from Kilburn to Euston seemed a lot more simple this time than it had when he arrived, and there were no predatory London girls to enliven it with blow-by-blow accounts of encounters with their boy-friends. He would have found it difficult to respond to, or get excited by, the wriggling buttocks, in any case. His bruises were still painfully stiff and after a night in Mary Duggan's arms his libido was temporarily stilled.

The journey from Euston to Holyhead was also dull, with no frightening new case to keep him on the edge of his seat, and only the sodden winter countryside of England to bid for his attention. He read and dozed until he reached Holyhead. Even then, with no reason for an additional *frisson* of fear, Michael yawned his way onto the ferry after a careful tour of inspection of the railhead.

The ferry crossing was less agonising than its predecessor, though Michael's stomach registered the first lurch of the boat as it pulled away from the dock. Wearily and palely, he stumbled to his feet and hurried to hide himself away for the rest of the journey. But the action of his stomach didn't still his mind. There was a lot to think about.

He was glad to feel solid unmoving land again when he arrived at Dun Laoghaire. But the train also swayed as it chugged into the city. So he was still pale and wobbly when he went to report.

It wasn't a place to be wobbly, though. Here the greeting was completely different from the one he had received in Kilburn.

This was a true Irish house, alive and lived in and full of noisy folk. There were lights on and people were moving about behind the blinds. And, when he rang the bell, the door was flung open as if he was expected and welcome.

A stranger was at the door. But he was smiling broadly. "Come in, Michael, and well done," he said. Others were coming out to shake his hand, fling their arms round his shoulders and congratulate him. Including Fallon – and Michael let him see his reluctance to take the offered hand. And including Cathal Linane. Michael took *his* offered hand timidly, though, for once, his mentor seemed almost enthusiastic. "Good lad," he said simply, and Michael felt like a dog that had been patted and praised.

To the others Linane said: "I think we'd better give the boy a cup of tea and then hear his report as soon as possible. He doesn't look like someone who enjoys the bracing qualities of sea travel." There was an immediate laugh and someone hurried to get tea while Michael was ushered to a chair.

They listened intently to what he had to say about his trip, and about how he had beaten the Customs at Holyhead. There were some exclamations of delight and more congratulations, but Linane cut them short with an impatient gesture. Michael noted the frown and then let his eyes travel to meet those of Fallon. The big man was smiling as usual. "Damn him," thought Michael. "He could have ruined the whole operation."

Aloud he said: "It's nice of you to congratulate me, but I was just lucky. If we are to send more messages and loads of goods, we have to do more than rely on luck and spur-of-the-moment decisions. We have to plan." The smiles were fading – especially Fallon's – and he could see that the men around him were beginning to resent him, a mere boy, telling them their business. Recklessly he plunged on. He wanted them to know what he thought. "It's no use just sending people off to be caught at Holyhead and lose valuable materials. We must not just plunge them in, like you did with me, and hope they succeed. We must prepare them, tell them what to do to get past the Customs, and what to do if they arouse suspicion."

Fallon's face was like thunder and he was on his feet shouting before Michael had finished. "Ten minutes in The Movement and already the boy's lecturing us," he roared. "Telling me what I should have done. When I . . ."

"And he's damned well right, Jack," cut in Linane. "It *was* ridiculous. It *was* unplanned and it *was* only a stroke of quick thinking that got him through. He's been to Holyhead. He's made his delivery. At least we ought to listen to him." Fallon was still standing.

"For God's sake sit down, Jack, you look as if you've been taken short in your trousers," added Linane.

The others laughed and Fallon subsided. Linane fixed Michael with his cold eyes now. "You'd better tell us what you think we ought to do," he said dryly. The message was clear — put up or shut up.

Michael nodded. He couldn't speak for a moment. His heart was beating like a steam-hammer and he could feel that his face was flame-red. His mouth was suddenly dry. But his mind was clear. His hours locked in the lavatory on the ferry from Holyhead had not all been wasted. He coughed and took a swallow of the tea that was rapidly cooling in the cup beside him.

"First," and his voice sounded unnaturally high to him, "there are some other things I think we ought not do – apart from sending people unprepared into the lion's den." He caught Linane's cold blue eyes and saw there an intent look, as if the man were willing him to put his point over. "We shouldn't give them new shiny cases with obvious false bottoms and we shouldn't waste trips like the one I've just made to carry such small loads . . ."

"That's what we shouldn't do. How about telling us what we should do, while you're about it?" snapped Fallon.

"Jack, Jack," remonstrated Linane. "Let's hear what he has to say. It's more likely to be useful than you sitting there sulking."

As Fallon made to respond the man who had opened the door to Michael banged on the table.

"Order, please," he shouted. "Will you all stop squabbling and let's hear this report. Go on please, Michael. Take your time and don't feel nervous." He too glared at Fallon.

Michael did as he was bid. He swallowed another mouthful

of tea and started again – in a lower voice. "Well, the worst thing to me was not knowing where anything was at the other end. I think we ought to give every messenger a detailed plan of the layout of Holyhead – Dun Laoghaire as well, I suppose, though it's not so important."

"Don't you believe it, lad," interjected another of the group. "They'll be working with the Brits again, just like they did in '56."

The interruption didn't put Michael off. He was caught up in his ideas now. "I think future messengers should carry stuff in body-belts under their clothes instead of in cases, which are the first thing the Customs look at and the most obvious. You could get quite a lot in bags down your trousers." There were delighted hoots from the more uninhibited members of the committee, but he went on: "I think we should also use girls as messengers. The Customs are less likely to suspect them and they can conceal more . . ."

The noise reached a crescendo as nearly everyone but the chairman and Linane joined in the competition to make his own joke heard.

"You should send my girl-friend," roared one. "She's got dynamite in her knickers and her bra would carry a ton of jelly."

"It already does," cracked another.

"What would happen if you'd got a bomb down your trousers and it exploded?" demanded one grinning member.

"It would be a balls-up," said Linane drily. "And that's what this meeting's becoming. I've not heard anything yet from the boy that's even the remotest bit daft. It's all damn good sense. I think we ought to hear some more and not behave like a pack of kids as soon as he mentions trousers or girls."

The chairman banged on the table again. "Cathal's right," he ruled. "Let's hear the boy out, like I said just now."

Michael felt surprisingly calm as he started up again. "There are just one or two things more for the moment, though I'd like to think about it a little longer, and maybe come up with some other ideas. I'm serious about sending girls as messengers, though. I also think we should switch the messengers around as much as possible, so that the Customs men don't begin to recognise them. We should recruit teams of them, and give them as much preparation as possible before sending them off.

"But that's only the first stage. Messengers are only good for carrying small loads, and their fares must be balanced against the amount of material they deliver. I was looking at the lorries going over on the ferry. Their drivers are Irishmen. Some of them would surely be willing to help. Perhaps they wouldn't even need to know they're helping. A few packs of stuff inside an oil tanker in plastic packages, an extra box in the back of a sealed refrigerator lorry or an extra carcase or two, already stuffed, in the meat waggons. The lorries stop on quiet roads in Wales and while the drivers sleep someone removes the bits and pieces we've added to the load."

There were some knowing looks and nodding heads among the committee members as Michael continued: "That again is only a short-term measure. What we have to do in the next few weeks is prepare our own lorries and tankers. A properly fitted tanker could carry men and guns even and be driven by our own drivers."

He could hear the murmur of voices already beginning to discuss his ideas. He could sense the general approval of the men around him. He looked at Fallon and the big man, smiling again, gave him a nod and a wink. But the ideas were welling up and spilling over. He wanted to go on.

"That's only using the ferries," he said excitedly. "Once we get those moving we can look at the boats and the airlines. There's no way the Brits can stop things getting into their country the easy way, via the docks . . ."

"The only thing stopping us sending a mountain of material to England is that we haven't a mountain to send and the main war is in the North," Linane said drily. He smiled then to make it right with Michael for cutting him down and added: "Not that we don't need such sensible thinking and forward planning – only that we have to walk before we can run. Now, Michael, and this is picking up one of your earlier suggestions, I believe, could you draw a plan of Holyhead, showing Customs, police, the station and the surrounds?"

"I think I could, though it wouldn't be in scale detail," replied Michael.

"That's good," said Linane soothingly. "Now, why don't you go into the next room – you'll find some paper and pens on the desk – and do just that, while the committee discusses your ideas and a few more things."

Michael went, as he was told, to draw his plan. Just a rough sketch, they'd said, and, since Michael knew his artistic limitations, that was all he did. He bent his head low over it to check it and the lines undulated. He yawned. His ribs still ached. He hadn't slept much in the last few nights and then there had been the horrors of the sea-crossing. He congratulated himself on the apparent acceptance of his plan to recruit other messengers. That would mean that in future he would have only an occasional ferry-trip to make. He lowered his head onto his hands and closed his eyes. This was one time he did not dream . . .

It was almost dark in the room when he awoke with a start. It took him a few moments to remember where he was, and a few more for his eyes to begin to adjust to the gloom . . . the table before him, the lamp on the other side from him, the armchair by the fireside . . . he felt the back of his neck tingle as the dark shape in it moved slowly.

"Who's there . . . ?" he asked anxiously.

He wasn't completely relieved when the head of the shadow swung to look at him and Linane's thin voice said: "Ah, awake at last."

He sat in silence for a moment then asked: "How long did I sleep?" It wasn't important but it was something to say.

"I've no idea," replied Linane. It wasn't his sort of question and his reply might as well have been: "Do you expect me to care?"

The silence returned. Even in the darkness Michael was aware that Linane was thinking about what he wanted to say and that what he wanted was important.

"The others have gone," he said after a time. "They liked your report and the drawing, though they think you should go back to fill in more details . . ." Michael peered at the desk and noted that his sketch had disappeared.

"I think that's a good idea, too. Not immediately, but pretty soon," Linane added, and then paused again.

Michael nodded – and realised that in the darkness that was a stupid thing to do. He didn't turn the nod into a spoken acceptance, though. He knew that what Linane had said had only been in the nature of a footnote to a learned work. He just waited for the turn of the page so that he could read on.

Outside, above the distant rumble of Dublin traffic, a bird returning from its foraging twittered a welcome or a warning as it settled down to roost for the night. The silence returned for a moment and then it was shattered by the roar of a jet airliner flying overhead. As it ended Linane spoke again, his voice soft like the rustle of parchment in the darkness.

"They want you to go back just the once. Then they think you should recruit some more messengers as you suggested and get the whole delivery thing between here and Britain sorted out. So do I, I suppose . . . for now," he paused again, as if to underline the last two words. Then he went on, speaking quickly and carefully. "But I want that nonsense all settled even more quickly than they do.

"I don't want you to spend too much time lounging about Dublin getting bored and losing your usefulness. I don't want you to stay too long in Britain. I want you to get it right first time. I've more important things for you to do. God knows there are few enough with brains I can trust. I want you out of all this in months and up north, where you should be."

He slowed the rattle of words only enough to add extra emphasis as he went on: "And I want you to understand that you take your orders from me, report to me and me alone. You want to win this war. I want to win it the right way. I don't want it to be just another victory for the rich landowners and factory bosses. I want, for the first time, a victory for the people of Ireland."

Michael frowned through the darkness, trying to understand the strange things the man was saying in his intent mumble. "But the Council . . . ?" he said in a sort of question.

Michael could almost feel the burning stare of Linane's pale eyes – even in the darkness. He could see the tense question-mark of his mentor's pose in the armchair.

"Council," the tone was mocking. "Let me tell you about the

Council. There are some who just missed the last fight and have regretted it ever since because it was a good fight – and there's nothing a certain type of Irishman likes better than 'a good fight and we'll all shake hands afterwards and nothing's changed'. You heard them in there with their street-corner jokes and jollities. God help them, the fools.

"And there's some who dream of getting the Brits out of 'auld Ireland' and being sung about in the ballads of the future as great heroes.

"And there's one or two who think just a little bit further and recall the old turncoat Eamon De Valera, the President who was like a king but started out as a peasant. They can see themselves standing in his shoes.

"And there's some who serve another master altogether, a master who isn't Irish or Brit. Some fella from a long way off across the ocean, who wouldn't mind if the Brits took a hammering, even though they're supposed to be his friends, as long as he had a say in the way things were run when they left.

"No, my lad, you can't serve the Council. Because there is no Council. Just a bunch of private armies, all with different policies. If we get rid of the Brits, that will be when the war really starts. I want you to serve me, to be part of my war for a different Ireland when we've got rid of the old enemy. I want you to be my eyes and my ears wherever you go – and my right arm when we discover the traitors. I want to win that war too. I want to fill the new all-Ireland Dail with people who care about people – not just two dreary sets of representatives of the same old order of imitation-English squires from a century ago. Even in England they have two parties that represent slightly differing points of views and pay at least lip-service to the people."

Michael wasn't sure he understood all that Linane was saying, but he found himself nodding again and again, pointlessly in the darkness, as the strange, cold passion of the man got through to him and stirred him. Linane wasn't asking him to join his private army, he was telling him that he was conscripted and had no choice. Michael accepted the little man's mastery as if there were no alternative. He could think of nothing else to say but "Yes".

Linane sat up abruptly and switched on the table-lamp. The spell was broken. "Can't think why we're sitting here in the dark," he said. There was a faint smile on his thin lips and a hint of colour in his sallow cheeks. He leant back in his chair and gazed into the fireplace, as if deliberately easing the tension.

"You'll want to go home for a day or so, I suppose?" he asked, and his voice was no longer compelling. "Well, maybe you should start tomorrow. But don't tell too many people what you've been doing, and don't bring back too many. After that it will be full speed ahead."

Michael nodded again. "OK," said Linane. "Now you'll want to clean yourself up and come with me to get something to eat. We're supposed to be meeting Fallon in an hour at some new restaurant he's discovered. He's a great man for eating and drinking, a great charmer. He's a good friend of mine too . . . so he says." And suddenly the chat had gone cold.

Michael didn't know why. At this stage, he was too caught up in the excitement of the things to come to register the chill with anything more than a flicker of a frown. He was to go into action soon. He was needed up north. And first he was to go home for a few days. He would see Tina again – earlier than he had expected. He might even be able to recruit her and Sean to his messenger teams. And, of course, he would see his mother.

There was little in the meal with Fallon to disturb his joy. Linane greeted Fallon like a good old friend, despite the things he had said earlier – and Michael began to wonder if he had heard correctly. Fallon, sulks and anger apparently forgotten, was a jovial and helpful host, guiding Michael through the unfamiliar eating-out rituals so unobtrusively that he never had to feel embarrassed. The only indication that there had been any trouble between them came at the start of the meal. As Fallon peered at the wine list, Linane said: "Don't worry about that, Jack, I'll just have a bottle of beer." "So will I," said Michael. Fallon paused only for a second in his perusal. Grinning broadly he told them: "Sorry, I'm not letting you gang up on me again. This time I'm in charge. And you can't celebrate a great success in tepid bottled beer." He ordered something that sounded incomprehensible to Michael, but tasted better than it sounded. Nothing more was said about the earlier battle and bad temper. Michael might almost have believed that that and the things Linane had hinted at about Fallon were just some wild fantasy in his own mind if he had not walked back to the meeting house alone with the thin man.

They walked in silence at first. Then, "Nice meal," said Linane (Michael sensed that he wasn't supposed to answer or comment), "I just wish I hadn't felt as if I was shaking hands with the devil, or that, like Titus Andronicus' missus, I might lift a tureen-cover and find the heads of my sons – if I had any."

He made the remarks almost as if he was soliloquising. But then he stopped suddenly, and in the dim light of the street lamps Michael could see his intense, almost theatrically agonised expression. "Damn it, you can't see, and I shouldn't be talking to you like this. That man is my friend. And yet there's something wrong between us – enough to make me scent trouble, perhaps even before it's there. Michael, I know he's up to some sort of treachery. Watch him for me – watch him for yourself. Tell him nothing I tell you, pass on none of your orders or instructions. Let me know what he says to you; what he tries to find out; what you find out about where he goes and whom he meets."

Linane stopped abruptly and then, uncharacteristically, punched a fist into the opposite palm. "That's it," he said. "When your messengers are organised and they aren't rushing to and from Britain they can watch Fallon. In shifts, changing regularly so that he doesn't begin to recognise them. Two at a time, reporting everything he does and everyone he meets. He's sure to slip up, sure to . . ."

Only then did he notice the horror in Michael's expression. Michael had felt the cold shivers begin to run down his spine as soon as Linane started on the patently hypocritical line about Fallon being his friend. Caught up in his new ideas about using Michael and the messengers as a private spy network, Linane had not spotted his protégé's change of attitude. He smiled and put a placatory arm round the boy's shoulders. Michael wanted to pull away, but instinctively knew better than to antagonise his master.

"Sure now, you're worried. It's not sporting and all that.

He – being me – should talk to Fallon, his friend, about it, man to man . . . except this isn't a boy's comic or a tale of the Knights of St John. This is a war . . . and a dirty bloody war. If Fallon is doing what I think – and I won't tell you what it is for the moment – the last thing to do is warn him and put him on his guard . . ."

"And what if you find out something about Fallon to prove you are right?" asked Michael truculently.

"Then I shall know, me boy," said Linane, nodding wisely.

Not for the first time, Michael wondered about the unexpected theatricality of Linane. Here he was, a cold unemotional man, with his arm about his shoulders, nodding and winking and putting on a ferociously fake Irish accent, as he did when he tried to impress with his sincerity. Michael would have laughed – but what they were talking about was no laughing matter.

"But what will you do?" Michael persisted.

"Knowing is a lot. Feeding false information or no information of any value to the spy is a lot more. Finding his contacts, informants and helpers would also be useful. This is war, lad, and to win it we must be as ruthless as the enemy and the people who want to dabble in our war for their own ends. It's most important to know. If you want to help me win this war, this could be your chance to make a real contribution."

"And what if Fallon is not 'up to something'?"

"An extra bonus for our side. Fallon's got a head on his shoulders despite the laughing-boy act. I'd be very grateful if you were to find out that he was really on our side, of that I can assure you."

Michael nodded – even while he told himself: "But not nearly as grateful as if we found out he was not. You've decided and you mean to prove it." At the same time Michael wondered at his own cynicism. He was learning the adult world too fast. You said one thing, thought another and did something else altogether. He would have liked to have protested. But Linane was not a man to oppose.

It was also true that, if Fallon was a spy inside The Movement, detection and rendering him harmless was vital. Michael joined the grown-ups. It was his first surrender. He would never see it that way, of course, but he had just turned his back on the memorial in the village square.

So he just nodded again. "I would be able to start that pretty soon," he said. He watched Linane's face. The thin lips twitched into a smile, but there was a new watchfulness in the eyes, as if he had caught on to the vibrations of some of Michael's ideas and suspected that he was not being totally frank. Maybe he had surrendered too soon and too easily.

"I know you won't let me down," said Linane.

They walked on, Linane's arm still about his shoulders.

CHAPTER XV

But next morning all the intricacies of spies and counter-spies were forgotten as Michael set off for home.

"Give my love to Tina," Fallon called to him gaily at the coach-station as he waved him away.

And, briefly, as he warmed again to the man, Michael felt bad about the unofficial side of his mission. That was all in the distant future though. Now was the girl he loved, whose name Fallon had so cleverly remembered. The past and another girl called Mary were sunk without trace.

In Tina's arms that night, when they eventually escaped her family and his oddly cool and undemonstrative mother, he even forgot about being the Black Irishman. He was just a gentle, considerate lover, returned from a perilous journey – eager but not aggressive. As if by consent they walked to their first hideaway at the back of the church – and the old stones would have shuddered, if they had been able, at the innocence of their lust. They kissed and loved until it was very late and the walk home seemed a long way. Then Michael spoke about his mother.

"Why is she so . . . queer?" He struggled for the right word to sum up the coldness he couldn't understand. They had never been devoted and demonstrative like other families. But this time his mother had been icily distant. Her biggest emotional display so far had been in opening the front door to him when he knocked. Mrs Foley had wept and hugged him; Tina had literally bounced with excitement; Uncle Gerald had grinned broadly all the time and couldn't be prevented from singing the first six verses of some ancient song about a returning hero; the boys ran about, yelling louder and louder; Sean and Liam

Barry had appeared as if by magic, slapped him on the back, asked how was his uncle in Britain and started in with all the gossip. But his mother had just gone about making tea and serving cake as if nothing had happened.

Tina didn't need him to use the right words. She had seen for herself and had also noticed Michael's reaction. Now, assured and reassured of his love – or so she thought – she asked: "And do you think it's so different to the way it always was?"

"What do you mean?" he protested. But it was not a strong protest. He was remembering. And, yes, in those days before the so-recent dawn of growing-up there hadn't been a great deal of affection. There had never seemed to be time for it. There was always so much of the routine of food and clean clothes and school and homework. He couldn't remember if his mother had ever kissed him. He thought perhaps she never had.

When they walked back, their fingertips brushing as their arms swung, Michael told Tina of the Council's plan for the teams of messengers.

She stopped walking then . . . waiting. He said no more.

"You mean you want me to join?" she asked at last.

"I mean it would be nice if you were to come to me in Dublin and maybe make a few token trips."

"I'm not sure I could do it, Michael. I'm not very brave."

"You wouldn't need to be brave about that. The bravest thing you'd have to do would be to tell your mother you were leaving home."

"No, I'll just tell her." Michael noted the change of tense. "But don't expect me to do anything too daring." She paused, and then her eyes twinkled and she seized his arm in hers and put it round her. "It'll be nice to be with you all the time." She tilted her head up and kissed him, still happy and feeling very daring and naughty. "I could get the Pill there and we could make love every night."

For a moment Michael had an image of a motherly figure saying to her small son: "And if you're a good boy, you can have a sweetie." But the image faded quickly as he returned her kiss.

For the remainder of his "leave", as he called his visit, he spent his days carefully sounding out the possible reactions of his friends to the messenger plan without revealing what he was really doing. Finally, he settled for asking only Sean to join him, and his most constant ally accepted.

Michael's nights were abandoned to much more hectic and less subtle pursuits as Tina and he explored the fields, hedgerows and barns in search of privacy, a state that is more often an illusion than a reality in a small town community, as the girl discovered when she finally broached to her mother the subject of her departure to Dublin. In her opening statement she was careful not to mention Michael. But her mother wasn't fooled so easily.

"Thank God for that," said Mrs Foley. "At least the two of you are serious and you won't stay on here with me wondering which of the local boys will take up where Michael left off. I can't see why you don't marry him. But then, I suppose what I think doesn't count. You young ones. You'd better not let your Daddy hear about it, though – if he hasn't already. One or two have told me about seeing the pair of you sneaking into Fitzgerald's field."

There was a lot more like that, with the occasional token protest from Tina.

"When will you go?" the mother asked finally. And Tina's heart leapt as she read in the question tacit acceptance of her plan.

"Two or three weeks from now."

But her enthusiasm was dampened by her mother's next words. "I'll have to get your father to agree though. So promise me you'll be more careful about what you get up to with the lad. If your Daddy hears the gossip he'll know why you want to go to Dublin and all you'll get is a leathering, a lecture and a visit from the priest. If he hears before Michael goes he'll probably tan his hide too . . . By the way, talking of the priest, what will you do about Confession on Sunday? If you don't go to Mass, Father Flynn will ask questions. If you confess to him first he'll give you a huge penance and he'll probably have words with your Daddy and Mrs Sullivan."

It had all seemed so simple behind the church or in the fields. She knew there that she loved Michael and wanted to be with him. What they were doing didn't seem very wrong at such times, and the hint of danger from the possibilities of discovery or pregnancy just added more excitement to the already overwhelming experience. But now the talk of her Daddy, the priest and Confession made her love seem dirty and crude. Suddenly there were tears in her eyes and the mother put her arms round her, to comfort her.

"Don't worry, my little one. Don't worry. I'll sort things out for you, don't fret. I'll get round your father. But you'll have to think of some way to avoid the priest."

She rocked her pretty young daughter against her ample bosom as if she were still a baby. Though her apron was damp, Tina nuzzled her head into it and felt safe.

She was still tearful when she met Michael though, and she burst into tears as he drew her into his arms, sobbing out her problems as he tried to kiss them away. Finally she stood away from him and moaned: "Michael, what are we going to do?"

"I can think of something," he said cheekily, nuzzling her ears.

She pulled the short hair at the back of his neck, lifting his head. "No, I mean about the priest and that. If my Daddy finds out he'll kill us and there'll be no trip to Dublin – probably for either of us."

"If he's killed us I suppose we won't go far," he chuckled. She reached down to punish him and they wrestled for a moment. "OK, OK, I give up," he gasped. "No. No. Look, if I tell you a way to get round the problem of the priest will you stop?" She looked up at him, all attention, and he took the chance to break away and run off a few paces.

"That's cheating," she said with a pout.

"I got away and so I don't have to keep to any old bargain," he jeered and put out his tongue – the committee in Dublin would have been hard put to recognise their earnest new subordinate, Linane would have wondered if he was going crazy to trust a face-pulling kid and Michael himself would have been ashamed at the loss of his new grown-up status if he had thought about his actions.

Tina advanced menacingly towards him. "Right then, my boy. First I'm going to beat hell out of you and then I'll go to Confession and tell Father Flynn that you forced me to make love with you the first time and have been blackmailing me to continue ever since." But suddenly it stopped being a joke and she felt the tears welling again.

Michael was beside her in a flash with his arms about her. "What's wrong?" he asked anxiously. "Come on. It's not so bad and I really do know how you can get round the problem of Confession."

"It's not that . . . It's just all the scheming and lying and pretending to cover up – and I don't want to cover up. I want to shout loud: 'I'm Michael Sullivan's girl and I'm going to live in Dublin with him.' Why have I got to feel dirty and bad?"

"You're not, you know you're not," said Michael.

"Am I so awful, Michael, to let you make love to me?"

"You're not awful . . . You're not awful," he said. "But I do know what you can do about the priest. You just go up to the school on Saturday morning and ask to speak to Father Hodgson, the English Priest. You say to him that you are so worried about something that has been happening that you want to make an immediate Confession. He may grumble about it a bit, but if you then say you don't want to make this Confession to Father Flynn because he's too close to your family, he's sure to hear you."

"I thought you didn't like Father Hodgson because he's so spiteful about the Irish," she argued.

"I don't and he is. But that will also work for us. He'll enjoy the idea that you don't entirely trust Father Flynn – and that you're right not to. He'll also be delighted when you tell him that I'm the one who has led you into sin. It will confirm all the bad things he has thought about me, particularly since I left school and ruined his plans for me to go to Dublin for higher education."

"That's marvellous, Michael," said Tina admiringly. "And did you just think all that out?"

"Yes," he said with a mock-modest air. "All by myself. Sean told me Mary Malone did the same when she first went with a boy."

"You haven't been talking to Sean about us, have you?" demanded Tina indignantly, and Michael put his arms up, as if to defend himself from her fury.

"What do you think I am?" he answered. "Of course I don't talk about you to him. He told me about it months ago."

Pause for reconciliatory kisses. Then Tina asked: "Why must I go to him on Saturday?"

"It's the day before Sunday, of course." Seeing the slight movement of her fist clenching, he went on hurriedly: "It's also the day the English Priest is free and there – and I shall not be."

"You mean . . ."

"I mean I have to go back to Dublin on Saturday. I was intending to tell you. So you won't have to make a false Confession. You'll be able to tell him, nearly honestly, that you don't intend to do it again, because you won't know when you'll see me."

Then, catching an anxious look in her eyes, he shook his head sadly. "Tina . . . You know damn well you're coming to me in Dublin. I've told you I just need a few days to find somewhere to stay and to sort out a few things. I'm not my father." He was angrier than he had expected – or the moment of doubt deserved. Tina bit her lip and, though she understood, felt the flash of answering anger in her.

They walked home in irritable silence soon afterwards. "Sorry," he muttered as they stood by her door. But it lacked conviction. However, since they were young, the anger between them was not to last. When they met again next day it was as if nothing had happened. And when he left on the Saturday there was no thought in his or Tina's mind that he might not send for her.

She waved goodbye to him. Then she tidied herself and walked to the school. She found Father Hodgson unexpectedly in the gymnasium. He was not in the anticipated pious pose. He was sitting with sleeves rolled and jacket discarded, scrubbing at some item of sports equipment with a brush and with an open tin of leather-wax on the floor in front of him. His thin face was flushed and his even thinner hair was fluffed round his balding head like that of a baby vulture. He hadn't heard her approaching because he was deeply immersed in his task and whistling tunelessly between his teeth. He looked up, startled. For a moment they shared confusion.

He recovered first and nodded to the bench opposite. "Tina

Foley, isn't it?" He didn't wait for her reply. "I wasn't absolutely sure. But then, I've not had much to do with the girls' school or the village either, I suppose. Pity, I won't get the chance now . . . Or is it?" He was recovering his more normal approach to the isolation and strangeness he had been made to feel in the village. He surveyed the leather ball he had been working on and then flung it down. "Irish mud seems to have a special clinging quality, sticks like glue. Maybe they should export it." He smiled his thin smile. "Don't see why not. It's not as silly as burning it. The only people in the world who have been working systematically down the centuries at burning their country." Seeing her puzzled expression, he explained: "Peat, peat. Makes Stalin's scorched-earth policy look juvenile." He sighed, and Tina wasn't sure whether she should laugh or react indignantly. She compromised with a look of blank expectancy.

"Anyway," he went on, "what can I do for you? You didn't come to hear me make bad jokes at your country's expense – or to gaze at me admiringly while I try to add a few more weeks' life to the battered and ill-used sports gear of this penurious establishment." He raised his head and gazed questioningly at her.

Even though his cold blue eyes stared at her steadily, she couldn't share the awe of him that his boys felt. She smiled. "I wonder if you will hear my Confession please, Father?"

He looked startled. "Surely that's something for your parish priest . . ." he began. Then he put a hand up and scratched his head, trying to hide a faint smile. "Have you been talking to Mary Malone, by any chance?" he asked sharply.

"No, Father," she protested. "It's just that I wanted to confess urgently." She remembered what Michael had told her to say. "I've been so worried about what I've been doing wrong. And I didn't want to make this Confession to Father Flynn because it would be like talking to a member of the family. I'd be too embarrassed."

The priest eyed her narrowly for a few moments. He sighed again. "You Irish. A terrible people you are, an' all. Charm the birds out of the trees, so you would."

Tina was again puzzled about how to react to his mock-Irish

accent and what must have been a joke. But he was reaching for his jacket. It could be a good sign.

Then he stopped with his jacket in his hand. "You're sure you haven't been talking to Mary?" She shook her head vigorously. He seemed satisfied.

"Right, follow me. And if you speak a word of this to another soul," he added in a sepulchral voice, "may St Theresa blow out all your candles." She still wasn't sure whether she should laugh.

He pulled a face and shrugged in parodied despair, muttered something about saving her poor ignorant Irish soul and strode off towards the chapel, with her scampering to keep up with him.

If the lead-up to it was bizarre, the Confession was even more so. After the usual preliminaries, through which he yawned, he demanded suddenly: "So, what is this terrible sin that can't wait until tomorrow, and which you suspect poor old Father Flynn will rush around gossiping about?"

Tina gawped. "Come on. Come on, girl," Father Hodgson urged. "How many times? Who was the boy? It's a pretty common sort of sin, you know. Half the world's at it and the other half is thinking about it – and we think humanity has progressed from the apes. It's hard to believe – especially in this benighted swamp of a country."

Terrified, Tina began all over again: "Father, forgive me for I have sinned . . ."

"Yes, I know. That's what we're here for – and we did all that."

"I have committed the sin of fornication," . . . she had rehearsed carefully in her mind what she would say.

"I realise that. So has everyone else but me and a couple of other priests who take our vows seriously. I've already asked how many times and who was the boy."

Tina was so hot she thought she would suffocate or burst into tears. But she dared not do either with the little priest there, just behind the screen. She could imagine the piercing blue eyes glinting and the cynical grin on the thin lips.

In a tiny voice she replied: "I think it's eight times and the boy is Michael Sullivan . . ."

"Speak up..." he roared. Then, more conversationally: "The young rogue. Where is he now?"

"Dublin," she answered without thinking.

"And still dreaming of driving the English out of Ireland, no doubt. He's too intelligent to be such a fool. Ah well. Three Hail Mary's and ask the young villain why he didn't come and see me during his visit to the village. You can also tell him from me I'll be in Belfast before him. I'm being transferred to the North in a week or so. If he gets there, tell him to look me up."

"Belfast," she gasped and then remembered where she was and completed her Act of Contrition.

After a pause, Father Hodgson mumbled a quick blessing. She heard him leave the box and walk away. It had been strange, but she couldn't imagine why Michael hated the little man so much, for as she left the school chapel she realised that her Confession had been so odd because the English Priest had been at least as embarrassed as she.

She wondered if he and Michael would eventually meet in Belfast. She smiled at the thought. She wouldn't have done so if she had known how the two men were to meet...

CHAPTER XVI

So Michael, Tina and Sean went to Dublin to form the nucleus of a special team with – as far as most of the committee were concerned – a limited number of objectives and an unclear future. It had been a good selling job by Linane, who had a clearer view of what he wanted from his "country cousins".

And they started off according to their brief. They made a number of messenger trips – though never again to the house in Kilburn. Michael prepared detailed drawings of all the main entry ports in England, and he and Sean began to establish a string of safe houses and contacts there.

When they were not travelling they were happy in the place they called home. They were like a small family. Michael and Sean both worked, starting out early in the mornings for their part-time jobs at firms run by sympathisers of The Movement. Tina played at being a housewife. And for her, if the days were boring, the evenings were a joy, as they all sat round the television or shared drinks and a lot of laughs. The best time of all was when she and Michael said goodnight to Sean and retired to their room with its big brass bed. She could lie in Michael's arms and love him and go to sleep with her lips an inch from his. The only faint shadow over her sky-blue life was that Michael always had a hundred reasons why he could not discuss the wedding. She didn't mention it often; there seemed no hurry and they were happy.

Michael also had few bad moments. He was kept too busy.

But one came when he sent Tina to England alone for the first time. As soon as she started out for Dun Laoghaire, he began to fidget and worry. By the time the ferry was due to dock in Holyhead he was pacing the floor and unable to concentrate on anything but his fevered imaginings.

Tina had been taken at the docks. She had been dragged away for questioning by brutal British Special Branch men. They took her to a shed in the docks, stripped, tortured and raped her until she confessed all she knew. He pictured her tied to a chair, with a series of interrogators taking it in turn to torment her.

When it became clear that she had not been raped in the Customs shed at Holyhead his masochism found another nightmare. She arrived at the safe house he had directed her to in Birmingham and immediately fell in love with the landlord, a good-looking laughing fellow. Michael's fantasy of their love-making tortured him in his sleepless empty bed throughout one night, at his work next day and when he reached home again.

Though her expected coded message arrived that evening, he still couldn't relax. He paced as he pictured her lips meeting the landlord's for the thousandth time. There was nothing in the code to indicate that she wasn't enjoying a passionate encounter. She could be fiddling with the top button of the man's shirt now, in that teasing way of hers, gazing up into his eyes . . .

"For God's sake, Michael, will you settle down," said Sean in desperation. You're as twitchy as a mouse in a cage. Up and down; up and down. I swear I'll scream and cut your throat if you pace the floor just one more time."

Michael shrugged, grinning foolishly in his surprise that someone had noticed his agitation. "I just can't help worrying," he explained lamely.

Sean stared pointedly at the telegram on the table between them. "Look, if that girl can face her mother and the English Priest in the same week and still get her own way, she's more than an equal for the bloody Brits. Come on, now. She's all right. You'll see her again in three days." He nodded towards the television set. "Normal transmission will be resumed after a short interval, God help the silly cow. Can't think what she sees in you or why she's running around after you, when she could move in with a handsome young feller like me." He ducked the bread roll Michael flung at him. "Sure and maybe I'll even offer to make an honest woman of her, since you don't seem to be doing anything about it. That'll win her . . . ugh."

He grunted as Michael's fist thudded into his ribs, covered up and crouched. They sparred for a few seconds until Michael jumped back with a yell holding his groin. "You're a dirty fighter, McDade," he yelled.

"That's right. And I have to be, with sneaky fellers creeping up on me while I'm giving them sound advice and all."

They grappled again, wrestling this time, collapsing to the floor in a flail of arms and legs, until they crashed against the table and brought it down on top of them with knives, forks and the debris of their last half-dozen meals.

"Oh God. You're a destructive bugger, Sean," growled Michael, disentangling himself from the rubble.

"Well, I'm in the right organisation then," countered Sean.

He reached out to a dark spot on the rug in front of the fire, dipped a finger in it and licked, mock-speculatively.

"Ah, it's OK. It's jam. I thought for a minute there you might have wet yourself out of fear of the furious McDade." He grinned broadly. "Do you want me to help you to your feet? I might have been a bit too rough for you."

Michael surveyed the wreckage dismally. "Herself will go crazy when she sees this," he said.

"It's all right, Michael. You've got three days to clear it up, if you don't go barmy first. That's if she comes back at all to a slob like you. And I can always tell her you didn't mean it, but that you went wild with passion when you got those three sexy young birds home and had to . . . have . . . them . . . one by one on the table."

The pauses were to catch his breath as he dodged some of Michael's next fusillade of stomach-punches. But suddenly Michael gazed into the fire and the shadows descended on his face. "I hope she is all right," he said. He had just pictured Tina mock fighting with a good-looking laughing fellow in Birmingham.

"Oh Christ. Not that again," growled Sean. "I thought we'd been through all that. Come on. Let's clear up." He gestured at the wreckage. "Then I'll take you round to Barney's and we'll have a drink or three. That'll make you forget – especially since you can't hold your liquor."

"OK. First one under the table at Barney's gets the girl," replied Michael slyly.

"You're on . . . No . . . Wait. Don't you mean last one under the table?"

"I know what I mean," said Michael, who also knew that there was more than a glimmer of truth in what his friend said about his capacity for booze. "And we've got a bargain. You agreed." He stopped suddenly, remembering. "But I thought you were supposed to be meeting some American girl you picked up?"

"I was, but it doesn't matter. I could do with a drink."

Michael looked at his friend in amazement for a second. "She must be an ugly old camel," he said. "I've never known you pass up the chance of a hit." Then he caught on. "Look, if it's for me, forget it. Go and meet your old camel – and don't blame me if it drops off after."

"No. Come on, Michael. I don't want to leave you alone like this."

Michael was touched by his friend's consideration but he couldn't accept the implication of charity. "Look, you go on. I'm all right, I tell you."

"I know," said Sean. "Why don't we just go and have a drink first, anyway? I can meet her later."

It seemed like a good compromise at the time.

In Barney's, Michael felt the creamy black drink warming and relaxing him – taking the sharp edges off the world. He felt the smile freeze on his face, as if his cheek muscles had seized up. He leant back in his chair and listened to Sean's voice, though he didn't bother to register much of what he was saying. But, after a couple of drinks, Michael realised that his friend was asking him something. He was going to telephone the American girl.

"I'll get her to bring her friend along. We can have a pleasant drink."

"Fine, fine," said Michael airily, willing to agree to anything.

Sean went away and returned. Then, it seemed only seconds

later, Michael was introduced to Helen and Lisa and found himself bowing with courtly grace over their small red hands, while they giggled and exchanged frantic eye-messages. The evening began to disintegrate over the next few glasses. Quite suddenly Michael found himself raging furiously at Lisa – she was the larger of the two girls, fair-haired and inclined to flush round the ears when she was irritated. Her ears were flushed. Michael didn't really notice as he tried to put the clear thoughts in his head into sensible words – and failed. So, to get his point over, he shouted.

"Of course no woman's the equal of a man. For God's sake, show us your muscles then. Come on! Let's put it to the test." He settled his elbow on the table, with his hand raised in the arm-wrestling position. "You're my equal. Show me."

Through the blur he saw the look of disgust she threw at the ceiling, the rest of the bar, her friend and Sean. "Oh Gahd. What is he . . . some sort of gorilla?" she moaned. "I don't need this."

"Michael. What are you doing? Why don't you cut it out?" Sean was snapping at his heels like a puppy. Helen, the other girl, pretty, slight and with hair nearly as black as his own, was anxiously plucking at his sleeve as if to attract his attention.

"You make me sick, the whole lot of you. Sick. The whole world makes me sick. Mongrels and moaners and yapping curs . . . Women who think they are men and men who are afraid to be men." He was standing now, swaying and looking down at them. He felt like a colossus among pygmies – a Black Irishman. "You disgust me, all of you, disgust me . . ." he roared and lurched away from the table. Someone was scrabbling after him . . . plucking at his sleeve . . . Like that girl, but he knew it wasn't her. He turned. "Get away from me, sheep," he bellowed and swung his fist as if to push the pursuer away. A red-head jerked on broad shoulders. Michael felt the jarring pain go through his hand and wrist. Then Sean was catapulting backwards onto the nearest table. Michael didn't care. He turned again and shambled to the door. He flung it wide and stood on the threshold swaying. He looked back and a small dark figure detached itself from the kaleidoscope of confused colours and shapes and glided towards him. He felt an arm on his waist. "Lean on me. Let me help you," a voice was saying softly but insistently.

"Don't need anyone . . ."

"Hush up now. I know that. Just a friendly hand."

"Don't need any . . ." he grumbled on and on as she guided him gently away from the noise and confusion into a mist, whispering, whispering and once, he thought, though he couldn't be sure, crying out sharply . . .

He woke suddenly. His head ached, his mouth felt cracked and dry and full of tongue, he was sweaty and every muscle ached. His stomach was bad too. He groaned, rolled over in the big bed . . . and felt a small figure beside him. Her arms went round him. "Are you all right?" she whispered her query. And why was she whispering when there wasn't anyone else around?

"No," he croaked. "I think I'm dying. Water." And, "Oh God, what is she doing here?" he thought. He felt the pressure of her arms ease as she lifted herself from him. She was naked too. Had he? He couldn't have in that state. Could he?

"If you're dying it's no more than you deserve," she said in a soft, serious way, so that he wasn't sure whether she was joking or not. "After what you did to poor little Sean – not to speak of what you did to me."

"I couldn't have," he told himself. To her he just groaned.

"I'll get you your water, though you don't deserve it, you wild Irishman." Now there was a definite hint of a laugh in her voice. "Then you can go and clean your teeth and use some talc or something before I get back into that bed with you. You smell like a brewery."

He did as he was told, feeling sheepish and still worried. That girl . . . his and Tina's bed. But he returned and was comforted by her arms and the gentle roundness of her.

She was gone when he awoke in terror, a red-haired figure leaning over him, shaking him and holding a huge carving-knife to his throat.

"Now it's my turn," snarled Sean – and Michael registered his friend's puffed and swollen eyes. Slowly Sean turned back the bedding, wrinkling his nose as he did so, and let the knife-point slide downwards an inch from Michael's body. "And now

I'm going to cut it off, you mad bastard, for what you did to me and to those poor girls."

Michael couldn't speak. His eyes watched, hypnotised, as the knife kept moving and the little piggy eyes, in their mounds of black, brown and blue swellings, glinted insanely. Sean let out a final wild cackle, lifted the hand holding the knife and then swung it down again. Michael closed his eyes and tensed, waiting for the bite of steel . . . and his friend whooped. "God, you should see your face! Thought your last hour had come, so you did."

Michael lay, letting the trembling stop, feeling the sweat cooling.

"I suppose I deserved that," he said finally, when he could trust his voice.

"I suppose you did," said Sean. But he was laughing still over the success of his joke. "And I was just getting used to the shape of me face when you decided to change it. Christ, that was a blow. I thought you'd broke me neck and all. Still it didn't do me any harm in the end. Very concerned about me was Lisa . . ." Michael groaned inwardly. He was about to hear the minutely-detailed account of another of Sean's conquests. He looked at his friend's rearranged features and sighed. After that, the least he could do would be to appear to listen.

"She just had to put me into her own 'little-old-bed' in the 'pensi-own' where she was staying and nurse me back to health, pillowing my poor sore head on her snowy white bosom. Very nice it was . . . the bosom. Only trouble was, just as I start taking a real interest she goes all stiff in me arms and says, 'I can't. No, I can't.' I was amazed . . ."

Blow-by-blow it was to be. Michael covered his eyes and stretched, only to roar with laughter as Sean went on: "It was the picture of Mary with the little red light shining on it. 'I can't,' she says, 'not with her looking at me.'"

Laughing hurt, decided Michael, and he tried to stop to sympathise with his friend. "All that," he pointed to the bruises, "and you still didn't get it."

"What d'you mean . . . didn't get it? 'Course I did."

"But how? You didn't drag her out onto the landing or something like that . . . ?"

"No. 'Twas easy. I just turned Mary's face to the wall. Should think so too. As a virgin she'd have glowed as red as her light if she'd seen what happened after that. Fantastic, it was . . ."

There was much more of the same, and Michael pretended to listen while he rehearsed his answer to the question that was sure to come sooner or later. What could he tell Sean? And, with Tina due back in a couple more days, what dare he tell him?

And there it was, the question he feared. "What about you? How did you get on?"

"God alone knows. I can't remember a thing. Must have gone out like a light. But she isn't here now."

Sean shook his head pityingly. "You don't remember a thing, eh?"

"No. Nothing."

"You're a poor hypocritical, lying thing, so you are, Michael Sullivan."

"Why?"

"I was in her room, remember, and she didn't get back there until but half an hour ago, looking like *she* knew what had happened to her. And then I came here and turned back the bedclothes. You're a terrible man, Michael Sullivan, with your own true love only two days gone into fearful danger. You put enough booze aboard you to sink a battleship – and that poor little thing. You could have injured her."

"Not such a little thing," smirked Michael.

"I thought you couldn't remember? What a liar you are. Anyway, you'd better get up if you're going to work today – not that you'll be much good to any boss after a night like that."

Michael was glad, then, that he had invited Sean to join his (and Linane's) private army. He wasn't so sure about it when Tina returned from her journey.

Sean tormented him by almost mentioning the night with the American girls in a dozen ways when Tina was with them.

"Thought I saw that little dark American, He. . .nry," he'd say, or, "They're asking down at Barney's about that nice little Yankee you pulled . . . on the second day of the Leopardstown races. How much did you win?"

Each time Michael had to splutter an answer while Sean went on to flirt outrageously with Tina, putting his arms round her or tickling her, until Michael was able to catch his eye and scowl or raise a clenched fist.

But the torment didn't last. There were more trips and then they had to begin recruiting for their team. Sean was especially keen on helping when they decided to find a couple more girls. And a whole group arrived unexpectedly from Northern Ireland.

It was a time of fun. The trips to England were an easy enough thing for them by now – like punctuation marks to make sense of it all. Michael didn't let his double dose of guilt interfere too long with the loving, carefree days with Tina.

But reality was marching along the roads of Ulster behind the banners of the Civil Rights marchers and in the gangs of Protestant bullies whipped up by Paisley and Craig to attack them. Reality was at its coldest in the frosty authoritarian words of the Unionist leaders about the Roman Catholics who were setting out to ruin Northern Ireland.

And it beckoned sharply to Michael when Linane summoned him to an urgent meeting. The little man seemed almost happy when he greeted Michael.

"The pot is coming to the boil nicely," he said. "Soon we'll be able to move in and give it a stir. So there's only a short time for what I want from you in Dublin before you go north."

Michael hoped it wasn't the instruction he had been dreading most since his meal with the little man and Fallon on his return from his first British trip. It seemed like a century earlier.

"You know what we discussed before you went home and started recruiting your motley army? I want to start on it now."

Michael looked blank, pretending not to understand.

It was not a game Linane was interested in. He ploughed straight on. "Apart from you, does Fallon know any of the others?" Michael still looked blank. "C'mon, boy, has the marital bliss, or whatever it is, addled your brain?"

"I was just thinking," said Michael sullenly.

"Look, Michael, we've discussed this before. This is war and war is not nice. If you want to win, you have to do things you don't like, that don't fit in with your own idea of the Queensberry Rules. You like Fallon. So, God help us, does everybody else. But I believe his circle of friends has just grown a wee bit too wide. We have to find out, and we don't do that by asking him."

The terrible thought struck Michael again. "And if we find out that you're right?"

Linane surveyed him with raised eyebrows. "What do you think we'll have to do?" He met Michael's challenging stare coldly until the boy dropped his eyes. "But first we have to find out," he added. "And that's why I asked if Fallon knew any of your team apart from you."

Michael wondered briefly about the description of "your team". It was suddenly being made to appear as if it was all his idea. Perhaps it was. He couldn't remember enough of what had happened at the committee meeting now. "I'm not sure. He came to pick me up from home, you remember. He saw Tina. I don't think he could have met Sean, then. The others are certainly all clear."

"Could he have met Sean here in Dublin?"

"It's just possible. Besides, with that red hair he does stand out a bit. If he'd seen him, just out of the corner of his eye or something, he might remember. Even if he just saw him a couple of times now he might get suspicious." Michael was already thinking and planning as if his objections to Linane's idea had never existed.

"Then you know what to do. Don't let Sean do any of the watching or shadowing, though you'll need him to help organise and keep track of things. Keep well out of the way yourself. But I want to know everything that Fallon does, who he meets, where he goes . . . everything . . . for the next few days."

Michael nodded. He was ready for his first grim task of the war.

Linane was going on. "I want to know which man he buys his newspapers from; the fellow he chats with in the bar, or walks past and brushes against in O'Connell Street; the man who stands and gazes at the water with him on Bachelor's Walk; who kneels beside him in St Patrick's. Make a note of every one.

Your team must pick up the magazine he has just put down on the bookstall, the paper he has dropped in the gutter. There are dozens of ways of passing messages – even the way he leaves the curtains on his bedroom window may mean something."

Michael nodded again. He was becoming impatient. He had probably watched as many spy films as Linane. "And how long are we to keep it up?"

"I don't know. A couple of weeks should do."

"And what if we *don't* find anything?"

Linane's thin lips twitched with the phantom of a smile. "Then you haven't watched properly . . ." he waited until Michael's angry protest nearly burst forth and then went on, "or there's nothing to find."

Michael tried again to voice his objections to the assignment. "What do I tell the others?"

Linane grinned. "They're your team," he said. "I expect you'll think of something. You don't want me to tell you everything, do you? If you do, maybe I should be running the team and not you."

Michael still wasn't happy but there seemed no further means of dissuading Linane from the plan without irritating him even more.

"And how often do you want the reports?"

"Once a week will do, unless there's something really significant. If there is, call me at once. Do this well and I'll know you're ready for the North. It's about time we moved some more of our own people up there and your crowd could be useful in the next few months."

The promise of action in the North – against the real enemy – filled Michael's mind immediately, as it was expected to.

He nodded again. This time more enthusiastically, as he began to grapple with the problems of the watch on Fallon. It would give him a chance to test some of his recruits. At times during a long surveillance they would have to think for themselves.

He left Linane soon afterwards and the little man then ushered in his next caller – a girl with a Northern Irish accent.

Michael began rounding up his private army. One of the

Northern Irish group, a strongly-built girl with incredible long shining hair, the colour of a newly-opened horse-chestnut, proved difficult to find. Her name was Maire Walsh. When Michael reprimanded her she seemed almost to enjoy his rough words, letting him know that she accepted them meekly from him though she would not have done so from any of the others.

He scented trouble from her but there was other business to attend to.

He told the group: "It's an exercise. But that doesn't make it something we can take lightly. If we want to do something really useful in this campaign, we have to prove we're up to it. If Fallon once spots us, or suspects what's going on, we'll spend the rest of our lives regretting that we weren't considered good enough for the real action. I don't think I could live with that. I want to be there in the thick of the battle, and to claim my honours for the victory proudly, not to know always that I didn't do much and I didn't deserve the praise and recognition that will come to every member of The Movement after the victory. I want the Brits out of Ireland – and the only way I can see them being forced to go is if as many people as possible join in. I want the Brits and everyone else to know that I helped to get them out. That's what this exercise is about – showing if we are fit to join the battle."

Some of it was a true reflection of the way he felt. But he saw Tina and Sean exchange amused, mock-mystified glances. He was going to have trouble with them later. But he plunged on with the detail of the mission.

The team made their way out into the night. The first couple were to stand outside Fallon's home until they picked him up, entering or leaving. They were to telephone in if anything remarkable happened.

Tina busied herself making cocoa, Sean looked at the racing pages. Neither spoke until Tina returned from the cooker and sat down with her drink. She set it beside her chair carefully and, as if responding to a signal, Sean put down his newspaper. They turned in unison and peered at Michael as if he were some sort of rare zoological specimen. He half expected them to stand up and inspect him. He tried to concentrate on his drink. It seemed essential to force them to make the first move.

Sean spoke first. "I think the most important part of friendship is the trust, don't you?" he asked Tina, turning away from Michael and speaking as if he were not there.

"I do. I do," she confirmed.

"I mean, it's like there shouldn't be any secrets from real friends. No secrets and no surprises . . ."

"Like in a marriage or a love-affair, you mean?"

"Or a love-affair that's going to turn into a marriage."

"A love affair that *was* going to turn into a marriage," Tina corrected.

Michael groaned. "For God's sake, you two. I'll tell you what I can."

"Tell us what?" Sean asked. "We weren't expecting you to tell us anything, were we, Tina?"

"No . . . nothing . . . After all *we* trust you," said Tina.

"Yes, *we* trust *you* . . . like good friends should . . ."

"And we're sure you wouldn't try to keep any secrets from *us*."

Michael groaned again and they raised eyebrows at each other. Sean bent to pick up his newspaper and Tina reached for her cup.

"D'you think the rain will keep off for the fellas who're out there watching Mr Fallon?" Sean asked Tina.

". . . Just for the exercise, mind," she added.

"Look, come on, I'll tell you," said Michael. "I was going to anyway."

"But we wouldn't expect you to, seeing as it's a special secret," said Tina. But she and Sean settled forward in their chairs, listening and intent while he explained.

"But who does Linane think Fallon's spying for?" Tina asked the obvious question and frowned as Michael admitted that he didn't know.

She shook her head. "Perhaps it is an exercise after all," she suggested hopefully.

Michael shook his head. "No. Linane means it. He thinks Fallon's up to something. And we'd better find out what it is."

"Maybe it would be best just to invent something. Might save a lot of time," suggested Sean. Obviously he liked the idea of spying on Fallon even less than Michael had done.

"And what would you invent?" demanded Tina scornfully. "I think it's awful. Mr Fallon's a nice man and here we are setting out to sneak and spy after him as if he were a criminal." She broke her temporary alliance. "And you, Sean McDade, how can you suggest we just make something up about him?"

"I wasn't serious," said Sean lamely.

"Well, it's a serious matter," Tina continued, her face flushed – pretty she was too, thought Michael, even then. "We're accusing Mr Fallon, the straightest man I know, of working for someone else . . . of being a traitor, is it?" She'd put the word to it finally, and they all sat silent for a moment. "And your Mr Linane says it, so it must be true," she went on, glaring at Michael, "Your Mr Linane, with his sharp tongue and his sneaking ways, says, 'Get Fallon'. So we have to do it. If you ask me, he's the one we should be watching. If you ask me, he just wants Fallon out of the way. And who's next after that? How long before he decides he wants you spied on, Michael? How long . . ."

"That's enough, Tina," Michael snapped. "That's enough. I didn't ask you. I shouldn't have told you either, and wouldn't if I'd had any sense. Now be quiet, both of you . . ." he raised a hand and waited while their protests subsided. At last he went on: "We're in a war and in an army, as much as if we wore a uniform, and you've got to start understanding it now, before it's too late. So we obey orders. WE OBEY ORDERS . . ." he raised his voice to silence their protests . . . "because we don't know enough about what's going on to do anything else. Linane does know and, whatever you may think of him, he's the man who will win this war for us. So there'll be no arguing about our orders, disobeying them or . . ." he looked hard at Sean . . . "inventing something."

They were quiet now, and Michael felt that he had to fill the silence. He strode to the fireplace and turned, hands clasped behind him. "Yes, this is war," he began, "and, as in any war, there are unpleasant jobs which, nonetheless, have to be done. Jobs which . . ." A snort from Sean stopped his flow and he looked up to see his two friends contorting their faces to try to suppress their giggles.

"It's no laughing matter," he roared and they doubled over

as they caught each other's eye. "Idiots, I . . ." and then he laughed with them.

"Point of order, Mr Chairman," croaked Sean and leapt to his feet waving his arms, before collapsing feebly against Tina, who clutched him. They danced round together. "Point of order, Mr Chairman," they chanted in unison. Michael stood, alternately laughing a little and clenching his fists in anger at their mockery. "I'll . . . I'll . . ." he spluttered, and then they swept him into their circle and made him prance with them.

When they subsided, Tina broke the circle and strutted theatrically to the fireplace. "Pray silence for Michael Sullivan, T.D., member for Screeb and Ballynahinch, who will give us his address on the horrors of war."

Michael grabbed her as she and Sean screeched with laughter again. "My God, what I'm going to do with you?" he roared.

"What are you going to do then, Michael?" she drawled with a sensual sway of her hips and shoulders.

"He's going to have you followed," yelled Sean.

And they laughed . . . and then they stopped laughing . . . partly because they had laughed enough, mostly because it wasn't funny any more. They drank their cocoa, Michael and Tina went to bed and Sean prepared himself for the first telephone watch. Together in their big bed, Michael and Tina cuddled close. Yet still they felt lonely.

CHAPTER XVII

Michael's watchers worked hard. Theirs was no nine-to-five job. They watched and followed and stalked Fallon, throughout the days and nights. They stood freezing in doorways while he ate and drank. They huddled miserably under raincoats with the water dripping off noses and hair, down sleeves and under collars. Faithfully, they recorded every move and meeting, every meal he had, every cabbie and shopkeeper he spoke to, even, despite their shock, details of the girl he saw regularly and took home twice. She worked in an office between Trinity College and the National Library.

The watchers kept their spirits up and almost enjoyed the job, believing, as Michael had told them, that it was some devilish test of their morale and endurance. Sean and Tina slogged through it, not unhappily at first, but gradually responding to the tension and irritation Michael showed.

At the end of a fortnight he delivered his dossier to Linane grimly and silently, certain that there was nothing to report. Linane accepted it and his verbal summary with a blank frown.

"Everything's here?" he asked, and Michael was relieved to see that he obviously believed it was. To Michael's expressed misgivings about the success of the mission he replied, almost lightly: "Don't be too quick to see failure, my boy. If every move is recorded here, so are the false ones. It will just take a little time to sort out the patterns and find the mistakes. Maybe he's a bit cleverer than you expected. It's in here!" He slapped the dossier. "Oh, there's something all right. And you've done well, all of you. He doesn't appear to have noticed a thing." He paused then, and that faint ghost of a smile flitted across his face. Michael realised that they were to receive Linane's version of a reward.

"Yes, you've done well. And next week I hope you'll do as well again. Soon you'll be going up to Derry. That'll be the real thing – though I'm not saying this isn't." He patted the folder again. "But you're all to have some special training first: to learn a bit more about explosives and such. You should have done the basics at the Fianna. This is just to teach you to be real soldiers. You'll be near Monaghan for a week, and then go on to Buncrana in County Donegal. They'll teach you a lot of things. But maybe the most important will be discipline. You see, the first and most important part of this campaign is the waiting..."

"Waiting...?" Michael blurted out. "But..."

"Yes, waiting, Michael. It isn't time yet. This is not going to be another repeat of the '56 fiasco, when everything was ready except the people of the Bogside and the Falls Road. This time we'll let the nice liberals of the Civil Rights Association, the Paisleys and the Craigs, even that 'thoroughly decent chap, what', Terence O'Neill, and, of course, the British, do our work for us..."

This was too much for Michael. "The British... you mean if we wait long enough they'll just pack up and sail away when we ask them?"

The pink spots were beginning to show on Linane's cheeks, a warning Michael was usually quick to heed. "No, I don't mean anything as crass as that. I don't need anyone to tell me what I mean, either. And if I did need lessons in strategy, I wouldn't get them from an ignorant country boy." Linane closed his eyes and pursed his lips, as if taking control of himself. "No, of course, you don't know what I have in mind and you are young enough to be in a hurry..." It was as if he were explaining to himself as well as to Michael. "Look, it's a simple matter, and historically, perhaps for the first time, the moment is right for us. The Catholics in Northern Ireland have realised at last that they are not getting their share of the gravy. They can't get into the police, the administration, even into jobs as simple as driving school buses. They're at the back of the queue for housing and social benefits, though they're the poorest. They don't stand a chance of getting their own people into Stormont or even to run the local council in Derry . . ."

"Yes, that's what the Civil Rights Movement is about. But . . ."

"Right. Now, I know, and you should know, that marching and getting your head smashed in is not going to change the minds of bull-headed Prods like Paisley. But the Civil Rights crowd doesn't know. So they'll get their heads smashed in – for a time. O'Neill will wring his hands and the Brits in their Parliament might even start asking questions about the nice little racket their quislings in Belfast seem to be running. Then O'Neill will make some meaningless concessions that will please no one – especially not his own side."

Linane lifted his hand as Michael went to interrupt again. "Just listen a minute, Michael, and you might learn something . . . O'Neill will make his concessions, Paisley will bellow like a bull. The Unionists will kick out O'Neill and get someone just as daft, maybe Major Chichester-Clark, if we're lucky. And so on. And all the time the trouble will be getting worse and the Protestant bully-boys will start raiding across the Falls Road and burning down the homes of good Irish Catholic folk – until they really need us. Only then will we move – when we know there's an invitation on the mat and a base to fight from. And that's when we'll win. So, now you know, Michael. And if you keep your mouth shut and your eyes open you'll see it all happening."

"You're sure?" said Michael dazedly.

"No. But if my brothers and some of my young assistants don't cock things up too much between them, there's a good chance that some of it might go that way. And the first thing that you'll do, to make sure you don't cock things up, is shut your mouth about our plans – not even that girl Tina is to know. The second thing you do is report to Captain Carson on Monday and he'll give you your instructions. The third is enjoy the training. It's fun."

As Michael went, a girl rapped at Linane's door.

For most of Michael's irregulars the training *was* fun. He, Sean and some of the girls enjoyed the tough physical effort they were forced to make, under the direction of a former British Army Commando Sergeant. And they quickly learned how to use the new weapons they were shown. Some of the girls also enjoyed the sensation they created in a predominantly male camp. Michael hoped that was all they enjoyed.

Tina hated every moment of it: getting up in the damp dawn; washing in cold water; dressing in an even colder tent, without much privacy from the eager eyes of the men; marching; exercising; climbing ropes which tore at her hands; splashing and crashing through mud; breaking her nails on recalcitrant guns; the coarse remarks of the men when they all sat together in the mess-tent – and most of all the lonely narrow bed at night, with Michael sleeping somewhere on the other side of the camp. She didn't want to be a soldier.

She wanted to be Michael's wife, to sleep in Michael's bed at night, with him in her arms, and to have his babies. She would follow him wherever he went. But she didn't have to be enthusiastic about exercises like this, which were meaningless to her.

She struggled through the course somehow, helped where possible by Michael and Sean – and occasionally by one or two of the instructors with an eye for a pretty face and an expectation of a little gratitude in return for their assistance. Tina knew how to use such helpers and string them along with unfulfilled half-promises, conveyed with a touch of her hand on theirs, by leaning on a supporting arm a moment too long, or letting her hair brush a cheek. She also knew how to avoid fulfilling those promises without causing offence. But she didn't know how to head off the anger she aroused in the girls, who noted her lack of enthusiasm, were jealous of her standing with Michael or were irritated by her blatant use of her femininity to make life more easy.

Maire Walsh was angry. At first she just watched, her eyes narrowing and her face flushed. Then she began to take care to counter some of the help the men were giving. Hers was the shoulder that crashed into Tina's back beside the obstacle-course pond and sent her staggering headlong into it. She was the one who carefully picked out the stiffest Sten and flung it to Tina to watch her struggle with it. She was the one who poured water on Tina's bedroll, let down the line on which her newly-washed clothes were drying and finally, in a contrived accident, knocked over her flimsy bed containing her carefully laid out possessions just before the final inspection.

When Tina protested she just shrugged and turned away.

"Aren't you going to help me pick them up, then?" demanded her victim.

"Why don't you get Michael or Sergeant Doyle to give you a hand? You can pay them back later. I expect you're going to anyway, milady," sneered Maire with a toss of her head.

"For God's sake, what do you mean by that?" Tina grabbed Maire's long red hair as she started to walk away.

The other girl, broader and heavier, shook her hand off and grabbed the front of her denims. "You know what I mean . . . with all your winking and slinking and making up to them for help. You poor wee helpless thing. Helpless, except when it comes to climbing into bed." She shook Tina once and then shoved her backwards so that she fell over the ruined bed.

For a moment she lay there, near tears. It was unfair. But so was the whole training camp. She leapt to her feet. She'd let that girl see what she thought. She strode after Maire. "I'll show you," she yelled and swept past to get to her enemy's bed.

She reached to throw it over but Maire grabbed her, lifted her by her denims again and pulled her close, so that the weather-reddened face was inches from hers. Tina could see the open pores on the girl's nose.

"God, you little sneak. I'm going to give you something you won't show any of your fellas," said Maire.

Tina felt her enemy's muscles tense and braced herself for what was coming. "Mother of God, help me," she whispered and then cried out as a fist smashed into her just below the breasts. The big girl swung and swung again and then let her go suddenly, so that she collapsed to the tent floor. She lay whimpering, feeling the hurt and the tears on her cheeks – and no one offered to help. She looked round at the others and most of them were turning away. They didn't seem to care. "Damn you, Maire Walsh, and damn all of you ugly old bitches," she screeched.

The big girl loomed over her, grinning nastily. "Haven't you had enough, then, or do you think one of the fellas is going to save you?' she demanded.

Tina cowered and tried to scuttle away along the floor. But lazily the other girl turned her over with a muddy boot. "Come on, girls, let's give the sex-kitten a lesson, shall we?" The big strong hands held her flat to the floor, and some of the others joined in.

Tina struggled but it was no good. First they took her boots off and then they lowered her denim trousers.

"Lookit them dainty little knickers. Wouldn't Sergeant Doyle love to see her now? Have them off her," ordered Maire.

"No, no. Please," whimpered Tina, wondering what they meant to do.

"Bring me that brush of hers," said Maire. And Tina winced before the hard tines smacked into her bare flesh.

She cried out, then drew in her breath sharply as she sensed the big arm being raised above her. There was a rhythm in it. She squealed as the brush landed, gasped as it was raised, tensed herself and then squealed again. She had stopped struggling. It seemed to go on and on. She was sure Maire had drawn blood. And then she heard the booming voice of her enemy. "She won't enjoy sitting down for a day or so."

"Nor lying down either, specially with one of her men," laughed another. But it was so unfair, Tina thought. There was only Michael. There were no other men. Terrified, she wondered suddenly if he thought the way these girls did. She murmured a silent prayer. As long as he believed her, she didn't mind what they did. And she realised with horror that they hadn't finished with her yet.

"We can make certain of that." It was Maire again. "Turn her over."

Giggling, they did, and spread her out as if they were preparing her for a lover. She shuddered and writhed as she looked up and saw the big red hands tip a bottle, and an even redder liquid ooze out and drip onto her. "Hold her still," the big girl ordered. The red liquid was sticky and seemed to be setting fast. Maire turned the bottle up to make sure Tina got it all. It was nail varnish, damn them.

"That'll make sure she keeps her legs together for a day or

two," she chortled. Then, suddenly, she and the others turned away. They seemed to have lost interest.

When she was sure they were gone, Tina sat up, reaching for her clothes. "I wouldn't put them on yet, love," said the girl in the nearest bed, who had not joined in the ragging. "Wait until it dries. 'Tis the best thing to do anyway."

"Hey," roared the familiar hated voice. "You on her side then, Connolly?"

"No, nor on yours either," said the girl calmly.

"Well, why don't you give her some remover, if you're her mate?" cackled Maire.

Tina looked up at the girl hopefully, but Shirley Connolly shook her head. "Remover would burn you to hell down there," she said. "I'm afraid you'll just have to let it dry and then get it off bit by bit."

Tina felt numb and helpless. But her unexpected friend was ready with more advice. "When it's dry, just put a towel on. That'll keep it off your clothes and such. And c'mon now. It's not the worst tragedy the world's ever seen. Let's just put your bed back together. Then you can go and have a shower soon as the inspection's over. That'll make you feel better."

Tina just nodded. She couldn't trust herself to speak. She and the other girl worked together to tidy up the mess of her bed. One or two of the rest also gave a sly hand, keeping a careful eye on Maire in case she noticed them.

When the wreckage looked nearly passable she just had time to dress before the inspection. It wasn't easy, as she told her helpers with a watery giggle. "I'm not sure if it's worse at the back or the front . . ."

"What a mess," growled Sergeant Doyle, eyeing her and shaking his head. "I'm not sure whether it's worse at the back or the front." He meant the bed. But Tina wasn't certain at first. She felt that he could see through her clothes to the mess Maire had made of her.

"I'm sorry," she whispered and sniffed back the tears.

"All right. All right. For God's sake don't cry at me. I won't be turning you over my knee or anything." He didn't know why the girls giggled. His remark hadn't seemed particularly witty. "Not that I'd mind, though," he said, emboldened by his triumph. Tina just lowered her eyes and blushed.

"Now there's a real girl for you," he thought. He couldn't imagine why she wanted to go and fight. Didn't seem suited for it at all. "We'll never make a soldier of you, girl," he said gruffly. Though it didn't sound like it, it was a compliment. To Maire it was a triumph: to Tina just a mild reproach compared to what she had feared – and she started to cry again.

Sergeant Doyle beat a hasty retreat.

And then Maire was standing at the end of her bed. Tina looked up defiantly. "Well," she sniffed.

"Well," said the other, nodding her head and smiling broadly. "So we've found something else you can do, as well as flirting with the fellas. Just cry at them and they'll go away. Maybe we should work you over whenever we've got any trouble with the men. Maybe we can use you against the English."

She was still smiling. She wasn't trying to be offensive. Tina gave a wry smile and turned back to her bed. She wasn't sure whether to sit or lie down on her stomach. Her legs were trembling and she felt exhausted. But there was no early call next day. She'd be able to sleep – if she could find a position that didn't hurt too much.

"Coming up to get some tea?" Maire asked, and it was a sort of olive branch.

Tina shook her head and decided to lie down. "No, thanks. I'm just too tired. I think I could sleep for a week."

"Suit yourself," said the big girl stiffly, and then, "it'll leave the way clear for some of us others then." She strode off.

"D'you want me to bring you back a cup of tea?" It was Shirley Connolly.

"Yes, please, and some cold cream, if you can find any." She smiled back over her shoulder, though her buttocks felt as if a brazier were suspended over them.

"I've got some in my bag. Should have thought of it before. D'you want me to send someone over to rub it on for you? Someone whose name begins with an M?"

Tina shook her head and pouted. "I'm sure it's against the

rules. There's always a rule. Besides, I don't think I'm in a fit state to welcome visitors."

"Not that one, anyway. OK. Here's the cream. D'you want me to tell him anything if I see him?"

Tina frowned. Was this girl going to talk to Michael? "Don't be idiotic," she told herself. And aloud: "Yes, please. Would you tell him I've a headache and had to lie down? Part of it's true. It's just a slight error in geography."

They giggled together, and the other girl went out.

She was stiff next day because of the bruises under her ribs. And her buttocks still tingled. So she wasn't delighted to hear that, as an added treat, they were all to march to the hill above Knockatallon. From there, many IRA border raids had been launched in the past, and they would be able to see into the North. Sean and the other boys were keen and eager, walking on ahead. Maire shared their enthusiasm, keeping up with them.

Michael stayed with Tina for a time, as she hobbled grumpily behind the rest. She couldn't see any point in rushing. It was just another old hill and it wasn't going to move away suddenly.

"You can see all the way over into Armagh," Michael told her enthusiastically.

"And that isn't going to go away either," she growled.

"But its owners, the Brits, are," said Michael. Then, after a pause, he added: "Oh, come on, will you. What's wrong with you today? God, you've made a misery of the whole week, and now you're sulking again."

She didn't want to upset him. But she couldn't share his present pleasure. "I'm sorry. I just feel awful today," she explained unhappily – but it didn't come out like an apology or an explanation.

He glared at her. "For God's sake."

"Why don't you go on with the others?" she urged hastily. "I'm just not good company now."

He stared at her hostilely for a second. "All right, I will, then," he said and marched off.

So he saw the North for the first time in the company of

another girl. Together, he, Maire and Sean peered into the misty distance and the boys, at least, imagined they saw all sorts of things – uniforms and wars and heroic victories.

More and more, that was the way it was to be. Michael, Maire and Sean led the way together, while Tina battled on behind. War and practice for it were not her specialities.

The next week at Buncrana proved that to her. With Maire's gleeful assistance she made a mess of most things. Maire swung across a chasm on a rope. Tina fell off it. Maire picked up the long-range rifle and put seven bullets in a target. Tina missed the target every time – though it was later found that the sights had been wrongly set. Maire shone at everything, while Tina failed miserably, mostly with a good reason. And Michael noticed. Suddenly she was the girl who complained, who couldn't keep up with the crowd, who always had an excuse.

"I don't know what's wrong with you, Tina," he said, and was to say a dozen more times.

In her misery Tina couldn't tell him. If she had confided her suspicions to him, she knew he would only have taken it as more sour jealousy. And she hadn't the confidence or boldness necessary, just to catch his eye one night and whisper in his ear: "Why don't you take me for a walk across the fields and give me a cuddle? I'm missing you so much." Instead, she went earlier and more tired to an uncomfortable bed, while Michael, Sean, Maire and some of the others sat in the bare but comfortable stone-flagged kitchen of the farmhouse they used as their headquarters, drinking tea, yarning and wrestling.

At the end of the week, the officer in charge at Buncrana sent for Michael.

"You've a good team," he said. "Most of them settled in quickly and learned how to handle the guns well. But I'm bound to say . . ."

Michael braced himself for the message he knew was coming.

". . . one or two would have been better left at home. I think you know who they are. In one case, at least, a lot of the problems seemed to be more bad luck than lack of application."

"Tina Foley," put in Michael.

"Yes, that's the girl. Charming, bright lass. It just didn't seem to go right for her. Besides, I gather there's a special reason for her being with you . . . ." He grinned and winked knowingly. "And she might be useful for other things, eh."

Michael had to swallow his anger and, unfairly, he blamed Tina for his embarrassment. So, that night, as she felt cheerful for the first time in days and prepared for the leaving celebration, Michael fumed. He hardly spoke to her when they met and she went to bed lonely and miserable again.

There was yet another shock for her in the morning when Michael gave them their instructions. They were to travel into Derry in small groups over two days, so that they did not attract the attention of the authorities. He, Sean and Maire would go first, to find the places where they were to stay with their symphathisers. Tina was to travel with another group on the second day. Her misery sat like a lump in her throat and chest as she wandered away to complete her packing without a word to him. Sean tried to bar her way and explain as she left the room. But she just pushed past him. As she sat on her bed later, surrounded by her bags, it was Maire who spoke to her.

"See you in Derry, then – that's if you don't get lost on the way. Don't worry about Michael, I'll look after him for you – keep your bed warm and all that."

Tina couldn't trust herself to reply. But she didn't cry until the other girl had gone. She didn't sleep that night either, as she tossed and turned in her bed, imagining all the things that might go on in Derry.

She would have been relieved if she had been able to go invisibly to the house where the three had set up their base. They sat with steaming mugs of cocoa, anxiously waiting for one to make the first move. They had discovered that they had to share a room. Michael was tired but thought Maire would like to go and undress first, for the sake of modesty. Sean suspected that Maire and Michael were planning to arrange the beds so that they could get together when he was asleep. He intended to stop them if he could. Maire was simply enjoying their uneasiness.

Finally, after a tense and uncomfortable wait, it was she who solved the problem. She stretched and yawned. "Come on, let's go to bed," she said. "I promise I won't look, if you don't."

The two followed her shyly to their room – "like virgin boys", as Sean was to put it later, when he reminisced about the "good old times". But the silence of the staircase didn't survive inside the room. Maire made sure of that. She strode in first, switched on the light, turned by the window, reaching for the bottom of her sweater to pull it over her head and challenged them with her eyes. Sean followed her into the room and stood dithering. Michael came third – and switched off the light.

"Ah, me shy little flower," she muttered from inside her jersey.

Sean giggled nervously and Michael said nothing. They stood for a moment, uncertain what to do next, both very aware of Maire's magnificent silhouette in the window. Michael stepped behind the double bed and began unbuttoning his shirt. Sean took off his jacket as if he were in the spotlight on stage and it was a G-string.

"What brave boys you are," said Maire, dropping her skirt tauntingly as she caught their attention. They bent again to their own undressing and she was silent for a few seconds. Then, she let out a whoop and leapt for the light switch, catching them both, literally, with their trousers down. Sean squealed and tried to hide. Michael made for the switch, only to find his way barred by Maire. They grappled.

"Ooh, you great passionate beast," said Maire, collapsing in his arms.

"Sean, for Christ's sake. Sean! Turn off the light," spluttered Michael.

"Oh yes, Sean, turn off the light," breathed Maire mock-sensuously, and twined herself round Michael.

"God, she's a bloody sex-maniac." Michael felt the laughter welling up inside him as he struggled free and plunged the room into darkness again. "And look at old Sean, cowering like a maiden. Let's get them off him."

They sprang at Sean together and they all ended up in a naked thrashing heap on the one bed, gasping and panting.

"You should have seen your faces when I turned on the light," she giggled. As she recovered her breath her grin widened. She reached out with both hands simultaneously and pinched. As they howled, she stood quickly and made her way to the furthest bed. "Mind, I might be willing to make men of you yet," she whispered.

They went to sleep relaxed after the release of their romp.

"It won't be so funny tomorrow night," thought Michael, just before he slept. "There'll be no fooling when Tina gets here."

And, when they met her, it seemed at first that he had been right. She was weary from her sleepless night and the trip over bumpy roads in local buses. For a moment they eyed each other suspiciously. Michael's hair was slightly ruffled, his brows puckered pugnaciously in a frown. He looked like a little boy who had been accused unfairly of naughtiness. She wanted to hug him. So she did. He relaxed in her arms and wanted her very much.

Even so, four in a room with three beds seemed an impossible arrangement. But four in a room it had to be at that stage. They did not have enough supporters for more comfortable arrangements to be possible.

That night, as they sat eyeing each other over their cocoa, it was almost like a repeat of their first evening in the house. Sean felt himself blushing as he realised what should be done. He hoped that someone else would suggest it, but knew no one would. He also wondered how to prevent Maire from creating a disaster. He saw the big girl start to stretch and seized one of her hands. "How about a walk?" he asked.

"A walk?" She looked at him in horror. "At this time of night? You must be crazy."

"I want to talk to you about something." Sean struggled on gamely, though he would gladly have crawled under the floorboards at that moment.

"Well, talk. We all know each other pretty well . . . especially after . . ."

"Look, it's about that I want to talk." He had to cut her off before she said too much.

She grinned nastily. "Oh, you mean my offer about making men . . ."

"If you like." He was desperate.

"Well, surely upstairs is . . ."

"I think you ought to go with him." Michael had caught on and had come to the rescue.

Maire realised what was going on – and that she was

outnumbered. It was too early in the game to show her hand. She grinned ruefully. She could still extract something from the situation, though. "Oh, yeah, I get it," she said, apparently stupidly, looking from Michael to Tina and back again. She banged her head with her palm. "God, I'm a fool. I thought you suddenly fancied me, Sean." She stared hard at Tina. "I hope you undress with the light out, sweetheart, or he might get a shock."

But when Michael and she were alone in the double bed together Tina had no time for embarrassment or worry, or even her own tiredness. "Michael, I love you. I love you. I love you," she whispered over and over again.

For a couple more days Maire accepted the back seat she was forced to take as Michael and Tina mooned about – as young lovers should after a quarrel and reconciliation. She grumbled about having to sit up late, made double-edged remarks which missed their target because the pair were so caught up in their rediscovered love, and prepared herself for the next phase of her campaign.

Then Linane arrived unexpectedly and unannounced ... and Tina was forced to join Sean and Maire on their late-night walk.

"I just hope we don't find *them* in bed together when we get back," said Maire.

CHAPTER XVIII

As usual, Linane wasted little time over social chat when he was left alone with Michael. "I think your lot are ready. As ready as they'll ever be, that is. I know all about the training and I'm glad you sent a couple of them home, though I gather there should have been one other going south . . . All right, all right, I know about her. I just hope you don't regret that decision when things get rough."

He paused and stared reflectively at his long pale hands, as if inspecting them for dust. "So I want you to start, just a few of the more sensible ones. Not Sean, I'm afraid – he's too obvious. I've got another job for him, anyway.

"As you know, there's a big Civil Rights March on. After the trouble at some of the others, the police are making noises that they're not going to let the Paisleyites and 'B' Specials get too rough with them. They've covered a good few miles so far, and there have only been a handful of stones. That's bad . . ."

"Don't you mean good?" asked Michael.

Linane sighed. "I think we've had this conversation before somewhere. I know what I mean. I mean 'that's bad'. Every Civil Rights marcher who gets away unscathed is a potential believer in the underlying decency and fairness of the police and the Brits – if there is such a thing. If this march gets into Derry and there's no trouble, I think we'll all have to go home."

"But, won't it mean the Brits are beginning to listen?"

"Possibly . . . or just that they're trying to prove to the world how decent they are and fooling our people up here into more complacent years of occupation."

"But I don't see . . ." Michael thought he did see, and he wasn't sure he was going to like what was coming.

"All right, I'll spell it out for you. The march must not get through without blood being spilled. Your crowd will see to it."

"How?" It was the question that left Michael with no retreat.

Linane produced a map from his pocket and spread it between them. "Here." He stabbed with his finger at a point a few miles out of Derry. "The road dips under a bridge and narrows. It's an obvious place for a Prod ambush and everyone knows it, including the police. But they've already been at work. Paisley won't be there, neither will Craig. There'll be a biggish local crowd and a few off-duty 'B' Specials. But without leadership they'll be puzzled about what they should do. The police hope they will be able to lean on them and persuade them to let the marchers through."

"And . . ." prompted Michael.

"And you'll be there to persuade them otherwise."

"But they won't listen to me . . ."

"Well, you won't be talking to them, Michael. In fact, you have to remember not to open your mouth for once. Actions speak louder than words – especially Irish-accented words among a gang of Protestants. No – 'He that is without sin among you, let him first cast a stone at her.' The upright boys in blue will get their agreement with the Loyalists to let the hairies through without violence. Back they'll go and they'll say: 'There you are. We've done our job. We've got you a free passage to carry your banners right into Derry. You see, we don't discriminate. We're fair and just.' And as the happy band strides forward to victory, the stones begin to rattle and someone starts smashing in their heads. Who'd ever trust a policeman again after such a betrayal?"

"I don't like it and neither will the others . . . attacking our own people . . ."

"Must you always argue like a sentimental Irish idiot?" roared Linane. "For a start, they're not our own people. Most of them are middle-class Queen's University brats, playing some idiot game in an imagined cause of justice and decency. Who the hell needs them? For a second, we don't want another bloody compromise with the Brits and a bit more gravy for the Irish in Ulster to keep them enslaved for another thousand years. We want the enemy out of our island, and it will mean more than just breaking a few heads to get them out. This place will be a smoking heap of ash, reeking with the blood of the people, before we win our victory. But win we will – with or without Michael Sullivan and his uneasy conscience."

"No, I understand all that," argued Michael earnestly, if not altogether honestly. "But I don't know if the others will agree." By the others he meant Sean and Tina, and he was remembering the battle over the decision to spy on Fallon in Dublin. He was also taking another step away from the village memorial with his name on it.

Linane shook his head in disgust, as aware as Michael of who was really protesting and why. "Michael, it doesn't matter whether they agree or not. Those are their orders. Those are your orders. This is an army, not a debating society. I've given an instruction. You will select your team and carry it out . . . or face the consequences."

"I never intended otherwise . . ." Michael tried to sound angry. "I was just considering the problems."

"Well, do you mind considering them silently." Linane concealed a grin and drew the map towards him again. "Now, this is where the main group of Prods are likely to gather . . ." he began.

Michael took his advice and silently considered the problem of how to deliver his new instructions. Linane had said something about counting Sean out of the action. That would dispose of one difficulty. In Dublin, though, Tina had been the main opponent to the watch on Fallon. Here again she was the enemy. Why was everything connected with her so difficult, these days? But there was an answer, also contained in what Linane had said at the start of their conversation. "Take a few of the sensible ones," he had said. The sensible ones: Maire and a few of the lads and that other Belfast girl, Connolly. He didn't even have to discuss it with Tina. It was such a simple solution. She need never know the real facts . . . but of course he was underestimating his lover-turned-adversary.

Linane caught the smile. "Obviously you've got it all sorted out at last," he commented cryptically, and for a moment Michael was startled into almost believing the man could read his mind. "So, who are you going to take?"

Michael told him – and it was Linane's turn to smile. "Good lad. Sensible choice," he said as he reached for his raincoat and walked to the door. "I'll be listening to my radio for the reports. And don't spare the heads of the hairies. Make sure a few of their girls get really worked over. You'd better tell Maire about that . . . And for God's sake remember not to speak to anyone at the bridge. Let Maire do all the talking. They'll kill you if they hear that accent."

He stepped out into the drizzle, turning up his collar as he went. North or south, the weather was still Irish. What was it Fallon had said that day in Dublin, when they still seemed to be fighting the same war on the same side?

"A fine soft day, as they say in Kerry," he called to Michael, who was still at the door. He was gratified by the boy's puzzled frown.

Michael stared after the slight huddled figure. "That's the man who is going to save Ireland, and I'll be standing at his side when he does it," he muttered melodramatically – and then looked round to make sure nobody had heard. There was nobody to hear in the dimly-lit street. He looked back after Linane. He was picking his way between the puddles, lit now by the yellow glow of a street lamp. He was already a long way off. "And I'll not be the only one standing at his side," muttered Michael, chuckling quietly to himself as he saw a flutter of skirts in a doorway. A girl, indistinct in the dark and at the distance, stepped out to join his leader. They disappeared together round a bend in the road.

Linane and a girl. He began to chortle. Then he stopped. It couldn't be. Not *that* sort of relationship. But who was she? He couldn't rid himself of an impression of familiarity. Perhaps he could run after them and find out. He took a half-step out into the street and a gout of water from the blocked and overflowing gutter above the door spattered onto his head. He retreated quickly. He had other things to think about without bothering himself over Linane's love-life or lack of it. Two of those problems were probably not far away now, and wondering if they should return home.

Sean would be easily headed off by being told to report to Linane for details of his own secret mission. He wasn't sure about Tina. He didn't know what he could tell her to convince her that what they were doing was right – particularly as he wasn't convinced himself.

He could lie to her. But how could he brief Maire at the same time? He kept rehearsing conversations in his mind and then realising the flaws. But he didn't have long to agonise. When the outcasts arrived, flushed with youth, joy and walking in the rain, he saw that Maire wasn't with them.

"What did he want? What did he say? Did he have a job for us?" The questions started as soon as he opened the door to them, and Tina's were tinged with anxiety.

"Come in. Get your coats off," he said, and hugged Tina to him to reassure her.

"Where's Maire?" he asked and saw, from the tightening of Tina's mouth, that it was the wrong question. Sean was telling him that the big girl had gone to call on her Belfast friends, but Michael could hardly listen as the wave of unhappiness swept over him again. He didn't seem capable of getting anything right with Tina these days. Damn it, why was she so miserable? Maybe, as Linane had said, he should have sent her home. He turned his face away from her, in case she read his thoughts mirrored there. But then Sean's explanation about Maire registered with him. He wouldn't have to give Tina a detailed account of his instructions. He smiled at his red-haired friend.

"Well, first, you've got to report to him in the morning for a special mission. He wouldn't give me details." It wouldn't do any harm to build up his friend's excitement and anticipation.

Sean questioned him further. But, since he knew no more about the mission Linane had in mind, he didn't have to invent a story.

"But what about us?" Tina finally put the vital question.

"Oh, ours is just a little practice run, really," he said evasively. "It's not important. Just a few of us. Not the whole team, you understand. We'll just go out, the few needed, to mingle with some crowds and do a bit of listening. I certainly won't be talking, with my accent . . ." His voice petered out under the accusing eye of the girl.

"Michael . . . ?"

"There's just a few of us going."

"You said that."

Sean fidgeted his way to the stairs, conscious of the tension. "I'll just go get out of these shoes. They're soaked through." He dashed away.

"Liar," thought Michael. "And traitor . . . And coward." He smiled nervously at Tina. But she just stared back, eyes narrow and mouth tight.

"You were telling me about the 'practice run'," she prompted.

"Oh. Not much to tell really. Just a few of us."

"Michael, don't dare say that once again. How many . . . and who?"

"Just six . . ."

She struggled to conceal her relief. It *was* only a few of them. She wasn't in disgrace or being sent back to Dublin . . . And she wasn't going to have to do anything. No fighting or shooting or blowing things up. She couldn't conceal the smile of relief. So she invented an excuse for it. "Did you see old Sean?" she said. "He looked like he'd been attacked by a plague of tinkers' fleas."

Michael laughed louder and longer than the recalled vision deserved. She stood up and he pulled her onto his knees.

"No, Michael," she protested as he kissed her. But she showed she was glad of his kisses until footsteps on the stairs made her move away from him.

Sean was relieved to see them flushed and smiling happily. They sat quietly, all three together, for a moment. "Will I make a cup of tea?" Sean asked, standing up suddenly.

"Cocoa, I think," said Michael, still grinning and unaware that the smile was fading from Tina's lips.

"Michael," she said quietly, "you didn't tell me who is going on the exercise tomorrow."

Sean stopped in mid-stride, half-way to the cooker. Michael turned quickly to face her.

"Oh damn," said Sean. "I left my keys upstairs. I'll just be away up to get them."

Tina and Michael collapsed, laughing hysterically, and, after a pause, Sean joined in. When the laughter had subsided to just an occasional round of snorts and giggles, Michael was able to tell Tina the names of the team. He told her as if he was having difficulty in remembering, starting with the intent to deceive, but then, as she caught on to his trickery, playing it up for laughs. After each name she looked at him ferociously and demanded: "And?" Each expletive conjunction was louder than the last until, after four names, she asked again.

"M...Me," he said and they laughed until the milk for the cocoa boiled over.

"You ... you ... bog creature," she spluttered helplessly. "AND?"

He shrugged and shook his head. "You have to know, don't you? But you know anyway. It's Maire, of course." He threw in desperately: "Linane's orders . . ." then inspiration . . . "he was worried about Sean's mission and didn't want him rushing back here, with me out of the house, to be alone with her and forgetting his duty."

Sean protested, blushing.

"And what about me being left here all alone?" demanded Tina. "D'you think Sean won't be rushing back to protect me and forgetting his duty?"

Michael heaved a sigh, the worst part was over. There was just one more problem for him to face: Maire would soon arrive.

As she walked in, big and confident and firing off questions, Michael told the other two: "Why don't you go up? I'll be along in a minute. I just want to brief Maire." He saw the troubled look return to Tina's face. But there was no help for it.

What he didn't realise and couldn't know as she started up the steps, followed by Sean, was the shape of the thought that wailed through her mind.

"He would never have sent me into a bedroom alone with any man – even Sean – two weeks ago," it went. "He has stopped loving me."

As she undressed, numb with her anguish and not caring whether Sean watched her or not, Michael had to grapple with his next problem. As he started to tell Maire about the raid, she let out a whoop and flung her arms round his neck. He let her kiss him excitedly, explaining to himself that while she did so she couldn't shout. She sat on his knee while he gave her details of the raid and talked her through the same objections he had voiced to Linane about it. Her eagerness for action quickly overcame her few qualms.

She bounced about excitedly as he outlined his plans. When he finished talking she turned and kissed him again, long and passionately. But there was still something he had to tell her.

He eased her away from him. "Look, don't say anything to Tina about this . . ."

She kissed him again and he realised that she had misunderstood as she whispered: "I won't, darling. I won't . . ."

"I mean the raid."

She sat up and looked at him questioningly. "You don't trust her then, Michael?"

He sighed. It was hopeless. How could he explain? "I'm not sure," he said. "I'm just not sure. And she isn't ready to go into action, yet." He cursed himself silently. It seemed that treachery was becoming a habit.

"Why don't you just send her back to Dublin?" whispered Maire, wriggling closer to him. "We'd be great together. We could fight the world and win."

Michael wondered in which film she'd heard that line. At the same time he could feel himself responding to the sexual invitation in her movements. But Tina was upstairs and he loved her, he told himself hastily. Even if things were going wrong between them and all he did seemed to make her more unhappy, she was his girl. This one on his knee, with her lips nibbling his neck and her hands inside his shirt, was not . . . At the same time there was no need to antagonise her. It would be better to lead her on just a little to keep her loyalty . . .

"In time. In time," he whispered in answer to her question about Tina. "I just want to make sure of a few things."

"This night, before the cock crow, thou shalt deny me thrice," he quoted to himself, and he felt Maire's hands teasing the hairs on his chest.

He kissed her. Then he tapped the front of her blouse with one finger. "Careful. I might just start pulling the hairs on your chest."

"That you won't. There are none," she said, sounding indignant. "But you're welcome to see for yourself." She pressed his hand against her, but he shook his head gently and withdrew it.

"Not now. With them both upstairs and needing to keep her sweet and with the raid tomorrow and all." It wasn't any sort of logic but it seemed to satisfy her. She stood and he followed her upstairs, watching the way she swayed and wondering if it might not be a good idea to send Tina back to Dublin, after all.

And he felt even more of a traitor as he crept into bed and felt the dear familiar arms go round his neck and the soft familiar body press close to his.

He didn't sleep well. But none of them did and in the morning they were almost glad to be up early and preparing. There was little laughter and few words and soon Michael and Maire were able to start out to rouse their fellow raiders...

CHAPTER XIX

A few miles from Derry a different sort of organiser was rousing his colleagues, shaking them out of dew-damp sleeping-bags and sending them to light the fires and start the routine of breakfast. As each tousled head popped up he greeted it – "Peace, it's time to start moving, Kevin (or Grace or Tim). We want to be on the road in an hour."

Donald, the organiser, was a big man with a gentle smile. Back in his own sleeping-bag, a plump, blonde girl was yawning and stretching and scratching her way into reality, also with a smile. Brenda, she was called. She reached outside the bag and was comforted to feel the worn carrying-case which contained her guitar. Maybe she'd be able to play it that night as they marched through the streets of Derry singing the old favourites: We Shall Overcome, This Land Is My Land, The Londonderry Air, Kevin Barry and She Got Up And Rattled Her Bin For The Specials Were Coming In . . .

". . . There's a green van parked on a street corner, with a pile of fence-posts, pick-axe handles, rolls of barbed wire and broken chunks of concrete in the back," said the instructions. "The keys are in the ignition."

Michael and his raiders found it, exactly where it was supposed to be, and got in. They drove in silence, fingering the fence-posts from time to time. Two of the boys had brought gloves. They drew them on and off their hands, fidgeting, until Michael glared at them. From time to time he glanced sideways at the girl in the passenger seat next to him. She was smiling confidently as she slouched at ease. She was a big girl, strong and useful to have on your side in a fight. The only trouble was that Tina should have been sitting there.

They had driven a few miles when he spotted a signpost and drew in to the roadside. They hadn't far to go.

"Let's you and me walk up to the top of this field and have a look," he whispered to Maire. They could be just a boy and girl walking if anyone noticed them.

"OK," answered Maire with an impish look on her face. "But you could look at me anywhere."

Michael also silenced her with a glare . . .

The marchers had set off, still ungluing eyes and stretching from their limbs the stiffness of days and nights on the road. This was the last day, but there was still no singing in the gruffness of the morning. That would come later, thought Brenda happily, as she stood beside Donald, clutching her guitar in one hand. She reached out and caught his wrist with the other. He kept his fist clenched for a moment in a sort of embarrassed resistance. They were at the front of the march, after all, and he wasn't quite as confident of the 'sixties morality as he tried to appear. Then he opened his hand and she smiled.

"Not far to go today," he said, for the want of some better form of acknowledgment of her.

The police Superintendent leading the escort was not so happy, as he showed by his answer to Donald from the side of his mouth. "Just as well, the rate we're going. Can't you hurry them up a bit? There's a big crowd at the bridge."

Donald caught his tension. "I thought the Prods said they weren't going to cause trouble? I mean . . ."

"That's what they said, lad. But I'd still rather get through there pretty bloody quick. Move them on, will you."

He was a new man. He hadn't been with them on the early part of the march. Donald eyed him suspiciously. But he signalled the marchers to move faster and, grabbing Brenda's hand, stepped up the pace at the front. They positively scurried along until they came in sight of the bridge and saw the waiting crowd.

"They may not be waiting to cause trouble," said Donald, "but they don't look as though they're going to cheer." The big, red, overfed, Northern Irish faces glared down at them with narrowed eyes and mouths twisted into snarls. Brenda clutched his hand more tightly as the police officer signalled them to stop.

Donald disengaged himself and with some of the other leaders stepped forward.

"Just wait there," said the officer. "I want to check that there'll be no trouble." He and his deputies marched forward to the bridge . . .

From a grassy slope a hundred yards or so away from the body of the crowd, Michael watched the men in peaked caps arrive and confer with the local Orange Order leaders, heavy farmers in tweeds. The two parties exchanged only a few words, the police visibly relaxing and feeling happier with their own kin than they were with the grubby, scarecrow collection they were escorting. As the policemen turned and walked back to the marchers, Michael signalled to his group to move into position. The two boys with gloves carried a loaded sack between them.

The eddy of movement they caused, as the police left the bridge, did not go totally unnoticed by Donald. He frowned and exchanged worried glances with his helpers. "Keep behind me," he told Brenda, who smiled at him trustingly.

"It's all right, they're just here to wave their own flags and shout some abuse," said the Superintendent.

"Only here for the jeer," said one of Donald's helpers, parodying an advertising slogan.

The Superintendent silenced him with a frown. "Just get this lot through as fast as you can."

"What about them?" Donald nodded with his head to the group who had moved into place while the police party were on the way back from their sortie.

The officer glanced at the bridge. Everything seemed the same to him. "They look all right to me," he said.

"Can't you move them back a bit?" suggested Donald.

"No." There was no room for argument in the blank refusal. "If you don't like it, you can stop your march. They've got just as much right to be there as you have to be here. Shall we get on with it?"

Donald looked at the others and shrugged. They had been promised no trouble. "OK. Keep close together and move fast.

Don't speak directly to the crowd or answer anything they say. Let's go."

They moved forward, eyes lowered, embarrassed and frightened – and alone. For the police suddenly dropped back. Donald flung a protective arm round Brenda.

Maire jigged excitedly beside Michael and lifted her fence-post into position.

"Wait," Michael hissed at her. And she lowered it a fraction. "Remember, I'll give the signal." He saw the light of joy in her eyes and sighed to himself. For a moment he almost disliked her. But then he had to concentrate as the marchers swung down the slope to go under the bridge, moving fast. The men on the bridge began to shout and chant, waving fat fists. The leading marchers were swinging close and Maire was plucking at his sleeve. He shook her off impatiently, staring fixedly at the first of the marchers. He was a big dark-haired man, whose face seemed more fitted for smiling than for its present worried expression. The man had his arms round a blonde girl. They were almost level with him. Their eyes met. And the man knew! He pushed the girl behind him and raised his hands in front of his face.

"Now," roared Michael and swung at the man's crotch. From the corner of his eye he saw Maire leap like an Amazon, whirling her club and bringing it down on the blonde head of the girl behind the big man.

From the bridge concrete chunks crashed onto the heads of the milling marchers. On the other side of the cutting, gloved hands tore away the sacking round a package and hurled a roll of barbed wire into the rearguard of the protesters.

The big tweedy men on the bridge tried for a few moments to stop the attack. Then they joined in with curses, hurling stones and bricks into the crowd.

Michael swung his stave again and again at each marcher who came within range. Beside him was a yelling fury, hitting, kicking and punching in time with him.

Not all the marchers fled or cowered in terror. One charged for Michael and caught him with a swinging punch. As he staggered the man leapt at him. But a stave was thrust between the man's legs and he fell before he could follow up his blow.

"Feel that, you bastard," screeched Maire, untangling her club from the man's legs and bringing it down on his head. Michael looked round quickly. The fight was raging and eddying about him and on the other side of the bridge the police were forming up. Two lads with gloved hands were sauntering away from the battle, up the grass slope, safe behind the line of uniforms.

Two of the others were disengaging themselves from the stone-throwers. He slapped Maire's buttocks as she braced them to bring down her club again on the man she had felled. As she looked round, he jerked his head to indicate to her that they should go and saw a flicker of disappointment on her face.

The police were marching forward in a disciplined line, cracking heads as they moved into range. Their instincts told them which heads to crack—as always.

Michael's group hurried up the slope and away from the battle. As they ran for the safety of the van, he stopped and looked back. Many of the marchers had broken out of the cutting and were regrouping under crumpled and tattered banners a little further on. Then, he saw a big black-haired man thrust his way through the last knot of fighting men, stop and swing a small blonde figure up in his arms. Even from where he was Michael could see, in the way he stood, the shape of anguish. As if drawn by magnets the man's eyes lifted to his and recognised him. Michael raised one hand and waved. Then he followed the others.

As he got in the van and started the engine Maire threw her arms round him, kissing him delightedly: "Wasn't it beautiful? Did you see the way that blonde slut's head split open like a flower? Oh, Michael, and did you see what I did when that fella hit you? I thought you were going down . . ." The others were all joining in now, yelling and slapping each other and telling what they'd done and seen. The babble rose to a crescendo and Maire kept grabbing him and kissing him. They were hysterical with delight over their victory. And he couldn't share the joy. He felt drained and numb.

"For God's sake. Get off me." He hurled Maire aside and turned on the others. "And shut up, all of you. We've got to get out of here." As he drove off he looked back at the slope they had descended a few seconds before and there was the big dark man with the blood-stained girl in his arms, striding towards them. The girl could have been Tina.

None of the others saw the man as Michael accelerated away. They were silent for all of ten seconds. Then they began again – "Did you see . . . ?" and, "When we dropped the wire on them . . ." and, "There was blood all over her . . ." – louder and louder. He couldn't shout at them again. He couldn't push Maire away as she put an arm over his shoulder and a hand on his thigh.

"And you should have seen Michael," she was speaking softly now, cooing her loving admiration and stroking him, tugging his hair gently, tickling his ears, leaning close. "He must have smashed a dozen heads. It was fantastic."

The others were all listening and nodding. His head was still spinning from the blow he had taken, as she broadcast his exploits. But he smiled and felt the nausea and anger lifting under her praise and caresses. She was right . . . they were right . . . it had been a victory. He looked sideways, taking his eyes off the road at last. She was glowing with triumph, her big breasts heaving with excitement. She was beautiful at that moment and he felt his own spirits soar. He let out a bellow of laughter and stopped the van. "God, and you should have seen old Maire," he roared. "She'd outfight any of you. Like a tiger she is, and she probably saved my life." He flung his arms round her and kissed her.

"Let's go and have a drink to celebrate," said Maire as they drove back into Derry and began to look for a deserted street in which to dump the van.

"Yes," the others all chorused.

"No," said Michael coolly – glad that his mind was still working in spite of his headache, the swelling on the side of his face and the disturbing persistence of the hand on his thigh.

"Come on, Michael. We deserve it and you can even invite Tina – if you really want her there," said Maire.

"No," said Michael. "Just think, will you."

"What do you mean?" demanded Maire.

"Think," he said, enjoying himself now as he drew out the pleasure of his superior knowledge.

"OK. We give up. You tell us why we can't have a drink to celebrate the success of our first big job," said Maire heavily.

"I suppose I'll have to spell it out for you – and you can take this as an order. There must be no celebration tonight, not for a few days yet and possibly never."

There was a chorus of protests and he felt his temper rising.

"There'll be no celebration because the people of the Bogside will have heard by now about the attack on the Civil Rights Marchers . . ."

"But isn't that what we want? People to know what we're doing," said a lad called Willy. Maire shook her head, frowning. She was beginning to catch on.

Michael smiled at her encouragingly. To his questioner he said: "No. We don't want people to know what we're doing. Listen, Maire's caught on, I'll explain it to the rest of you." He was proud of her again. "By now the Bogside is mourning the kids who were hurt in the attack at the bridge" (most of whom were older than he, despite his grand manner). "Soon, when they hear how the police apparently led the boys and girls into a trap, they'll be good and angry. That's why we did it. So you want us to blow the whole thing by roaring round the bars and getting drunk and boasting about beating in the heads of our people . . . the IRA on the same side as the 'B' Specials? For a start we'd have to run for our lives out of Derry. The Movement would be on its way out of Northern Ireland and the victory would be put back fifty years."

Most of the others were getting the message. Willy was still concerned about his celebration. "But when . . . ?" he began.

"Never," replied Michael. "This is a story we can't tell to anyone who wasn't there – and I mean that. Tonight we have to go back to where we are staying and mourn with the people about what we did. There's plenty to mourn, after all, and I would rather not have had to do it. And later this afternoon, when the marchers limp into town, I won't be there to see them. We all have to keep out of their way, in case any of them recognise our faces."

The others nodded, one by one, even Willy. But after they had parked the van, separated and started to walk to their homes in ones and twos, Maire took Michael's arm. "Maybe we can have a little private celebration of our own, tonight, darling," she suggested.

Michael looked at her – and she was still attractive. He recalled the way she had fought beside him at the ambush.

"The others will be there," he said lamely.

"Then maybe we should send them out for a walk," she said.

"Ach, come on, Maire. You know we have to sort things out and there's nothing much we can do about it at the moment." He had left the Black Irishman behind at the bridge.

"OK, Michael. I understand. But how do you think I feel . . . in the same room while you're in bed with another girl? Just answer me that. I'll wait. But don't ask me to wait forever."

Michael felt like replying that he hadn't asked her to wait in the first place. But again the memory of how she had fought beside him at the bridge came back and he realised that he would sooner have her on his side than as his enemy. He bent and kissed her. "You won't have long to wait," he whispered, sounding as if he meant it.

A few minutes later he began to think he had. Though they could not celebrate their victory, they still walked home feeling buoyant. But, as they stepped into the kitchen, Tina's accusing eyes turned to them.

"I'm surprised you can smile," she said.

"Why?" demanded Michael – and the question was a lie.

"You were at the ambush, weren't you? You turned the mob onto those marchers . . ." As Michael began to deny it, Maire took his sleeve and shook her head at him.

"I'm not so stupid as you think. It wasn't hard to work out what you were up to . . . My God, our own people, protesting about things *we* want changed, and you can do that. I suppose you're going to tell me it's some clever scheme of your precious Mr Linane. Well, I don't want to hear about it. And I suppose you don't think I know what you two are up to behind my back. Michael, I don't know what has happened to you. I thought you were a brave boy who wanted to save our country and do the best for the people. But now everything you're doing is rotten. Everything . . ."

"No," roared Michael. "Everything you're doing is rotten. All this whining and complaining. All this stupid nonsense on the course about not being able to do the things all the others could do. All this refusing to join in the fun. All this nagging when you don't even understand what we we're trying to do and don't want to understand..."

"I understand... that a Catholic girl from Belfast died this afternoon and that you, or one of your gang, killed her. That's what I understand..."

"Oh God... died." He looked at Maire. She too was shaken.

They both sat down. Maire began to weep quietly, hiding her face in her hands. He shook his head as if he couldn't believe it. "Dead," he muttered.

"Yes, dead," snapped Tina. "And you killed her." She didn't want to rant and rage at him. She would rather take his head in her hands and comfort him. But he had walked in so happy and smiling – with Maire – that she had to scream the news at him. "You killed her..."

"Shut up, will you, Tina? Give me time to think," he said wearily.

"Time to think... You should have done that before you went off to do somebody else's murders for them. If Linane wants people killed, why doesn't he go and do it himself...?"

"Starting with you, eh, Tina?" Linane's dry voice cut short her tirade. All three of them whirled, to see him standing by the door. He had walked in unnoticed while Tina ranted. Now she gaped and blushed.

"Maybe I'm beginning to understand why you've been so soft lately, Michael – the voice of your conscience over there." He fixed Tina with his cold stare and she remained silent. "Well, I came to congratulate you all. And there's no reason for you..." he nodded to Maire... "to sniffle. You, Michael, to look as if a tragedy has occurred. Or you, Tina, to sound off like some hell and damnation priest."

As she opened her mouth to protest he cut her short brutally. "I'll thank you to keep your tongue still. You are in an IRA house under IRA orders and I am your commander. You have already said too much and done too little. Provoke me and I shall have you shot."

Tina gasped and burst into tears. "Oh, shut up," snapped the little man. "You make me tired. I should have had you sent back to Dublin a week ago. It was only because this idiot seemed to need you around that I allowed you to stay. His morale is more important to me than your bleeding heart. That's why I came here to say thank you personally and to hear his report. Now, before you leave to let Michael and I discuss this, I have one or two things more to tell you, young woman. The first is that today *was* a major victory – a great start to our campaign. The death of that girl only adds to the success. And before you start snorting your righteous indignation at us I want you to realise, and that goes for the rest of you as well, that this one death will be nothing compared with what's to come. For the next few years Northern Ireland will be awash with blood – just as our country has been watered with the blood of martyrs for centuries and must continue to be so until the British have been driven out. It hurts to kill almost as much as it hurts to die. We may all suffer both pains in the years to come."

Michael felt a shiver down his spine at the last words. They sounded like a prediction.

"You, Tina, know why this raid took place. Only if we discredit the police and remove the chance of another meaningless compromise with our masters will we turn the protests into a battle, which we shall win, to get the English out of Ireland. I'm determined that we shall. I'd also have preferred it, personally, if that girl hadn't died today. But, since her death will help our cause, I salute it."

He paused. "Now get out of here, girl. I've explained myself enough – too much – for one day. Get out of here and get your mind in order before I lose my patience with you."

She went, meek and fearful. Linane caught the jut of Michael's jaw.

"Don't pout, my boy, it doesn't suit you," he said, almost lightly, when Tina was out of earshot. "If you think I shouldn't talk to your girl like that, you're probably right. But I haven't time for kid gloves and neither have you. In fact, all you have time for is to pack up and be ready to leave tonight."

"Leave, but we've only just got here," said Michael.

"Leave, is what I said." Linane was smiling mysteriously, like a conjuror about to pull a rabbit out of his hat. He produced the rabbit. "Just the six of you who were at the bridge will head back across the border now and join up with Sean in Buncrana. You'll pick up a car and some hand-guns there and he'll take you on to the bank he's been looking over in Donegal. You'll hit that, then move on fast to Castlerea . . . and so on."

"You mean we're to rob banks now?" Michael asked.

"Well, I'm not expecting you to force them at gunpoint to take *your* money. How do you think we're going to finance our operation if we don't do some fund-raising on a slightly larger scale than carrying collecting-boxes at Cork Airport, labelled Irish Language Society? Anyway, that's the idea. You hit fast and move on, changing cars whenever and wherever you can. Yes, lad! Steal them. Willy has a lot of experience with cars if his record's anything to go by. You'll be back in Buncrana in a fortnight, with any luck . . ." Michael shivered again. Was that also a prophecy?

Linane continued: "If you succeed, The Movement will be able to pay for the next shipment of arms. You'll see a lot of Ireland and, by the time you get back here, the heat will be off. What you haven't realised is that the police may be stupid but they're not so stupid that they won't smell a rat about the episode at the bridge. They'll also be good and mad about what happened to their reputation. They'll turn the place over looking for the wild Irish boy and the red-haired girl who led the attack. There's also the danger of betrayal while you hang about here – not to speak of the likelihood of some of your lads shooting off their mouths about their triumph."

"And it will be only the six from the bridge that go?" asked Michael, suddenly aware of a pair of new problems.

"That's right," said Linane with a crooked grin. "I'm afraid I'm going to have to break up the happy home for a little while. Besides, I've got some use for Tina here. I'll keep her fully employed while you're away, so that she doesn't have too much time to brood over her wandering boy being with that other woman."

Maire smiled happily. She reached under the table and put her hand on Michael's knee. At that moment Linane seemed like an angel to her. For two weeks she would have Michael to herself. But Linane cut short further expressions of her joy by sending her for a walk so that he could give detailed instructions to Michael.

As he continued his briefing, Michael wondered first how he would break the news to Tina, then, how he would keep Maire at bay for two weeks. Perhaps he would be able to keep his bank-robbers too busy for her to think of that sort of thing – and he knew there wasn't a chance. He wasn't too alarmed at the prospect. But what would Tina do, left here alone and angry about his journey?

She was strangely quiet that night as they lay in bed – but not passive. Maire was still out walking and it was just like those treasured, remembered times in Dublin. When Michael explained about the trip Tina was full of her love for him. It didn't matter about the other girl having all those opportunities to be alone with him. She knew he loved her and would come back to her. She had been behaving stupidly, being scared and possessive in a way that was foreign to her. The parting would serve as a punishment and a reminder to keep her head, she told herself. It could also be a chance to prove herself again. But trusting Michael was one thing. Acting like a fool was another.

She reached down between his legs. "I love you, Michael, remember that," she said and he thought, even in his dreamy loving mood, that there was something odd about the way she spoke. Then he gasped with alarm as her hand gripped him hard.

"No! Christ! What are you doing?" he yelped.

"Just warning you, Michael. This is mine and, if I hear of any fooling around with a certain big fat girl from Belfast, I'll rip it off, I promise you."

"You know I wouldn't," he squealed desperately. "Of course I wouldn't – Tina . . ."

"I know you would and all. So, promise me there'll be nothing like that . . . promise me." She gave another tug and twist.

"All right, all right. I promise. I promise." He gave a sigh of relief as she released him. "God, you're mad. You could have done me an injury." Then: "And what about you, here alone?" He hauled himself up onto one elbow and looked down at her, catching the flash of her teeth as she grinned in the darkness.

"Me . . . I'll do no worse and no better than you," she said tauntingly. "Oh."

He leapt on her and they wrestled.

She was asleep in his arms when Maire returned. He pretended to snore as he heard her undressing. He felt no stir of desire. She was a well-built girl – but she wasn't Tina. She was brave and tough – but she could never love him like the girl whose head lay on his shoulder.

"Goodnight, Michael, darling," she called softly as she climbed into her bed.

"Goodnight, Maire," he answered.

CHAPTER XX

Sean had done his reconnaissance well at the first bank they raided. They left with a wad of notes and no one in pursuit. The second raid, two days later, seemed as successful. But, by then, odd fractions of description were being tied together in Garda offices, patterns were becoming established.

Patterns were being established among Michael's team, too. Before and after the first raid they were all tense and watchful, carefully noting everything that happened. By the time they drove off at breakneck speed after the second, they had all realised how easy it was to rob small-town banks. While Willy demonstrated his driving ability yet again, skidding round corners on two wheels and whipping through the gears like a racing driver, Maire settled close to Michael, in the front seat, showing her speed and falling into their pattern. Her eyes shining with the excitement of the raid, she whispered her joy into Michael's ear, her arms round him. He was excited too. Another raid, another haul for the funds and another raid to come next day. Tonight they were to sleep in an empty cottage. There was no need to watch Wild Willy's driving. He could relax and enjoy the congratulations of this girl who was crazy about him.

Sean was waiting for them at the cottage, when they located it. He was grinning broadly and mysteriously as they tumbled out of the car and stretched their cramped limbs. He kept his hands tucked behind his back and didn't rush to greet them.

"What's wrong with you?" demanded Maire finally. "Don't you want to congratulate us? What in hell's name are you looking so smug for?"

He just went on grinning and still kept his hands hidden.

"What are you hiding there, fella?" she asked, as he had intended.

"Nothing for innocent young girls like you," he replied tantalisingly. "You have no use for this."

She advanced on him menacingly and, as he backed, flung herself onto him.

"Careful. Careful," he protested. "You don't want to smash this."

After a few moments of wrestling, he let her snatch the contents of one hand.

She held it aloft in triumph. "Christ, it's a drop of the Black Bush," said one of the others reverently.

"And another here," said Sean, holding up his other hand.

There were more yells of delight. But Michael stared at the bottles and kept his mouth grimly closed. He knew they wanted to celebrate, probably needed to work off some of their tension before tomorrow's raid, but it didn't seem right. It also didn't seem that there was any way he could reasonably stop them. There was an unanswered question though: how could Sean have afforded two bottles of fine old whiskey? He couldn't have paid for them unless he had used some of the money from the raids. Or had he stolen them during his reconnaissance of the next town they were to hit? Both alternatives were silly.

"Sean . . ." His cold voice cut across the noise of the others. "Sean. How did you get the money to buy the stuff?"

The smile froze on Sean's mouth. He knew the implication in the icy question. The blood came to his cheeks and he carefully put his precious bottle down behind him. "What in hell do you mean, Michael Sullivan . . . ?" he began pugnaciously, taking a stiff-legged step forward.

Michael smiled sardonically at the angry figure – and dealt with him. "What I mean is: how did you get the money to buy the stuff?" And as Sean began to advance more rapidly he barked: "You will stay there and you will answer my question, McDade. I'm in charge of this mission and I'll not have it threatened by anyone's stupidity."

"I didn't buy the stuff," growled Sean, hurt by his friend's suspicion and remembering the often-repeated warning about spending any of the haul from the banks, because of the danger that it might be traced. He knew the money had to be shifted in mysterious ways to The Movement if they were not to be tracked down.

"You didn't steal it?" There was disbelief in Michael's voice and Sean bristled again.

"Of course not. You know me better than that."

Michael had to control an urge to snort with laughter at Sean's injured innocence. Here was a lad who had just mapped out two bank robberies and he was mortally offended by the suggestion that he might have stolen two bottles of whisky. If he had done, it would have been dangerously stupid and would have warned people of the possible dangers. But that wasn't what was worrying Sean.

Still, Michael had to know, and the only way to find out was to continue with his role as prosecutor.

"Then, where did you get the bottles?" he asked, sounding impatient.

"I'd have told you, if you'd just waited," said Sean grumpily. "You know I'd to hand the money from the first job to a messenger I was to meet in the town before I looked over the bank! Well, it was Mr Fallon who turned up. And he was so delighted with the haul that he marched off and bought the two bottles. He said to give them to the lads with his compliments, to celebrate. Nice of him, don't you think? And him not knowing about all that checking up on him we were doing in Dublin."

Michael felt the cold shiver yet again. So many things were wrong that he wondered which question to ask first. And he wasn't sure the gift of the bottles was such a nice gesture.

"You didn't tell him about the checking?" he demanded. When Sean said he hadn't and began to expostulate, Michael cut him short with his next question. "He didn't buy the bottles with any of the bank money?" Michael remembered the way Fallon had mishandled his first trip to Britain. Mr Popularity Fallon, winning all hearts with a cosy gesture and plunging them into all sorts of dangers with his carelessness. Sean didn't know the answer, of course.

Fallon? What was he doing acting as a messenger anyway? Everything about it alarmed Michael. He asked a couple more desultory questions and then tried half-heartedly to placate Sean while his mind wrestled with his premonitions.

Sean and the others filed into the house ahead of him. His harshness had taken the joy out of them momentarily. And what could he do about these damned bottles? He didn't feel right about celebrating now. He wanted them all to be fresh before the next raid. He didn't approve of drinking in the middle of things. But Fallon, a member of the Central Council, outranked him and had cut the ground from under his feet. He couldn't object.

He asked Sean for his sketches and his ideas about the town and bank they were to hit. But his mind was in turmoil. They were waiting expectantly, his gang of bank-robbers. A great crowd. They worked well together. He couldn't disappoint them.

"OK," he said, with a forced grin, "Let's have a drink."

The tension fell away from them immediately. "Good lads . . . and lasses," he thought, still feeling gloomy. He must not let anything happen to them. He couldn't relax with them, though. Not tonight . . . Something was wrong.

One of them thrust into his hand a mug with a large slug of whisky in it, but he sipped from it while they all swigged theirs. He edged over to the gaping spaces where there should have been windows and peered out anxiously into the damp gloom of an Irish evening. There wasn't much to be seen out there beyond the weeping hedgerows. But there was the car, stolen that morning from another town. They'd left it, doors open, where it could just be seen from the road. Perhaps he could move it a little way, under the cover of those trees, and close the doors so that it wouldn't be damp and uncomfortable to ride in next morning. He took another swallow from his mug. The stuff wasn't having its usual effect on him. It was on the others. The girl, Connolly, was dancing with Sean. Willy was singing and the others, including Maire, were clapping in time. From time to time the big girl looked at Michael and frowned. She saw him move towards the door and was there as soon as he opened it.

"What's wrong, Michael? Where are you going?" she asked.

"Just to move the car under cover," he replied, trying to sound casual.

Maire sensed his uneasiness. "Come on! Why don't you relax? You're like a cat on hot bricks tonight."

"It's nothing," he said. "Nothing important, anyway."

"Tell you what," said Maire, taking his arm and leaning against him, tipsy already. "Why don't I come and help you move the car and you can tell me all about it?" There was a wealth of meaning and invitation in her voice.

He smiled down at her. Her red hair glowed in the dim light. He could smell the earthy scent of it as she leaned her head against his shoulder. "Sure. Why not?" he said. And none of the others noticed as they stepped silently from the old cottage.

As soon as they were in the car, Maire slid into Michael's arms and kissed him determinedly.

He ran his hands through her heavy long hair and held her close. "Let's just move the car up a bit," he whispered, "into the shadows up there."

She nodded soundlessly. But, while he fumbled under the dashboard to find the two wires that had to be joined, she held on to him. The engine spluttered into life and he eased the gear lever into place. She kissed his neck, nibbled his ears and slid one hand inside his shirt. He grinned as he rolled the car forward.

"Just wait a second or you'll have me driving through the bushes."

She stopped nibbling his ears, just letting her lips rest against his neck. And it was only fractionally less disturbing.

The shadow of the trees was over them now. He slapped the gear lever into neutral, yanked on the hand-brake and tore the wires apart in a series of frantic gestures. Then he reached urgently for another lever. She was kissing him eagerly on his mouth, his nose, his eyes. His fingers found the handle beside the seats, he pulled and they toppled down together, lips searching, hands seeking — "A little liquor is a dangerous thing," he muttered to himself, enjoying his own pun, then changing it. "A little yearning is a dangerous thing. A little Maire is a dangerous thing." Then he gasped and forgot puns as she pulled his head down to her bared breast. For a few minutes they both wrestled frantically with shoes and zips and elastic. Then they were free of all the encumbrances. He could feel on his back a cool draught from somewhere. There was a moment of peace and calm. No more need to wrestle and hurry as she stretched herself into the position of surrender and he lowered himself, to kiss her first and delight in the soft firmness of her, to feel the cool leather of the car seat on his knees. It was a moment to savour . . . and the unmistakable click of a rifle bolt sounded a few feet away. She tensed under him. She had heard it too. He held her still, stifling any sound from her while he listened. There was a soft whisper of voices, the swish of feet on grass and then the crunch of trodden gravel. They were moving away. He reached beneath him and put his hand gently to her mouth while he lifted himself, infinitely slowly, from her. Now he could hear, faintly, the sound of singing and clapping from inside the cottage – and more feet crunching on gravel. Armed men were moving all round.

At last he got his eyes level with the bottom of the rear window. They quickly confirmed what his ears had told him. Dark shapes. Uniform badges glinting in the last light. Some of them must have walked past, only yards from the car. The moment of lingering over his conquest had been fortunate. Breathlessly, he eased himself back to the driving seat. He could see Maire's eyes staring up at him and lifted his hand from her mouth, put a finger to his own lips and then signalled her to stay low. He located the two wires under the dashboard and prayed that they'd work yet again.

A voice barked a command, the door of the cottage was kicked open and the sound of the singing and clapping ended abruptly in a string of oaths and shouts. Michael drowned the whole chapter of sound by plunging the wires together and kicking the accelerator so that the car roared to life. He slammed it into gear and it roared forward, straight through the hedge. He prayed there were no hidden stumps in this section, cursed as the metal pedals bruised his bare feet, and wrestled with the steering wheel. He had no idea what was on the other side of the hedge. He hoped the ground was firm in the field. He hated the idea of running naked from the Garda if the car stuck. He felt the back wheels spin as they broke through the hedge, then they bit as he eased his foot off the throttle. They were rattling forward, bumping and lurching. He heard a rifle crack behind and slammed Maire flat in her seat as she tried to sit up.

"Go right to get to the road," she yelled.

He swung the wheel left. He was sure that was the way. "And why is it no woman can ever tell left from right in an emergency?" They bumped down into a hollow, skidded wildly, then stormed up the other side, through another hedge. He felt the car's tyres strike tarmac. They had found the road. But it was difficult to see and stay on it.

"Why don't you switch on the lights, idiot?" yelled Maire, sitting up beside him.

"And why don't you put some clothes on? If we're going to be arrested, at least you'll be decent," he cracked back. But he turned on the lights. He still hadn't heard any sounds of pursuit.

Soon he saw the main road. Once they reached that they would be safe. He pointed ahead and Maire nodded. She hurried with her dressing and then grinned at him.

"You'd better let me take over as soon as I'm ready. We don't want someone calling the Garda to tell them they saw a naked man driving a car."

He gestured to her to be quiet and she shook her head in disbelief. "Michael, we can talk now. They can't hear us from back there at the bothy, damnit." They changed places soon afterwards.

Back on the main road, safe in the early evening traffic, Maire slowed the car and pulled into a lay-by. She answered his unspoken question. "We can't just drive. We've got to decide what to do. What was all that about, anyway?"

Michael sat silent for a moment, gesturing her to silence too, as she went to repeat her question. At last he voiced the thought that had been lurking at the back of his mind, unwanted and unwelcome, since his first sighting of the armed policemen closing in on the cottage – and which might even have been there in his subconscious, making him restless, before that. It was a one-word answer.

"Betrayal," he said.

She frowned. "Who?"

"By accident or design, the man we were set to watch that time in Dublin."

Her eyes widened in disbelief, and then rearranged into a frown as if she were thinking about it and realising that it was possible. "Fallon . . . but . . ."

"Fallon, and not many buts. That wasn't an exercise in Dublin. Linane had reports. Now Fallon turns up here, hands out some free booze which he knows will throw us off guard and then, by chance, the Garda arrive to spoil the party. Even if he only paid for the booze with cash from the bank haul, that was criminal carelessness – and not the first time either."

"But Fallon's a big man – very nearly the biggest. Certainly the most popular. No one would believe it, even if it is true."

"I'm not sure of it myself," said Michael. "But now I'm suspicious. I reckon the others will be too."

"What about them?" asked Maire. "We can't just leave them, can we? I mean . . . I know what we're expected to do is call off the mission and leave it to The Movement to get them out . . . but . . ."

"Exactly," said Michael. "My guess is that they'll take them back to the town jail for the night and ship them out again early in the morning. We either get them out of jail or get them out of the van on the way from the jail . . ."

"Is that all we have to do?" interrupted Maire, her head cocked pertly.

And she still looked pretty, thought Michael, with her hair ruffled and her blouse showing "too many buttons and not enough buttonholes". He reached for one of the buttons.

"Michael, stop it, will you. Not here. We've got to think . . ." She flushed and couldn't conceal the smile that softened her features. "Damnit, if you get in there I'll have the pants off you again, main road or no."

He refastened the button – correctly this time. "Just doing it up properly, so I could concentrate," he said. Then, more seriously: "Just listen a minute, will you. We've got two machine pistols and an automatic, plus a crate of grenades, in the back there. If we can't get the lads out of a country jail with that lot, how the hell are we going to cope with getting the English out of the North . . . ?"

"But the orders were that if anything went wrong we were to send the 'abort' signal to Linane and get out."

That was the second time she had mentioned the orders, thought Michael – and how would she know those? Linane had only told him and possibly Sean. Sean had not spent more than a few seconds with her since they started on the raids. Then Michael shook his head in irritation at himself. The business of Fallon had made him ridiculously suspicious. But who could he rely on now? Tina had turned hopeless. He looked at the big flushed girl beside him. Here was one he could rely on.

He took her hand as he explained: "We're heading towards the town. Look there." In the opposite lane, going fast, a police car sped past in the direction from which they had come. After a few seconds another followed. He had seen several go by while Maire was driving. "They'll have a ring round the area a tadpole wouldn't get through by now. They'd never expect us to be going this way. While we're there, we call on our local man and find out a few things about the jail and the roads around the place. At least it will keep us busy while we're waiting to break out of the trap . . ."

She smiled and pressed his hand down on her thigh. "I can think of another way we could pass the time," she whispered, "and we wouldn't be breaking our orders."

There it was again. Sean must have told her, the idiot. "The orders were that I should use my head if there was trouble. That's what I'm doing," he said.

She leant against him. "Michael, I'm not sure . . ."

"You don't have to be. Just do as you're told," he said and kissed away her last protest.

He drove them into the town, found their contact and had a long private chat with him while Maire dozed, read a week-old newspaper and finally tidied herself up.

When Michael returned with the man he grinned at her efforts. "You might just as well not have bothered with all that," he said. "We're going to exchange clothes in a minute – at least, some of them. First we've got to move the stuff out of the car."

Maire did as he instructed without too many questions, gave him her dress, with some comment about how he could take that off her any time, and pretended to frown when he gave her a spare pair of his trousers and a jacket to wear. She tied up her hair and hid it under the black cap their contact produced, while Michael tied a headscarf on himself. When she asked what it was all about he replied laconically: "And nobody knew they were there."

At last they stepped out to the van that had been stolen and delivered to the front door while they were preparing. They drove off with a wave to their new friend, Rory. "He'll get rid of the other car and drop the loot off at the station."

She looked aghast. "You trusted him with the money. Are you some sort of idiot?"

"No," said Michael. "I don't have to trust him. He saw the guns."

That didn't explain much to her. But she could see it was all the explanation she was going to get. "And why the fancy dress?" she demanded. "You look less like a woman than anyone I've ever seen."

He took his eyes off the road long enough to squint at her. "Funny, you look just like a boy," he said. "Ouch! Get off, you crazy fool. You'll have us into a lamp-post." After a pause he added: "You'd better start practising sounding like a man, while you're at it. From now until we get out of this town you've changed. So, if you have to say anything, sound and act like a fella, OK?" He said the last few words in a high falsetto. She giggled, turned it into a leer and sidled across the seat towards him.

"OK, my little darling, I'll do just that," she boomed and slid her hand under his dress.

"Oh, you beast," he squeaked. "That's all you ever think of."

"But where are we going, Michael?" she asked more seriously. "And what's it all about?"

He explained, maintaining the falsetto: "We're going to jail. Rory told me that the crowd were brought in a couple of hours back and are being questioned there now. When the questioning stops – or when the Garda find their knuckles hurting too much to keep it up – we go in. The back way. Rory gave me a layout of the place. As for the disguises: no one has seen us as we are, and I don't intend that they should."

She nodded as they drove along a narrow deserted street

behind the high wall of what was obviously the police barracks. Michael stopped and then reversed into another street, which faced almost directly onto the wall. She looked at him questioningly.

He pointed to a lighted high window. "That's where they do the interviewing. When the light goes out they've stopped. Then we move fast. Meanwhile, we just keep out of sight in the back of the van."

She was smiling happily as they climbed into the back and settled down. She snuggled close to Michael. "How long do you think it will be?" she asked, apparently innocently.

"It'll be an hour or two yet," he said, suspecting nothing. "I just hope they don't talk. I'm worried about Shirley."

"Don't worry, my darling, she's smart enough. You've got something else to worry about now." Suddenly her voice was a booming bass again. "We've got some unfinished business and you'll not get away from me so easy this time, my little flower." She reached under Michael's skirt again

He giggled shrilly, still innocently playing the part. "Oh, stop it, you brute. I shall scream." But Maire had no intention of stopping. "Hey, hang on now," Michael protested in his normal voice. "What are you doing?" He tried to push her away. "We've got to watch the light."

"You watch the light," hissed Maire, playing no longer. "You've got me so steamed up. You're not leaving me like this. If we've got a couple of hours . . . Michael, I want you so much." There was a pleading sobbing note in her voice.

"But . . ." She kissed him and he slid his arms about her. He held her head back with one hand for a second. "Suppose someone comes, police or something."

"Suppose . . ." she grated. "Suppose . . . They'll be embarrassed and look the other way, that's what. Michael, I have to . . ."

Michael opened his eyes with a shocked gasp. He looked up immediately at the window. He couldn't see it. The light was out. He looked further down the wall. A dim orange light glowed in a window diagonally to his right. That was the night-light in the cells, which he had been told to look out for.

He reached over and shook Maire gently.

"Michael, darling," she sighed and turned round, reaching for him.

"Come on," he called urgently. "Time to move."

She sat up – and she was magnificent in the dim light, he thought.

"Time for action," he repeated softly.

She smiled briefly, as if she was fondly remembering some other recent action, and then started to dress in the clothes that were supposed to make her look like a boy. "No chance of that," Michael told himself as he also scrambled into his disguise.

He handed her one machine pistol, slung the other over his own shoulders and slipped the automatic into the belt of his dress. Then he broke open the box of grenades, filled his bodice with some, gave her a few others and finally put six more in a bag which he tied to the radiator of the van.

"Get out now," he ordered as he started the engine. He manoeuvred the machine carefully into position, pointing directly at a spot four feet to the left of the dim light. He slipped from the driving seat and fumbled in the bag on the bumper. Five seconds to go. The van rattled forward as he gave it full throttle. The noise seemed deafening in the silent street. Four seconds. Quickly he dropped the heavy empty grenade box onto the throttle pedal – three seconds – and leapt out into the street. Two seconds. The van thundered into the wall, which opened up round it in a strange, slow-motion tumult of bricks. One second. Michael covered his head and ears. The road seemed to leap and quiver under him. Though his eyes were tight closed, the searing yellow light of the explosion cut into his brain. Then he was up and running towards the gaping hole in the wall – and damnit, his trouser legs, which had been rolled up under his skirt, started slipping down. He slowed, slapped at them to push them up again and a bizarre heavy-breasted "boy" ran past him into the gaol, pistol at the ready. He followed, spluttering in the smoke and dust.

"Open up the cells. All of them. No matter who. Use grenades. I'll cover." He screeched his orders in his ridiculous falsetto. There was no time to laugh. She was moving like a machine, roaring "Keep Down" and blasting each door in turn. Sean was out. So was Willy. But where was Connolly? His eyes fixed on the top of the stairs. Here came the guards. Uniforms dishevelled – flung on in a hurry probably. He loosed off a burst over the heads of the staggering escapers. One guard fell, the others ducked back. Where was Connolly? A rifle barrel began to slide round the door at the top of the stairs. He took careful aim and it jerked back out of sight.

"Here, Sean," he screeched and flung the automatic to his friend. "Take this and cover outside."

The last cell was opening. "All outside fast," he roared. "Out, out, out," boomed Maire, backing towards him and pointing her gun along the corridor. The rifles were bristling at the door on the top of the stairs. He let off a long round and fumbled for the grenades in his dress top.

"Down, everyone, and out," he yelled – and thought, "Christ, this daft voice is going to give me a sore throat." He heard Sean's gun blast. "Help him, Maire. Remember the bombs." He shoved her out of the hole in the wall and heard the bullets start to whistle round him as he crouched. She let out a gasp but carried on running. He heard her machine pistol start up. Quick now. He pulled a pin with his teeth, counted two and flung it, ducking out of the gap in the wall. Sean, Maire and the rest were kneeling behind the van. Police were blasting at them from both ends of the barracks.

The grenades. Why didn't she use the grenades? He let off long bursts both ways and then began hurling his bombs frenziedly at every sign of movement. He lobbed a couple more into the hole in the wall, bringing down more debris.

"Maire, the bombs . . . the fucking bombs," he roared over his shoulder. There was no answer. He swung round to remonstrate. She seemed frozen in a kneeling position. Still and swaying fractionally. Silly cow. Not like her to panic. "Sean, get her gun off her and the grenades. Use them. Give the automatic to Willy."

Another fusillade of bullets and bombs, and he screeched above the noise: "That way. Run like hell."

They obeyed and he went to follow. But Maire was still kneeling, still swaying. He ran to her. "Let's go." But in a glance he saw there was no chance that she would go anywhere.

There was a dark hole in the back of the jacket he had loaned her. "My God, Maire."

Her eyes were wide and moist as she looked up at him, gasping. She was trying to say something. Then her arms, waving like seaweed in a tide, grasped him and pushed him away. "Get out of here, you daft bastard," she moaned and fell flat on her face with the effort of propelling him. Automatically he picked up her cap as it fell. She was right. He sprinted after the others.

"Round the corner fast." They went—and there was another van, engine running.

"Come on! come on! What's been keeping you?" yelled Rory. He gunned the engine as they scrambled in and drove off, van doors still flapping.

"Any of the bombs left?" demanded Michael sharply of Sean. "Give them here."

He stood in the swaying van, dropped the cap he was still carrying, took the grenades and edged to the open doors. The police-car sirens were close. As the first car rounded the corner behind them he pulled a pin and counted carefully before lobbing the grenade into its path.

"Got the bastards," yelled Willy and Sean as the front end of the police car reared and crumpled in a bright flash. Michael closed the van doors and sat down heavily. He was still wearing that ridiculous dress. He closed his eyes and lowered his head. There was too much to do. He couldn't cry. But the eyes, the eyes of her . . .

"And the only thing his friends have to fear is that, in following him, they suffer disaster by getting too close . . ."

There was a question he had to ask Sean, something about Shirley Connolly . . . No, questions. There was that business of Maire knowing about the orders. He looked at the other lads as they sat dejected, waiting for orders to let them know he was still in charge. The questions would serve as a start. There was no time for mourning now.

But which question first? The one about Maire? He could still almost feel the strength of her arms tight around him, hear the shouts of delight when they loved. More than that, he could see her, that dark circle in her back pulsing mockingly, pushing him away from her with the last of her strength, urging him to escape. How could he ask? Yet the voice echoed down the months . . .

"Those who pose as his friends and cross him will die . . ."

"Sean, Willy, what happened to Connolly? Why didn't she come out with you?"

He realised suddenly that he was still squeaking in his falsetto voice.

The two blinked and looked at each other, puzzled. Their expression said plainly: "For God's sake, you must know." He repeated the questions, speaking normally.

"They took Shirley to the women's section, separate," explained Sean.

Michael covered his eyes. Of course! What a fool he was! Why hadn't he thought of it before? They could have made time to get her out.

"Did she talk?" he asked. "Did anyone?" For the first time he saw clearly, his vision unclouded by the image of the dying Maire. They were bruised and battered. Sean's eyes were more swollen than they had been after he had punched him in Dublin. Willy's jaw seemed to be jutting at an odd angle and his mouth oozed blood. The others also showed signs of having been "questioned".

Their reproachful looks were an answer to his second question. "What about Connolly?" he asked.

"She told them she hitched a lift in a van a few miles out of town. She was from the North, going to visit her auntie in Dublin. She'd never seen any of us before in her life. She took the lift because there was another girl with us. That was all she said while we were there . . ." mumbled Sean. "They took her away and we don't obviously know what happened after."

She had thought quickly to suggest she wasn't part of the group. It just depended on whether they believed her. Michael wondered if the attack on the police station would have jeopardised her chance of being believed.

The driver had been twisting the van through narrow streets. Finally he slid it to a stop behind an old American Studebaker car. Michael glanced at him and he nodded.

"Right, all out," called Michael. "Thanks, Rory. See you in jail." The driver was going to make his way back home on foot. He reacted to Michael's half-hearted try at a joke with barely a flicker of a smile. But he waved as the bank-robbers got into the old car and Willy started the engine.

They drove fast for a few minutes, with Michael directing them. And, though the car hadn't looked too promising, it roared reassuringly every time Willy stepped on the accelerator. There wasn't a chance to test it fully as they soon arrived at the end of the tarred roads. Michael directed them along rutted tracks. And then it became clear that they couldn't drive on.

"Drive it through the hedge into that field as soon as you see a gap," he ordered. Then: "Right. We head almost due northeast in pairs, keeping away from the roads. We should be in the Monaghan training camp inside two days. Willy and Tom. You go first. We'll follow."

The two boys groaned. But they set off. Michael and Sean watched them in silence until they disappeared from sight. It was peaceful in the grey of the morning – and inviting to limbs already tired from the wildness of the night to stay where they were.

"Come on," said Michael. "We'd better get going while we can. Here, you'd better put this on your head to cover that beacon you call hair."

With a pang he handed Sean the black cap that had been used to cover another mass of red hair earlier that night – the cap he had picked up when Maire fell.

CHAPTER XXI

Three days later Michael sat in a room in a house near the Falls Road in Belfast, while Linane stood looking down at him.
"What the hell am I going to do with you?" he demanded.
"The Council have sent you their heartiest congratulations..." Michael perked up. Perhaps it wouldn't be as bad as he had feared when he was first taken to the house to see Linane. He began a hasty revision of his thoughts in the next couple of seconds. "That's because they're bloody fools," Linane went on. "Keep a low profile, I said. So you just blow down the back wall of a police station, tear open the cells, pin down a whole corps of Garda with machine-gun fire and rescue a gang of bank-robbers. Then you drive off, with half the Irish police and Army on your trail – and evade them. You're about as low-profiled as a Panzer division. Just go and rob a few country banks, I said, and this is what I get . . ." He slapped a wad of newspapers he held. "I instructed you that, if anything went wrong, you were to get out as fast as you could. Instead you mounted this lunatic raid and lost the best operator we've got. What the hell's it all about, Michael? Perhaps you might consider explaining before I have to tell the Council I couldn't pass on their praise because the Hero of Cavan had an accident with a pistol and his brains got blown out. My God, if that's what you do to the Irish, what on earth will happen if I ever let you loose on the Brits or the Protestants up here?"

Michael took heart from the last sentence. Linane, angry as he was, secretly admired his efforts. So Michael explained, carefully, from the moment Sean had arrived at their rendezvous with two bottles of whisky from Fallon, via his escape with Maire, to the final cross-country hike.

"So Fallon gave Sean two bottles of whisky and that night the police closed in," Linane summed up.

Michael nodded, tight-lipped and grim.

"And you decided to get the others out because of what they might tell the Garda – *and* because you were damn mad about the way they were taken . . . Are you thinking what I'm thinking about that?" asked Linane.

They stared at each other. There was no need to spell it out.

"Then perhaps Maire didn't die for nothing," whispered the little man. "Perhaps it wasn't all wasted . . ."

For a few minutes they said nothing. Then Linane sat down abruptly and smiled at Michael. "Maybe the whole damn thing wasn't so bad after all. People will know we're up to something, preparing something. Keep them guessing. And I suppose I can understand the raid. Are you sure our charming friend didn't spot your lads following him in Dublin? Pity poor bloody Maire had to die for him."

Michael watched his leader thinking aloud for his benefit and felt his irritation growing. There was something false here. Something odd about the way Linane was handling things. Maire . . . There was one question he needed an answer to in any case.

"How did Maire know about your orders to me and Sean?" he demanded, suddenly certain of the true answer.

Linane turned a crooked smile on him. "I told her, of course," he said.

Michael was astounded. "But . . . why?"

"Lots of reasons. First: you didn't expect me to trust you entirely, did you? She was my secret ears and eyes among your lot. Second: suppose something had happened to you on one of the bank raids?"

Michael was disarmed by his leader's frankness. "So you don't trust me?" he asked, lamely.

"I don't trust anyone. Trust is for fools. Fallon's one of my oldest friends. We joined The Movement together." Off the subject but not off the subject – enough to divert Michael though.

"Where is he?" asked Michael.

"Patience, lad, patience." Linane made calming gestures

with his hands – and Michael suspected something else was not as it should be. It really was the most difficult conversation.

"Where the hell *is* he?" he demanded.

Linane sighed. "You really are getting too smart, my boy. Well, if you must know, he's looking after things in Derry, for the moment."

"But Tina . . . ?" Suddenly Michael was worried. But in his mind he reproached himself with the fact that this was the first time he had thought about her since before the police raid on the cottage.

"She's doing all right, Fallon says. He told me to tell you he's keeping an eye on her personally." Linane grinned at the fury Michael showed. "Charming man, Fallon. Got a way with the ladies, they tell me . . . No, she's all right. Helped out with a bit of stone- and bottle-throwing a couple of days back. Very sensible, quite resourceful. She seems all right as long as you're not around."

Michael seethed at the thought of Fallon, the traitor, with his girl. But he also knew that Linane was deliberately turning the knife in his wound.

"You look like a man with murder on his mind," said Linane softly. "I can understand. But you'll just have to wait a little while. I'm not suggesting you should forget how you feel, just put it on ice for a few days. There's work to be done here . . ."

And Linane kept Michael busy. The weeks began to stretch into months. Michael and his group joined in as the marchers came and went, Catholic and Protestant in turn. They threw stones at first, then petrol bombs – sometimes at one group, sometimes at another. But they made sure they didn't get their heads smashed in by batons. Shirley Connolly joined up with them again, having been released by the police south of the border because they could not establish whether she had played any part in the bank robberies and because her parents were persuaded to visit her in the Republic and plead for her. She was quieter than ever when she returned, and she said nothing about her experiences in jail.

Michael himself became silent too, during these bad weeks. Seethingly silent, as Linane put it once to him. There were so many things to make him tense. Since the raid on the police station he had not been entrusted with a gun of any sort – and more and more often he saw the police, the Protestants and the "B" Specials beating and bullying his people. Guns were the only answer. But Linane paid no attention to his plea. "We must wait," he said always. Once he explained: "The British won't send enough troops in unless they're absolutely sure our people are in danger." That didn't make much sense to Michael. And he didn't stop to work it out. There was the other thing that made him angry. Tina was in Derry. So was Fallon. He received occasional notes from her, for what they were worth. They were always short and sounded happy . . . She was busy. She loved him and missed him but there was a lot to do. Mr Fallon said they would be able to get together again soon. He was running the operation there and was very efficient. Such a nice man . . . on and on about Fallon, damn him. The charming, efficient, kind Mr Fallon – the bloody traitor.

And it was in Derry that the major events were taking place. After yet another civil rights march outrage the police stormed into the Bogside, the people rallied and the barricades went up. Free Derry was born.

When there was action in Belfast, Michael hurled himself into the thick of it and urged his team on to greater and greater efforts. When there was none he would withdraw by himself, sometimes with a bottle. Sean quickly learned to keep out of his way then.

And Terence O'Neill resigned as head of the Ulster Government. James Chichester-Clark took over.

"No guns," said Linane repeatedly. "No guns," when the Protestant mobs grew more and more menacing, when Paisley and the wild men who supported him threatened to break through the thin protecting wall of police, drawn up between them and the Catholics. "No guns," when the people started moving away from their homes in fear. But, Michael knew where there was a gun – a relic of the Second World War, kept by one of the old hands in a secret place. Proudly the old man had shown it to Michael once. "I'll be ready for them when they come," he cackled, fondling the worn stock of the ancient Bren before replacing it in the cupboard under the stairs and locking the door on it.

And the night they came – as they drove the fighting Catholic people back, street by street, as police bullets rattled and ricocheted around the Divis Flats, as the mobs from the Shankill Road invaded Clonard, burning and looting – Michael remembered it. He kicked in the cupboard under the stairs at the house in Bombay Street and took out the gun. And he fought back. He blasted a swathe through attackers as his people ran before them. He fought a dozen lone rearguard actions and the people saw the tall black-haired young man with the angry eyes, wherever they seemed most oppressed. And when the battle was nearly over he handed the gun back to its owner. People who didn't know made the old man their hero. People who did know spoke only in whispers about the silent young man who had let his gun speak for him.

"Damn you, Michael, I said no guns," Linane told him in the morning after the attackers retreated exhausted – as the smoke from the burning homes made the sky hazy and the survivors picked their way among the wreckage, recovering their dead and injured.

"I don't know where old Danny got it," said Michael. "But he did a good job." He smiled at Linane.

"Since when has old Danny had black hair, or any other sort of hair?" demanded Linane.

"People get some very colourful visions in such a battle," said Michael. "Perhaps Danny was transformed into the Black Irishman."

"And the Protestants also had to cope with an army of Catholic flying pigs. If the pigs didn't get them with their tusks on the first dive they shit all over them. Come on, Michael, we know what happened."

"Yes, the *Belfast Telegraph* has the full report – and none of this fanciful stuff about a black-haired boy avenger."

"OK, Michael. Have it your way. We've too much to do to quarrel. And maybe old Danny, or whoever it was who disobeyed my orders about guns, did a good job in some ways, by not letting the thing get too far out of hand. But, if it had gone wrong and he'd won, I tell you there might have been a firing squad in operation this morning."

Michael was tired, especially of all the "if onlys". "But how could there have been a firing squad if there are *no guns?*" he asked.

"Go and get some sleep," ordered Linane. "We'll need it."

He's backing off, thought Michael, allowing himself a half-smile of pleasure. But there wasn't much to smile about in a small personal victory, he told himself as he looked out onto a city burned by hate.

So the troops moved into Belfast. "And they don't know their arse from their elbow," commented Sean disgustedly when he saw the young soldiers, fresher-faced and more boyish-looking than he, smiling gormlessly at everyone and gladly accepting the cups of tea the housewives gave them as they built their peace-line.

"They may be stupid but their masters in London know exactly what they're doing," said Michael.

He and all the others were even more disgusted when the graffiti began to appear on the walls: IRA – I Ran Away. "But we didn't run," they protested. "We stayed here."

"The people will know, soon enough, who their friends are," said Linane, when Michael told him how his team felt. "They're beginning to realise they need us. That's what the graffiti mean."

And the uneasy peace didn't last long. The Protestants started the new trouble by rioting when they thought the Army favoured the Catholics. And security reports began to reach the military about IRA arms arriving in the city. The searches of Catholic homes began and the cups of tea stopped. Linane chuckled as he drafted another anonymous note about an imaginary arms cache. And another group of the fresh-faced soldiers went tramping through people's homes.

The war went on gaining impetus, pushed and prodded when it seemed to be slowing down, nudged on by bomb attacks, blazing briefly with battles like that in the Short Strand when the IRA finally took to the streets, armed and ready, to smash back the invading Ulster Volunteers. The timing was nearly perfect. The Protestant invaders took the chance to move into the isolated Catholic ghetto when the British Army was too stretched to protect it. Michael and his gang and every other IRA group in the city were handed their guns at last.

They fought and drove off the invaders – and they established themselves on that one night as the people's only protectors.

Bloody from a grenade splinter that had scraped his cheek, bruised and tired, Michael was able to meet Linane next day feeling happy. Even his puppet-master allowed himself a brief outburst of euphoria – his lips curved upwards in what could clearly be recognised as a smile.

"You did well. It was right to wait, you see. Now you're all bloody heroes – especially you and Sean. St Michael and St John. Now we'll be wanting some martyrs, to make the simple religious souls of the poor content. Perhaps we can organise it."

He looked thoughtful and Michael wasn't altogether sure he was joking.

"Anyway, you've done so well I'll tell you about your reward now."

Michael's heart leapt even before he heard the rest of the sentence. He knew what the news was. But Linane paused sadistically, making him wait. "What is it?" he had to prompt.

"Easy now, easy now, lad," Linane's eyes twinkled. "It's only news of some girl, after all."

"Tina." Michael grabbed his arm. "What about her? What?"

Linane shook off his hands. "I suppose I'm going to have to tell you quickly if I want to save myself from injury. Yes, it's Tina . . ." Michael was practically hopping about in his delight . . . "She's coming up to join you. I think she might be useful here . . ."

Then, as Michael took off round the room in a dance of delight, Linane's soft addition stopped him in his tracks. "Fallon is bringing her with him when he comes to the conference next week." He watched Michael intently as he spoke. "I thought you might be interested in that. I have some sort of idea that you feel suspicious about Mr Fallon and his charm school." Suddenly his words were biting and angry. "Well, not more than I do, I tell you. And I have more reason."

"More reason than what happened in . . ." Michael began to protest.

"As much as you over Maire's death, more over a great deal else – and I have proof too." He paused as if he was thinking what to say next. Michael was too caught up in his own anger to spot the patently bad acting. "The trouble is that he has a good part of The Council in his pocket. If I demanded a court-martial they'd see it as some sort of power battle between me and the big fellow, and they'd back him. He seems to be a bit ahead of me in the charm ratings – as Tina will tell you, no doubt."

The last was an obvious pinprick. Michael noticed it but did not let it move him. He was angry enough with Fallon already. But he was astonished by Linane's next words.

"In the old days they knew how to deal with a traitor. He'd be taken out and shot. Sometimes I'm in favour of the old ways. What about you, Michael?"

Michael knew exactly what Linane was telling him, but he had to ask: "What are you saying?"

Linane adopted his long-suffering look. "Do I have to spell it out for you and upset your queasy little stomach?"

"Spell it out," said Michael stiffly. "No more conundrums." He wanted time to think, wanted to hear it from someone else, so that he could assess how he actually felt. It was one thing to be angry with a man – another altogether to think in terms of execution.

Linane must have realised what was going on in the mind of his protégé. So he explained carefully – about the Council and Fallon's influence on it; that the girl Fallon visited in Dublin while Michael and his team were watching him was employed at the American Embassy; about his certainty that Fallon was working for the American CIA, which in turn traded information with the British; that Fallon had almost certainly betrayed the gang to the Garda during the bank raids.

"Apart from yourself, Sean, Maire and me, no one else knew that you'd be staying at that cottage. I'm sure about myself and certain that Sean and Maire wouldn't want to turn themselves in to the police or die. That leaves you and Fallon as the suspects . . ." It was a typical piece of Linane's sardonic humour to finish off his exposition of the evidence. Michael acknowledged it with a groan.

Linane continued: "So we have a lot of good evidence that Fallon is our traitor. It wouldn't be enough to convince his friends on the Council, of that I'm sure. So *we* have to decide what to do. We could let the slow drip of information continue, and see every move we make headed off and smashed by the British."

Anticipating an objection from Michael he explained: "Don't think it can't happen. As soon as the Brits realise the CIA have a man planted among us, they'll find some tempting bit of information to trade for an introduction to him. He's in so deep with the Americans he'd have to accept his new British masters too. We'd be ambushed and hunted at every turn. It would be disaster and we'd lose this war, as we've lost every other in our history – because of betrayal.

"Then there are the other alternatives. We could raise our doubts with the Council – and face the fury that would bring down on us. We could pass the information about Fallon's arrival in Belfast to the RUC and let them arrest him – though he'd probably wriggle out of that because of his spy status and come back thirsting for revenge. We could turn him in to the Ulster Volunteers, with no certainty that the CIA hasn't some pull there that might get him away from them. Or we do our own dirty work . . ." He carried on mercilessly now. "If, like me, you see that as the only tolerable alternative, it has to be execution. Quietly, in a deserted street. One bullet . . ."

"But why execution?" protested Michael, though he knew the answer before he completed the question.

Linane explained anyway. "You're thinking of knee-capping or something like that. So we leave him crippled and he tells his pals: 'Michael Sullivan did it on orders from Linane.' Then we get ours too. We'd be able to have wheelchair races back in Co Tipperary, the three of us, for old times' sake. No. If he doesn't die, we can say goodbye to the war. Can't you see that, Michael?"

Michael debated the points desperately with himself.

"Can't you see that, Michael?" Linane insisted softly.

Michael let his eyes meet those of his examiner at last. "I see it. But I don't like it," he said.

"Nobody expected you to like it," growled Linane. "Do you think I like it? But there are such things as duty. And duty can be bloody cruel."

Michael nodded grimly and somewhere in his mind he pictured the scene differently—like something out of a poor quality American television film, as the hero in his foxhole looks at his buddy, in that manly way they have, and whispers: "This is war, pal." But he wasn't able to laugh. This was real.

Instead he asked: "How?"

CHAPTER XXII

The rain was bucketing down as Michael stood huddled against a wall, trying to peer at the door from which Fallon was supposed to emerge. The water cascaded from his sou'wester hat. The small proportion that missed the gap between his lumberjacket collar and his neck found the legs of his trousers and then his shoes. He had long before given up any hope of staying dry, preferring to wait in the only place from which he could observe and stay out of sight. But what was worrying him was that even from this vantage point he was unable to watch steadily. If he stared that way for long the rain stung his eyes and everything became blurred. He looked across enviously at Sean, who was out of the rain in a shop doorway, awaiting his signal. Sean didn't look as though he felt enviable as he watched anxiously – and damply.

Suppose he missed Fallon because of this rain. Suppose water got to his gun. Michael reached into his inside pocket for the hundredth time. The gun felt comparatively dry, just as it had done on all the other inspections – and as it ought, inside its waterproof cover. "Ach," he chided himself, "there's nothing to go wrong. It's all planned."

Afterwards he would go back to his room, where Tina would be waiting, and he would be able to forget it all in her arms. He hadn't seen her since her arrival in Belfast earlier that day because Linane had arranged it carefully that he shouldn't. "The execution is the first priority," he had said.

Michael thought he could read, in what was unsaid, the real thoughts in Linane's mind: that he would not be able to concentrate on the killing if he was preoccupied with Tina; that he might let something slip to her (as if he could tell her something like that); that he might act more swiftly and precisely to carry out his orders if he were anxious to get back to her quickly.

He peered out into the rain again. Was that a dark shape by the door? He drew a dripping hand over his face and eyes to clear them and looked again. It was not. But had Fallon slipped out while he was wiping his eyes? He shook his head and another cascade from the hat hit his neck and trouser-legs. At this rate Tina would have to nurse him through pneumonia as her first act in their reunion. Perhaps there would be no reunion. Suppose Fallon had his bodyguard with him and they won the shootout, killing him and Sean. Linane would be able to explain it all away, Michael was sure.

A burst of light came from the door he was watching as it opened and then closed behind two figures. A burly dark-haired man and a slighter one stood on the step, turning up collars, chatting. Fallon and Linane. Michael was puzzled for a moment. Then the two set off in different directions. He signalled to Sean, who emerged quickly from his shelter. They moved silently after Fallon, passing Linane, who did not look up or acknowledge them.

Fallon walked fast for a big man, bending into the wind, one hand clamped to his hat. He seemed intent on his battle against the elements. Michael gestured to Sean to keep back. He might still look round. There might be a sudden lull in the rain. It was too important to take chances. And . . . there . . . he was right. As Fallon turned the next corner in the road he glanced back. It was just a slight gesture, the gesture of a man skilled in survival. You heard a sound, caught a scent, a sign of movement, or just had a feeling down your spine. But you didn't look back directly and tip them off that you knew they were there, or even suspected that they might be. You waited and as you turned a corner, you glanced sideways – enough to catch the tiniest movement, a change in the pattern of the shadows, some other confirmatory hint. And then you paused under an awning to shake some of the rain off and stamp your feet. The trackers, if they were good and came from the same jungle, would have dropped back a pace or two beyond the perimeter of your visual range, would have adapted their step to a loping, padding gait to avoid the scuff of feet on pavement, picking their way to avoid the tiny pools. Michael and Sean had. But they knew it wasn't enough now. Fallon knew they were there, though he didn't know how he knew.

There were one or two more confirmatory moves by Fallon – breaks of step, pauses, hesitations. Next would come the breakaway bid. Round a corner into an alley. "It's as well I checked the route earlier," thought Michael. "Here's the place." He signalled to Sean to stop as Fallon disappeared from sight round a sharp corner. He heard or half heard the footfalls of their quarry as he speeded up. He wasn't absolutely certain but he had to make a decision. He broke into a run. Sean followed. There was the alley mouth on the right. He made an imperious signal to Sean to stay with him and ran . . . past it. Sean made anxious signs. He shook his head. Fallon was not ahead. He knew that as well as his partner. But you didn't gallop straight into the mouth of a trap, especially if you had the advantage of better knowledge of the area. He ran only a short way. Then he slowed abruptly as they reached another opening on the right – an alley that ran parallel to the one he was sure Fallon had entered. He walked along it a few yards and stopped level with a gap between the houses. He smiled to himself and sighed. He could hear that he was right. He gestured to Sean to retrace his steps and block the entrance Fallon had bolted into. Then, after another confirmatory pause, he hurried on. He knew the two alleys eventually joined a cross street. He went fast and silently. Certain now. Closing in. Right turn, right again. Face to face with the man.

He heard the relief in Fallon's voice. "Michael. Is that you?"

"Yes, Mr Fallon," he said softly.

"God, boy, I was almost ready to kill you back there. What the hell were you doing, following me like that?"

Michael watched as the burly figure before him slipped something back into his inside pocket.

"Just shadowing you, Mr Fallon," he said, stepping closer.

"But why? What . . . ?" The instincts were working again. The ready smile faded.

"Don't reach into that pocket again, Mr Fallon."

"Michael. What the hell? . . . Why, Michael? Why?"

"Why" rhymed with cry and dragged out into a long wail as the silenced gun in Michael's hand recoiled once, twice, three times, giving its stifled apologetic cough after each jolt. Fallon seemed to topple slowly, like a big old tree struck by lightning but reluctant to fall.

He lay, mouth open and still. Blood trickled from the gaping mouth, but quickly spread and dispersed in the flow of rainwater. Michael was turning and walking away before Sean pounded up, gun ready after hearing the shots.

"It's over, then," he puffed.

"Yes. Over." Michael didn't look back. Couldn't look back. Over. He didn't wait for Sean. Didn't even know if his friend went with him. He ran blindly and determinedly to the place where he knew two arms were waiting. She was there. Loving at first, cradling his head. Puzzled, as he sobbed in her arms, on and on through the night. She didn't know what was wrong and he couldn't tell her. It wasn't the blood or the death. He already knew a lot about them, accepted them as constant companions. It was the face that stared up at him, even from the cushion of Tina's breasts, with the question on its lips and in its eyes. Why? Why? Why? Was it asking because it did not know why . . . because the sentence of death was wrong?

Tina asked why too, during the night. Why was he racked with sobs? What was wrong? Why didn't he show his love for her in the usual way? Soon after he went to sleep next morning she went to the kitchen to make herself a cup of coffee – and found out the answer. She turned on the radio to hear if there was any clue in the news to what had caused Michael's distress. There was.

"The body of well-known Provisional IRA leader, Jack Fallon, was found in an alley-way in the Lower Falls area, late last night. He had been shot three times at close range," the bland unemotional voice announced. "The killing was thought to be the work of a rival group within the IRA. No one has yet claimed responsibility."

And there was much more about the late Jack Fallon . . . where he came from, his work within The Movement, his performance in Derry.

Another faction within the IRA? A faction called Michael Sullivan? Or was it Linane, she wondered?

She asked when Michael woke and he evaded her questions, his head rolling like that of a boxer on the ropes.

"Why did he have to die?" she demanded.

"It was decided."

"By whom?"

"People in The Movement."

"Which people? Fallon was a hero over what he did in Derry—a bigger hero than you, Michael Sullivan."

His head stopped rolling. "It was decided, that's all," he snapped.

An experienced in-fighter would have recognised the moment to break and move back to the centre of the ring. Tina crowded in again.

"Who decided, and who did the killing?"

"Tina, if you were supposed to know you'd have been told. You weren't and you won't be by me. I understand orders and discipline. Besides, why in hell's name are you so mad keen to know what and why and who about Fallon? What was he to you? Your boss, or more than that? Tell me that, girl. Tell me that."

"Michael, how can you ask why I'm concerned? Are you mad or something? I worked with him in Derry. I know what he was and what he did for The Movement there. He was no more of a traitor than I was unfaithful to you."

"But he was, Tina. He was."

"Oh Michael. You're so wrong."

This time he didn't answer her. But, suddenly, there was an appeal in his eyes that she couldn't have resisted a few weeks before. Now she could almost see the gun in his hand as he walked up to the unsuspecting victim. See the blood spurt, even while he smiled. She dodged the reaching hand.

"Jack was a good man," she said, and the use of the enemy's Christian name was like a stab-wound to Michael. He went out then without another word. He went to walk first and, eventually, to report to Linane as they had arranged. It had been deliberately decided that they should not meet immediately after the killing or early that day. Linane could then be genuinely unaware of Fallon's death and seriously question the first person to inform him about where and when and how.

"Don't expect me to thank you, Michael," he said. "Jack Fallon was my best friend. Sometimes duty isn't easy to accept. Now there are things to do. We have to get our revenge on the SAS bastards who did this."

Michael looked at him amazed. "What?" he said stupidly.

"That's right. The British Army did it. No one else could have known that Fallon had left Derry. We grab an officer tonight and let them have him back in a sack in the morning. Use your head, boy – and close your mouth. Here's what you do."

Michael listened in horror. Logically, he could understand the need to do it and recognised the propaganda value. Even though the officer they would grab would not be one of the crack secret force, no one else but they and the Brits would know it – and who would believe the Brits? It was brilliant as usual. But how could Linane, with his best friend dead only hours, use his still-warm body as a propaganda weapon? His best friend.

"Take Tina as the decoy and have Sean with you for back-up", Linane ordered.

"But . . ." Michael began to protest.

"But what, Michael? I'm sure Sean won't mind killing another Brit."

"It's not Sean," Michael blurted out stupidly.

"Oh. I see," Linane looked wise. "Tina's upset about her boy getting it last night. Tina has conscience-trouble. Tell her about orders. Tell her that if she fails again, I'll deal with her – and with you for not controlling your troops."

Michael left to carry out his mission.

"It's not Sean," he had said. But when he reached his friend's room he learned otherwise. A half-empty bottle stood on the bedside table. Sean sprawled on the bed, his face nearly matching his hair.

"What's it feel like to be a bloody murderer?" he slurred as Michael stepped into the room. "A hired gun. Who you going to murder tonight, killer?"

Michael eyed him coldly. He wasn't going to get much sense from him, it seemed. But he had to try. "Keep on like that and it might even be you," he said. It was the wrong thing to say. He caught, first, the hint of genuine fear in Sean's eyes, and then the acted-out terror. Neither was amusing. Nor was the next phase, as Sean slumped back again in his chair and caressed his glass as if it were one of his conquests.

"Michael," he said, owlish wisdom in his voice. "You used to be something special. I'd have followed you anywhere . . ."

"Except to the top of a certain mountain," cut in Michael.

Sean raised his head slowly to meet Michael's gaze. "That was the time," he said admiringly. "You were special then. Maybe even something like the Black Irishman. But that was when you made your own decisions. Before someone made them all for you. Can't be the Black Irishman if you're running round getting your orders from someone else. Doesn't make sense, does it?" He looked up at Michael, the thread lost in his drunkenness, smiling stupidly as he tried to remember what he had been about to say. "Anyway, I can't come killing anyone tonight, Michael. I couldn't even hold the gun straight." He giggled inanely.

Michael reached out and ruffled his friend's unruly red mop. No one else could have said those things to him, and not even Sean would have been allowed to if he had been sober. No one else. Not Linane, however important he was. Not Tina, especially now. Michael walked away, wondering at his own forbearance. Was it because the things Sean said were true?

Certainly the last thing Sean had said was true. There was no chance of him going anywhere except to bed. And now Michael faced an even bigger problem – Tina. After Sean's reaction, what could he expect from her? Perhaps he should go straight to Shirley Connolly and ask her instead. She wasn't Linane's original selection because she wasn't as pretty as Tina. But surely there must be an English officer somewhere who was lonely enough to find her beautiful?

But then Michael realised what he was allowing to happen. Because of some drunken nonsense from Sean and a temperamental outburst by Tina he was allowing his authority to be challenged. He was allowing personal sentiment to stand in the way of duty. He had been given a task. He must carry it out.

He marched back to Tina, determined to make her play her

part in the job they had to do. She recognised the look about him as soon as he strode in and confronted her. There was something about the set of his jaw and the defiant challenging tilt of his head as he stood over her, daring her to object to his instructions, that melted her heart. She couldn't let him see how much she loved him, even now. So she accepted her orders meekly but coolly. She understood them in a way. It was clever to use even an internal execution to score off the Brits. The man she would be luring was only another member of the occupation Army. As a fighting soldier he must expect to face danger and even death.

Michael was amazed by her submissiveness. Later she was to surprise him again. When, with Willy, he sauntered into one of the Army pubs, he spotted Tina immediately. She sat by the bar, looking into the eyes of a young officer, tilted her head prettily, prinked nervously at her dress, let her hand brush his sleeve as it came up, blushed demurely. In a hundred ways she flirted and drew away. In everything she was the shy young country girl admiring the brave warrior and waiting, with a fearfully fluttering feminine heart, to be swept off her feet and led into some mad adventure. The young idiot was as caught up in the performance as Michael. It was a consummate acting display, inspired by the fact that Tina knew Michael was watching every move closely. She leant on her young soldier's arm as he led her to his waiting car later. And she hoped Michael was bursting with jealous anger. She let the young man settle her in her seat, lean over and kiss her; let his hand brush the swell of her breasts as she responded to his kiss, and watched in the mirror over his shoulder as two pairs of eyes stared hard from another car, parked close behind. She lingered over the kiss and then drew back enough to whisper in the young man's ear the time-honoured half-promise, "Not here, my darling, someone will see us." She directed him out past the badlands of the Lower Falls to a secluded spot – and the car lights in the mirror told her that her act was still being watched. She let one hand rest lightly on the young man's thigh as he drove, leant her head against his shoulder. She had to keep him – and the watchers – occupied. And when the car stopped and the lights were doused she let him sweep her into his arms and kiss her eagerly, his hands beginning their search, until that other car was stationary close by, its lights also doused.

"Will you excuse me a moment, my love," she whispered. And when he frowned his surprise she added, tormenting him again: "I'll only be a moment. There are things a girl has to do."

She slipped out of the car and flitted away in the darkness. And his erotic fantasy came to an abrupt end with a cold pistol-barrel against his neck and a hard voice ordering: "Keep still while I put this over your head." Then: "Right, move over to the other seat."

His body was found thirty hours later, across the border in Monaghan, hands on the steering-wheel of a car he had never owned, that was tilted nose-down in a ditch. It was hard for the authorities to convince anyone that the young man was just an ordinary officer.

By then Michael and Tina, excited by their adventure and the erotic promise she had made herself act out, had fallen into each other's arms, in bed. But somehow it was unsatisfying.

CHAPTER XXIII

They tried to rekindle the happiness of Dublin in the drab and gloomy atmosphere of Belfast. They failed. But there were many things to do in the crusade Michael believed he was fighting. There were bombs to plant, soldiers to shoot, riots to begin. Under Linane's careful tutelage Michael began planning and carrying through his own operations. And it was good to be on his team. There were few arrests, few failures. Michael's reputation, inside and outside The Movement, climbed steadily. Linane approved most things – except Tina. As the coldness grew between Michael and his girl, so did the little man's complaints about her. It was true – or it became true – that there were fewer and fewer operations in which Michael felt he could use her. Sean was horrified by what he saw happening, by the tears he saw Tina shedding that Michael didn't notice. And when she asked him in her anguish: "What's happening to him, Sean?" he couldn't find an answer that made any sense to him either.

Linane asked Michael a similar sort of question at one of their meetings. "What's happening to Tina?" he demanded. "She doesn't seem to be doing much these days. Not even baiting traps for sex-happy young soldiers. And that was one of the few things she seemed to do well. We can't keep too many passengers up here, you know, even if they are the girl-friend of that brave young Irish hero, Michael Sullivan, the one who escapes every ambush and trap the Brits set for him. Seems a pity a bright young fellow like him can't find a use for a pretty girl for the good of Ireland."

For a moment Michael hated the grinning face of Linane as much as he mistrusted him when he adopted this bantering manner. But he gritted his teeth and refused to rise to the bait. "I'll use her, don't worry," he said. "The time has to be right, that's all."

"And when will it be right? Or mustn't I ask?"

"Soon. Soon." Michael wriggled desperately.

"It ought to be. And what had you in mind for her?"

Michael snatched the answer anxiously from what had been said before. "It's what you were talking about," he said. "You know, using her as bait for the soldiers."

Linane frowned and tilted his head quizzically to show that he was interested, and also to force Michael to flounder on.

"Look, there's lots of Belfast girls going out with the soldiers now – and not just Protestant girls either."

Linane nodded.

"Well, that's no way to make them feel they're in a hostile place. They can forget a lot when they're getting love as regular as their rations." Michael blushed as he spoke.

"Sure and I can see in you the making of another Irish bard, the way you tell the stories so beautifully," the thin man said. "Another Padraig Pearse or Sean O'Casey. Tell me more. You're making music."

There was a hint of approval amid the sarcasm and Michael responded. "So what we do," he said, "is poison the arms of the willing girls . . ."

"I wouldn't have thought it would be the arms we'd be poisoning. The randy young buggers wouldn't be too worried about that. More like something else we might have to poison – like a Venus Fly-Trap. D'you like that? Operation Venus Fly-Trap we'll call it. Our little Irish Venuses will trap the buggers by their flies."

Though Linane was enjoying himself at his expense, Michael just waited for the silly puns to peter out. But not patiently. He realised that he had a good idea.

Linane noted his growing impatience and said: "OK. Tell me about your scheme. But try not to be poetic this time. I think you'll go down in history – if you live long enough – as a warrior rather than a bard after all."

"Right. So if, suddenly, apparently willing young girls were to start leading their ordinary soldiers into ambushes, the Brits would have to do something to protect them. Sex would have to be put off limits . . ."

"And the British Army would suddenly all get tired wrists and not be able to fire their guns . . . Is that what you mean?"

"No, it isn't . . . and you know damn well what I mean."

Linane suddenly dropped the flippant mood. "Right. Do it."

"It would also help stop some of our people thinking these young soldiers aren't bad fellows by themselves . . ." Linane was nodding fast and with irritation. "And we wouldn't be able to use someone who they already have on their wanted lists. That was why I was keeping Tina back from a lot of work."

Linane frowned at the last but he quickly cut off any more explanations. "Look, you can stop negotiating, Michael. I've already accepted the idea. It's a good idea. D'you want me to give you the Pulitzer Prize as well? Just two things: start it soon, and don't waste too much time or too many resources on it. It is a side-show, even if it's a useful one. There are a few other developments we can talk about later. Let me know when you're going to start."

They parted soon afterwards and Michael then had to overcome Tina's objections.

Again, it wasn't as difficult as he had expected. She had realised that she was not being used on operations and was eager not to give Michael any more cause for coldness. She wasn't delighted at the idea of luring young men to their deaths. But she had done it once and she quickly understood the reasoning behind the plan. Sean was there as Michael explained and, for once, some of the old fun atmosphere they had generated together in their innocent Dublin days seemed to return.

Sean began it, as he had so often in the past, when he said to her: "Right, and how about a cup of tea to celebrate, my little Irish temptress?"

Tina turned up the collar of her blouse, peered over it and slunk mysteriously towards him. She stroked his face, leaning back against him: "Oh no, soldier boy," she breathed in a heavily accented purr, "let us make heem" (she pointed to Michael) "go for the tea, leaving us together, so that I can worm the secret plans out of you. My passion will soon make you drop your guard."

"We're not having any of that here," snarled Michael, in his best Ian Paisley imitation. "None of that Papist plotting and dropping of guards or trousers by old Red Socks."

Sean collapsed in hysterics and the other two looked at him amazed. The joke hadn't seemed that good. Sean saw their amazement and, rolling over speechless, tugged at his trouser-legs helplessly.

"He's taken you literally. He's trying to rip his trousers off," said Michael to Tina.

"It's the strain, poor thing," she replied.

Then they both roared simultaneously as Sean succeeded in pulling up one trouser-leg. He was wearing red socks.

There was a lot more acting and laughing and fooling, until, in the end, Tina felt like weeping. For she realised this was only nostalgia and that things could never be the same between them again. That night she and Michael made love tenderly once more. And again she had to fight off the tears.

In the following weeks she succeeded twice in luring young soldiers to a less than glorious death on a battlefield different to any they had imagined.

The two young soldiers were killed and left hanging from lamp-posts with their trousers round their ankles and placards tied to their chest announcing: "Death to the despoilers of Irish womanhood." Each death was followed by Linane's grace-note of a young woman, known to be a frequenter of the soldiers' bars in each case, being found with her head shaven, tarred and feathered.

For her third venture, Tina set out for a bar that was popular with British NCOs. Michael and Sean were to follow her after a few minutes. They sat in the tense silence that preceded most operations, trying to look casual and not to fidget. But both jumped as if they had been shot when the door burst open and one of Linane's messengers panted in. He thrust a note into Michael's hand. "It's urgent," he gasped.

"Stop present operation. S and M go to Sector 5 at once with guns. I'll meet and explain," it stated.

"But . . . God . . . What?" Michael gasped, and Sean took the message from him. He put his head in his hands too. The messenger frowned his amazement.

"Come on, fellas. We've got to go. It's a big job."

"Look. You go. I'll try to get Tina out of that bar," said Sean desperately.

"It says S and M. And anyway, how can you march into a British Army bar where half of them know your face better than their own granny's? We've got to go," said Michael.

"But Tina . . ."

"I don't know. For God's sake, I don't know." He shook as he shouted the last words. Then: "Maybe Willy or one of the other lads . . ."

But Willy and the other lads were gone when they detoured to the safe house where they stayed. Michael hurried up to Linane when he reached their rendezvous. All the familiar faces were there and a lot of others too.

"Tina was already out on the job we'd fixed up. We couldn't get her back," he said.

"So," Linane shrugged.

"So she could be in trouble," Michael shouted.

"Or not," said Linane. Then, as if suddenly losing patience, he told Michael icily: "Look, I know about your special relationship with Tina. Some of the time it is almost useful. Just at the moment it is a pain in the backside. In about twenty minutes from now a prison van will come along that road. We are going to stop it and release two of our comrades, who have been tortured by the Brits. Now, if you think that, at this moment, I'm going to worry my head about some fat English Sergeant putting his hand up your girl's skirt, you've got to think again. If she's any good, she'll sort out her own problems. She doesn't have to fuck with anyone, not even the Army of Occupation. So, just get on with the job we're doing and stop bleeding all over my jacket."

Michael retreated. It seemed as if his commander was right.

In fact, on all the major points, both of them were wrong. No prison van appeared that night. And five miles away – it might as well have been five thousand – Tina cast her eyes towards the door of the bar for the hundredth time and wondered where Michael and Sean could be. They had not appeared. There had been no signal.

"Looking for something, darling?" asked Sergeant Burns.

"No. What would I be looking for now, with you and the Corporal here to look after me?" asked Tina, letting her hand fall on his forearm. Michael must be out there. She must have failed to hear his signal because of the juke-box blaring out NCOs' perennial favourites – "So Long, It's Been Good To Know You", "We're Saying Goodbye To Them All" and "The Quartermaster's Store". She tightened her fingers on Sergeant Burns' muscular forearm. He was a big man, over six feet, with a face like a wood carving – all strong lines and sharp edges. His complexion was like well-burnished leather. He had gained that and his experience of women in Singapore, Malaysia, Egypt and Africa. This was one of those girls who didn't quite know whether she wanted what she was going to get, he decided quickly. A bit timid. Might try to back out at the last minute. But be they Chinese or Irish, he and his partner Joe Sime, Slimey Sime the men called him, knew a few things about girls who tried to change their minds. He winked at Sime.

"I know what you're looking for, love," he said with a knowing leer, slipping an arm round her waist.

"Who said I was looking for love?" she said pertly, turning her head against his khaki-clad shoulder. "Are you saying I can't get it for myself?"

He guffawed. "Hear that, Joe?" he demanded. "We've got a cheeky one here, no mistake. Have to teach her a lesson, I can see."

"Ooh, what will you do?" She play-acted fear.

"Just you wait until we get out of here, darling. You'll see. Meanwhile, like I said, I know what you're looking for – another drink."

She thought of protesting. But there was no point. He was going to insist. "You clever man," she said, sliding her hand up his arm until she was almost facing him. He moved quickly and, before she could dodge, he was kissing her. She heard Sime order another round, while she pretended to respond. Sergeant Burns' lips were, like his face, leathery. When he released her, she blinked and reached for her glass. Another double. She felt dizzy already. They all clinked glasses and she shuddered as their big red hands touched hers during the toast.

"Here, I'm feeling a bit left out. Don't I get a kiss?" demanded Sime. "Just to say thank you for the drink, like."

She turned to face him. Sime was short and black-haired. He had a lot of hair, thick eyebrows, black hair on his forearms, a dark stubble on his chin. There were even fronds of black hair in his nostrils, she saw as he moved in for his kiss. But his lips were softer than the Sergeant's. He forced her head back, holding her tight and sliding his tongue into her mouth. She had to work hard at being nice to him.

"Oy, that's enough, Joe. You said a share. There won't be any left if you go on," chaffed Burns.

There were more drinks and more kisses. When she stood she felt unsteady. The skin on her cheeks felt taut and numb. She tottered to the window and peered out. She could see nothing remotely like a car with Michael and Sean inside. Where were they? Where was Michael?

"Lookin' for something, darlin'?" Sime was closer to her. He let a hand rest on her buttocks as she leant forward.

"Just to see if it's raining," she said. "Don't want to get wet going home, do I?"

Sime pulled her round to him. "You don't have to worry about that, darlin'. Sergeant Burns and me will look after you." He drew her close and kissed her again. She closed her eyes. Where was Michael?

"One for the road, love?" called Burns from the bar.

"Oh, yes." It would give them a few more minutes to get here. But – she looked at the clock on the shelf behind the cash desk – they wouldn't come now. A sudden inspiration. Just one chance. "I won't be a second," she called and headed for the door marked "Women". There *was* just a chance. But there was one door and the window had only a small flap that opened. But perhaps . . . The door was partly hidden from the front of the bar. The lights were low as they were the last customers. She might just get to the street on that side without them noticing. She took off her shoes, feeling the stone of the floor cold on her feet. She edged the lavatory door open and slipped towards safety . . . and a hand reached out from the shadows, catching her arm.

"Going somewhere, darlin'?" It was Sime.

"No, no. Just out to the truck. You did say you were taking me home."

Sime kept a hold on her arm. "'Ere, Sarge. Little Tina was just going out to the truck. I'll take her out, OK? Can't let a lady go unescorted, can we?"

He led her out to their Land Rover and she was almost glad of his arm to steady her—except that she felt like a prisoner. He opened the door.

"In you get, love," he said and helped her in. She thought it was the back, though, by now, she wasn't quite sure where she was. But he didn't close the door behind her. He followed her in, bore her to the floor and began kissing and fondling. She tried to push him away, shaking her head to avoid his lips, whispering: "No! Don't!" His hands were everywhere. She didn't want him to touch her like that. Why hadn't Michael come? Perhaps he would arrive to help her after all. The driver's door banged. Could that be him?

"Oy, Joe! What you up to, back there? Can't you even wait a minute, till we get round the corner, at least?"

"Oh, I can wait, Sarge—but only for a second or two. Trouble is, our little Tina doesn't seem friendly any more. Do you, love?" He jerked her head up close to his by the back of her hair. "Do you, love?"

Had to keep them friendly and unsuspecting, silly really. Course Michael was coming. Just round the corner. She swayed her head and giggled. She didn't have to act that part. "Course I'm friendly," she said, spreading her arms.

"Good girl," he said accepting the invitation to kiss and pushing her flat again.

The Land Rover was moving over uneven ground, bouncing her against Sime's hard body. He was very muscular and she could tell that he liked the bouncing. She didn't. Wished it would stop. He was taking advantage to wriggle in closer to her. The van stopped moving—except for the roof, which kept racing past. She concentrated on a dark patch on the canvas, trying to stop it. But then the van really rocked as Sergeant Burns climbed over the front seats. She felt his body plop down beside them on the floor.

"Why don't you just turn round here and give me a kiss

too, love," said Sergeant Burns. "Joe's had more than his share."

Tina frowned and tried to keep her head from lolling as she lifted herself up on her elbows. Michael would be here any minute.

"Little kiss," she lisped. She remembered the formula she had used before with the young boys – much younger than these two. "Jusht a li'l kiss. Then I have to go and . . . and . . . get myself ready."

"You don't have to go anywhere, darling," said the Sergeant, pulling her head towards his and kissing her hard. He slipped his hand inside her blouse, pulling it out from her skirt waistband. His fingers were hard on her flesh. Sime was doing something too. She couldn't keep up with them. Her clothes seemed to be all falling away. Every time she reached for one thing, another disappeared. And the wooden floor of the van was rough on her shoulders.

"Splinters," she gasped once, loudly, to make herself heard over the gasping of the men as they moved her back and forward, zipping and unbuttoning.

"Aah, poor little thing. That won't do, will it," said the Sergeant, lifting her again. "Put one of them blankets under her, Joe. There. That better?" He lowered her gently. "There."

"I have to go . . . I have."

He blotted out her protest with his hard lips. Pressed her down with his hard body, levered with his powerful legs.

She twisted her head away from under him. "No, no. You can't. No . . ."

"Hold her still, Joe, just a minute. She can wriggle all she likes then. There . . ."

She cried out. He was a big strong man. It wasn't supposed to be like this. And Michael hadn't come. Why hadn't he come? It was all his fault. And there was nothing she could do.

"Michael, Michael," she wailed once or twice while the big man lifted her to him in fierce joy, kissing her, running his hands over her. She almost felt she liked him for a moment – he was just like a little boy with a cream bun. She ran her fingers through his hair as, at last, he gasped and bucked and then lay still. Like a naughty, dirty little boy. Well, now she could go home to Michael and lie down and go to sleep.

"Finished, Sarge?" asked Sime. She had forgotten about him in all the turmoil.

"Yeah. Think she enjoyed it too. All that fuss." He slapped her bare bottom playfully.

"Move over then, sod you. I can't wait all night."

Tina gasped. Sime couldn't mean . . . But he did . . .

She fought back the tears as she struggled back into her clothes later. She was sober now, and they were driving her home. The sky was growing pale.

"Couldn't let you walk when you've been such a good girlie, could we?" said the Sergeant.

"That's if she could walk, after that lot," guffawed Sime contentedly. "You really gave it to her, Sarge, specially that last time."

"You were on form too, Joe." Sergeant Burns was happy. He could hand out a little praise. "Here, but what a juicy little piece our Tina is." He squeezed one of her thighs appreciatively, like a greengrocer with the best oranges. "Wouldn't have thought she had it in her."

They were discussing her as if she were a football match in which they'd both played well. She didn't feel able to speak. If she had tried she might have cried – and she wasn't going to let them see her cry. She signalled for them to stop about half a mile from the place where she and Michael were staying. It gave her a noble feeling to remember the rule her IRA instructors had drilled into her: never lead the enemy to a safe house.

The two soldiers were letting her out.

"Goodnight, darling. Come up the bar again soon. We'll look out for you." They both said things like that, sounding sincere. Nasty, dirty little boys.

She couldn't stumble or cry while they were in sight. She walked stiffly upright, controlling her knees and tear-ducts, both of which were tremulous. For a little while she kept going. They might come back. She couldn't really believe they had gone and her ordeal was over. Then, as the sound of the Land Rover receded to near inaudibility, she thought that at last she was safe. She slumped against the nearest wall and wept bitterly. But one thought began to bring the tears back under control. Now they wouldn't make her go out snaring soldiers again. In fact, it was as if she had suffered a war-wound. When she was better she would be able to resume a normal life with Michael, and neither he nor The Movement would expect any more of her than that she should love him.

A door opened briefly beside her and then slammed closed. People in these parts had learned not to inquire too closely into the grief of others. But it reminded her that she had to go on. "Never draw unnecessary attention to yourself, unless it is part of your duty to do so," they had taught her.

Weeping, staggering, shuffling, she covered the last few yards to safety and banged on the door. "Michael. Oh, Michael. Come to help me," she prayed. She never dreamt of any other reception than that of a sympathetic lover.

The door burst open. And it wasn't Michael. It was Shirley Connolly.

"Oh, my God," the Belfast girl blurted out. "Oh Tina, what have they done to you?" Then the girl flung her hands to her mouth. "Quick! Let me get you upstairs and clean you up. Mustn't let Michael see you . . . ."

As Tina tried to grasp what the other girl meant it was already too late. He stood at the end of the passageway, glass in hand, Sean and Willy and some others behind him. But all she saw was the look of disgust on Michael's face. All she heard was his rejection as he said to her: "Couldn't you even cope for one evening without someone to hold your hand? For God's sake, get her out of my sight and clean her up. She's filthy, fouled. She smells like an Englishman's urinal – and that's what she is."

He turned away, meaning to stride into the back room. But Sean blocked his way. "You're not going back in there, you pig. She's your girl and you're going to look after her. You got her into this. Now you can help her, poor cow."

Pity and horror, that was all she merited, it seemed, from her own side. She wished she could be swallowed up as Sean and Michael scuffled over her and the others just stared. Even Shirley was holding her arm as if she was something nasty to be carried to the dustbin.

Sean pushed Michael again. It was more of a double-handed punch to the chest than a push. As Michael staggered back he roared: "Go on. Show you're a man. Go and look after her, you bastard . . . Take her . . ."

But he got no further. He should have known better. He should have been watching Michael's eyes. At first there had been surprise. Now there was some other light as he stepped back from another push, let Sean topple forward, just off balance, and hit him with the wildest and wickedest right-cross any of them had seen outside a boxing ring. But this was no ring. Sean crashed against the wall head first, slid down it and lay inert. Michael took a step towards him, one foot drawn back. Then, as if with an incredible effort, he stopped himself. It wasn't Sean he was smashing. It was Tina and the Englishmen who had taken advantage of her stupidity.

"Get them both out of my sight. I can't stand filth," he growled.

CHAPTER XXIV

Everyone rushed to do as he ordered. He wasn't surprised. It was what he expected at that moment. But it marked the beginning of another change in his relationship with his team. Sean and Tina had been close friends as well as fellow soldiers. Maire had been lover and protector as well. Now that was all over. Maire was dead. Sean and Tina had failed him. The others were there to do as he commanded, whoever they were. Something decent in him had ended its death-throes as Tina stepped in from the night, tear-stained and sex-tainted. It had started dying a long time before. It had collapsed under repeated blows to his conscience from the trip to London; the American girl in Dublin; the tracking and trailing of Jack Fallon; the attack on the Civil Rights Marchers; the affair with Maire and the way he sold out Tina; the bank raids; the police-station attack; the execution of Jack Fallon; the trapping and luring of troops; the lying and conscience-twisting; the killing and bombing and maiming. He couldn't cope with the accusing eyes of his girl any more. He didn't want to see Tina ever again. From now on it had to be different. Cold, ruthless and always with a purpose. Who needed humanity? "Who are you going to murder tonight, killer?" Sean had asked. He hadn't answered then. Now he knew the answer but didn't need to voice it. It was: "Anyone who gets in my way."

Shirley took Tina to the bathroom and went through the ritual of cleaning her and putting her to bed in a fresh nightie. "Cold-creamed and comfortable," she said in an effort to cheer the miserable wretch who lay, snivelling ceaselessly. "It'll all seem different in the morning."

It was a pious hope that neither of them really believed. And they were right not to do so. Tina wept on and off for two more days. Sean called on her and sat at the foot of her bed, silenced by her misery. But he wasn't the one she wanted to see. That one didn't go near her. But surely he would have to see her some time? With that thought, she began to pull herself together. There were no physical reminders of her night of entertaining the troops. She was worried that so many of the others knew what had happened and that even Shirley seemed to be avoiding her – as if what had happened had been her fault. But once Michael took her back under his wing again they'd soon forget.

On the third morning she decided to make a start on her own rehabilitation. She'd buy herself a scarf and some perfume so that she'd look and smell nice for Michael when she saw him again. She noticed as she stepped out that there seemed to be an unusually large number of women and girls about. But she took no notice until she turned a corner and looked back. They were hurrying after her. She couldn't understand it. But she could see their faces twisted with hate. They were shouting something. She began to run. She kicked off her shoes, dropped her shopping-bag. What were they shouting? She half turned her head to see if they were gaining . . . as a woman stepped out of a doorway and punched her in the stomach, knocking the breath from her. The woman stood over her. She could see her through the tears of pain as she tried to scramble up; see her raising her foot gleefully and bringing it down to grind it in her groin. "Shirley? Why?" she moaned. And she heard the answer in what the women surrounding her were chanting. "Soldiers' whore," they screeched. "We'll show the soldiers' whore."

They beat and punched her and tore at her clothes. They were stripping her and she was helpless. "Haven't I had enough?" she wailed.

"If you haven't had enough men by now, you never will. But they won't want you when we're through with you," panted one.

She was naked now, bruised and battered. "Give me the scissors," snarled her chief tormentor. What was she going to do with the wicked-looking long-bladed scissors she thrust at her head? Tina tried to draw back but there were plenty of hands to hold her still. The scissors snipped and Tina was almost relieved as she felt a chunk of hair fall. But the scissors kept on cutting and chopping until there was no more hair to crop and her head was bleeding from half a dozen places. And still they didn't let her go.

"Have you got the stuff?" There was a flutter of movement. Something else was being passed through the crowd to the women around her. She sniffed and slumped in their arms. Tar. Hot tar.

"Spread her out, now. She likes it hot down there. Let's see how she takes this."

Tina screamed. She could smell the hot tar—and her own flesh burning. The woman in charge grinned down at her. Though she was on the edge of consciousness, Tina remembered another time when a woman had puddled a sticky mess into her pubic hair. It seemed such a long while ago.

Suddenly the woman above her let out a bellow of laughter. "Hey, girls! How about setting this in the tar and turning her into one of those English-soldier rams she likes so much?" She held up a broom handle . . .

And then there was the distant sound of police sirens. The women around her stirred uneasily, diverted from their tribal passion.

The woman in charge tried once more to rally her troops. "If I set it in her and we pour the tar . . ."

The sirens sounded nearer. There was no doubt they were heading this way.

The head witch threw away her broomstick. "Drop the placard on her and let's piss off quick," she shouted. Her advice wasn't needed. Most of the others had already gone.

Tina lay and waited. It didn't seem long before she was being lifted gently into an ambulance and driven off to the hospital by serious-looking young men. In the hospital there were more of them. These were young Protestants. For so long they had been teaching her that the only good Protestants were dead ones. Yet these men were good and not dead. Her shocked and muzzy mind wrestled with war's perennial problem: if the enemy were not all bad and your allies were not all good, was there really much difference between the two sides after all? It was almost like a conversation she had had with Jack Fallon a few months before. After she had put to him a similar equation to the one she was now putting to herself, he had answered: "If you can ask that, I don't know what you are doing in the IRA. We all know, despite some evidence to the contrary, that there's no Englishman as good as a dead Englishman. Modern teaching goes on to suggest that we should kill as many of them as we can and complete St Paddy's work of driving the snakes out of Ireland." He had laughed then. "But you're probably right. I worry a lot about what the English might do to me, but much more about what my friends are up to, behind my back."

If he had been joking about his friends, and it wasn't always easy to tell with him, it was a joke that had gone sour.

Despite her pain and misery, Tina wondered if Michael would also fall foul of Linane. For, instinctively, though she had no real evidence to back her suspicions, she knew that Linane was the man who had ordered Fallon's death. She suspected a lot more besides, and when Michael came to see her she would tell him. She put her hands to her battered scalp. He wouldn't like her if he saw her in this condition. It was a pity she hadn't bought that new scarf before the women had caught her.

But would he come at all? The awful thought hit her. How could he be seen with a woman who was marked as a collaborator with the Brits, a soldiers' whore? Was he big enough to overcome that?

He didn't come. And in the silence from him and all the others she could only read one message. She was not wanted any more. She must go back home.

She wept and kept on weeping. Exasperated, the doctors explained that her injuries were not much more than superficial. Her hair would grow again. She was lucky they had not used the broomstick on her or poured the tar over her head and body.

Finally, on the third day of her misery, one of the young doctors shouted in frustration: "Look, you're bloody lucky. We've had maimed and injured in here you wouldn't believe. Other girls who've gone with soldiers and been caught have ended up permanently disfigured, needing plastic surgery. All you got was a tiny smear of hot tar in your pubic hair, for God's sake. And if you're whining because you think you've got no friends, just ask yourself who in the Ardoyne called the police. He's got to be a brave man, who cares for you a great deal. And . . ."

He went on but she didn't hear the rest. He had just spoken a line of poetry to her. "A brave man, who cares for you a great deal . . ." She smiled softly and the amazed young doctor stopped his tirade about her blessings. He wondered what he could possibly have said to change her outlook so drastically.

And a few days later the same doctor, who was assumed to have some special way with her, now that she was concentrating on her recovery, brought another smile to her face. He told her that a man had telephoned three times to ask about her condition. Each time he had rung off before they could ask if he would visit her or send her a few things she needed.

"Michael. It's got to be Michael," she told herself.

Not many miles away, the two things that had brought Tina back to life in the hospital were the subject of discussion between two other people.

"Michael," said Linane, his thin lips pressed tightly together in that intent way of his, "have you any idea who tipped off the police about Tina?"

Michael blinked. The whole thing didn't seem worth investigation. He said so. He realised he should have kept quiet as the little man's cheeks flushed.

"Michael, I sometimes wonder how you've survived so long without brains," Linane began. There was much more like that. It also carried the message that, though what had happened to Tina seemed unfair, it was the only solution to the problem she presented to The Movement. Michael couldn't keep her with him after what had happened. There was nothing else they could use her for. So they might just as well get some propaganda out of her . . .

It was Michael's turn to be furious. "You mean you turned those women on her?" he roared, standing menacingly over his leader. That was a mistake too.

Linane's voice became silky. "Sit down before you go too far, Michael Sullivan. We don't need another court-martial yet."

Michael sat, but seethed. Linane stared at him hard, forcing him to drop his eyes. "Look at me, Michael Sullivan. Now I'll explain this and then you'll answer. On your answer may depend your life. You see, nobody in my Movement" – and Michael noted the personal pronoun with astonishment – "talks to, or has anything to do with, the Protestant police, unless they're at the other end of his or her rifle-barrel. No one has even to think of them as something to be used to put right a wrong . . . in any circumstances. The police are our enemy and you know what it means to collaborate with the enemy."

Michael pretended irritation. "For God's sake! Do you think I don't know that? How many of the bastards have I killed? Do you think, after what they know about me and I know about them, that there's any way I could pick up the phone and call them?"

"All right, all right. You've answered my question. But someone called them."

"It could have been anyone."

"It could have been one of ours. If not you, Sean perhaps."

"No! He'd never contact the Brits. I'd swear to that." Michael could reply to that with absolute certainty. Even though he had become a good liar he didn't enjoy it. And he knew that neither Sean nor any of the others could have called the police.

"Well, he has been telephoning the hospital to ask about her."

Michael sat up, astonished. "He's what?"

"I don't have to repeat what I just said. Just take it that I know, and that he's not being very bright about it." He lifted a hand to still Michael's next protest. "Look, I know there's nothing dangerous in what he's doing. It just doesn't seem right. No one else is to contact her, except you."

Michael began to protest again.

Linane continued, talking him down. "I know your stand on this. But you must write a brief Dear John letter, enclosing her fare to Dublin and a few pounds besides. Tell her to go there and find a job as soon as her hair has grown. Until then, no calls, no visits – by anyone. Pass the word on."

But there were suprises for Tina during her stay in hospital.

The first was a visit from Father Hodgson, the English Priest. Her mouth dropped open when she saw him hurrying through the ward, his thin hair standing up fluffily, his thin lips set in a sneer. He could almost have been Linane in clerical clothes, except that his sneer seemed to her to be a defence. Linane's was bred out of the certainty that he was superior. She was glad to see the priest and said so.

Clumsily, Father Hodgson told her: "And I'm angry to see you here like this. Michael Sullivan has a lot to answer for. But this is just about the worst thing, so far."

He saw her eyes mist over and realised his mistake. "I told you I'd probably see you again, didn't I? That'll teach you to listen to your priest." He hurried on, avoiding subjects furiously and obviously until it was nearly time for him to go. She was glad, in any case, to see him and hear news from home about her family and friends. She had been prevented from contacting them for so long because of the need for secrecy.

But at last he had to ask: "What about Michael? Is there any way I can get in touch with him?" He saw her eyes. "No, I suppose not, me being English as well. Not that that means anything. Pity. I've followed his career with . . . not interest . . . horror would be a better word. I hear a lot of strange things that don't get to the security forces, even though I'm English. But I still think I could help him . . . You don't. Oh well."

He bit his lips for a second. There was obviously something else he had to say that was worrying him because of the effect it might have on her. At last he blurted it out. "Look, I'm sorry to have to say this, but someone has to. I don't see how you can ever get back together with Michael and I expect you will have to leave Belfast to be safe. See me before you go. I might be able to find a good job for you in Dublin. I have a few contacts. Or there's always a refuge in the Church. God is there to help us and we are all His servants, though it's not always easy to remember that in this terrible town. There's always room for someone to give their service in a practical way."

And Tina remembered that as a little girl she had treasured the dream of being a nun, a cool, loving Bride of Christ—as portrayed in an RTE soap opera. She almost laughed, though that would be rude to this man, who was trying to be kind and hadn't needed to make the effort to visit her. But her . . . a nun . . . after all that had happened. She wasn't fit to be the bride of a man now, let alone of Christ. It didn't seem to matter really, since the only man whose children she would have wanted had been irrevocably taken from her. She knew that she would never see him again when she left the hospital, unless he was shipped home in a wheelchair. And, if that happened, the man she received would not be her Michael. He had disappeared a long time ago, the way the Black Irishman sometimes did, according to Uncle Gerald's tales, leaving a warped dwarf in his place. She didn't cry. She felt too numb for such things now. She just thanked the English Priest politely for his offer and lowered the shutters on the world where people lived.

Her next surprise was a letter. She didn't recognise the big, clear, notice-board writing, which spelled out Miss Tina Foley on the envelope. It aroused her interest enough for her to open it and turn to the signature. It ended: "Yours sincerely, Sergeant Burns." She giggled . . . "Yours sincerely, Sergeant Burns." It was ludicrous. She had to read his message, even though he was also the author of all her troubles.

"Dear Miss Foley," it began, and she had to stifle another giggle, "I hope you will excuse me writing to you like this, but I heard about what happened to you and think Sime and I might have been responsable. I'm sorry for that. It was never our meaning to get you into trouble. We were just having a bit of fun, the three of us. I just can't understand these people behaving the way they did. Sime and me have had a few drinks with girls all over the world and nothing like this has ever happened before, though some funny things have. Anyway, if you want anything whilst your in hospital or need any help when you come out, please let me know [he gave an address]. I shall come up and give you a lift when your allowed out. It's the least I can do. Yours sincerely, Sergeant Burns."

She shook her head over the marching clichés of the letter. So, what they had had that night in the truck was "a bit of fun". He obviously believed girls liked that sort of thing—or maybe those he'd met all over the world, in the dingy bars near the barracks, did. But he seemed to mean well in his clumsy soldierly way. "God help us all, if they are to be our masters," she added to herself.

His letter was soon forgotten, in any case, when she received the rest of her mail that day. This time she did recognise the handwriting on the envelope and she didn't need to look for the signature as she tore it open eagerly. But she would have had to search a great deal harder to find the humanity in it. It was very short and very cold. There were no grammatical or spelling errors. The punctuation was correct.

It read: "Tina, You are instructed to leave Belfast as soon as possible after your release from hospital. Do not go to any of the houses you have lived in here to collect personal belongings. I enclose more than enough money to get you home or to Dublin, where you could find work. Do not try to contact me or any of the other people you have met because of me in the last three years. M."

What a fool she had been to cling to hope. She didn't cry. It was what she had really expected. She just lay silent and sleepless in her bed until morning, when people started organising her exit from the hospital. She had no bags, only the clothes she had been wearing when the women attacked her and a scarf that one of the nurses thoughtfully provided to cover her shorn head. But it still took hours. It was midday when she left. She walked as if she were sleeping. She had no idea where she would go or what she should do. Out of the front door, down the steps . . .

"Oy, Tina. Come on! I'll give you a lift, love. You look a bit tired."

It was Sergeant Burns. He helped her into the truck.

"Haven't you got any luggage?" he asked.

She just shook her head.

"Where you going, then?" He started the engine.

"I don't know. Dublin, I suppose." That seemed to be where everyone wanted her to go.

"Well, you are a funny one. Still, after what happened, it might be a good idea to get out of this place."

He prattled on as he drove and she answered "yes" or "no" whenever he paused long enough. It seemed to satisfy him. At the station he told her to wait in the truck while he went to find out about the trains. He came back a few minutes later, shaking his head.

"No go," he said. "There's bombs on the nine o'clock and

they've held it up in the middle of the main line. They defused one. But they think there might be others. They daren't move it until they've looked it over thoroughly. They don't think there'll be any more trains today."

She tried to concentrate.

"Where will you go?" he asked.

She stared blankly at him for a moment. Then she answered vaguely. "Maybe a hotel. I've got some money."

He frowned. He didn't approve of people spending good money on hotels. "Haven't you got nowhere to go?" he asked.

She shook her head and fought back the tears. "Do not go to any of the houses you have lived in here . . ." Michael had instructed her.

"Well, you know what you're doing, I suppose," he said, frowning as he wondered what he could do with this blank-faced misery of a girl.

"Always a mistake to see 'em again," he had told Sime years ago. "A few drinks to get 'em warmed up, a bit of the other somewhere quiet, take 'em home – never leave a lady in the lurch, son – and that's your lot."

Then he came up with his usual answer to problems. "Let's go and have a little drink while we think about it, love."

He smiled happily, now that he had found an answer – it was that cream-bun look. She thought of asking him to set her down here. But if he wanted his "bit of fun" it couldn't make any difference to her now.

"Come on, cheer up, love. The world ain't come to an end yet. Nothing a few drinks and a bit of a laugh won't put right."

She smiled mechanically. What a terrible man he was.

"That's better, love. Feels a bit strange going off to a different town. Christ, I should know. I've been in enough of 'em."

He reminisced over the drinks about some of the strange places he had been posted to – many of which she had never heard of, or didn't recognise from his military-style pronunciation of their names.

"Give us a kiss, love," he said every so often. "Just to show there's no hard feelings."

She did. Why not? It seemed to please this strange world-traveller, who saw places in a very different way to the guidebooks. It even gave her a temporary sense of belonging somewhere. And she was interested in his tales. He had been in the Army a long time. She asked him how long he still had to serve.

"Due out next year. Feel a bit odd, I suppose. I'll miss the lads. Never had time to marry. Sometimes wonder what I'll do." He looked almost sad for a moment. Then: "Give us a kiss and let's have another drink."

She was staggering again when the bar closed and he led her to his truck. "Come on, love. Let's find that hotel." He gave her a broad wink. "Give you something to remember old Sergeant Burns by. Nothing like a bit of fun after a little drink, eh?"

It seemed odd going into a bedroom with someone who wasn't Michael. Odd taking her clothes off and climbing into bed with a man whose Christian name she didn't even know. It was a bare little room to suit her numb mood. Still, it would be a shame to spoil this lonely man's only approach to closeness with other people . . . his "bit of fun". She giggled when he tickled her, squealed when he squeezed her breasts, sighed and gasped in time with him. It seemed to please him. And, when he left her that night after promising to pick her up in the morning, she wept . . . for the last time. It wasn't fun. There was no fun without Michael. He would be killed by someone like this strange Sergeant Burns, who had fought in wars all round the world, who knew everything there was to know about fighting wars and whose morale was so professionally hardened that it was unbreakable. The only thing that could upset a man like him was the news that he might not be allowed to fight any more wars.

He was a terrible man and he meant to kill Michael. She didn't want to be there when it happened. She didn't want Michael dead, even if she couldn't have him alive.

CHAPTER XXV

The headline in the *Belfast Telegraph* proclaimed: "Black Michael's bride in hanging mystery".

The story began: "A twenty-year-old girl, found hanging in a Belfast hotel late last night, has been identified as Tina Foley, the former mistress of top IRA killer Black Michael Sullivan.

"Miss Foley, a native of . . . in the Republic, was found dead, hanging from a light-fitting. She had booked into the hotel during the afternoon with a man who left later that evening."

It went on to describe how Tina had become a victim of the tar-and-feathering campaign. How the man who had taken her to the hotel had been an Army Sergeant. The editorial imagination began to work on that. Sergeant Burns was suddenly described as a possible British undercover agent, who had been infiltrating "Sullivan's select group of wild killers". It then gave a score-card of Michael's exploits. They didn't have to invent many to make it impressive.

Michael was not impressed. He couldn't understand how Tina could have done such a thing and brought such bad publicity to The Movement. He was the big man in Belfast and knew it without a newspaper having to tell him. The suggestion that his girl had been going off to hotels with British soldiers and had been tarred-and-feathered for her fraternising was another matter entirely. He sought out Linane grimly.

"Did you see this, Cathal?" he slammed the newspaper down in front of his master. "What the hell did you tell them that for? There was no need. You'd done enough to her. And what do you think it does for me, making me look like some dumb Paddy joke, my girl sleeping with soldiers."

Linane went pale. He noted the use of the Christian name

but made no mention of it. He did silence his protégé with a roared: "For God's sake, Michael, what's wrong with *you*? Do you think I did it personally? Do you think I've nothing better in my mind than trying to score some sort of pyrrhic victory over you? The bloody fool girl did it herself, that's all . . ."

"And one of your devious plots has gone wrong. But I'm the one who takes the stick for it. You're a bloody fool, Linane," shouted Michael. He shouldn't have said that. He recognised the cold shadow that came over Linane's face.

But there was no immediate response other than a soft: "And that I'm not, Michael." He paused. "Anyway, there's no use shouting at each other about it. What we have to do is decide whether we can still turn it our way . . . a martyr's funeral . . . she'd used some clever trickery to lure another of their spies into the open . . . he killed her with his bare hands when she refused to let him touch her sexually . . ." He was getting caught up in his new plot.

"No," said Michael, just loudly enough to interrupt him briefly.

"A sort of Irish Mata O'Hara . . ." Linane sniggered. But his voice tailed off as, at last, he looked up into Michael's face. "Oh well, perhaps not. I doubt if we could really sell that one. Maybe we should just leave it—*Black Michael*." He grinned.

A faint frown wrinkled Michael's brow even as he nodded. Linane was being unusually meek. He didn't normally let people win even tiny victories over him. That was why, since Fallon's death, he had dominated the Council. It was also why so many of the other top men hated him.

"Anyway, while you are here, there's a job I need two of my top men to work on," Linane continued. Michael noted but ignored the blatant flattery. "And it will take your mind off this mess. The fellows who put the bomb on the Dublin train two days back cocked it up. It didn't go bang. I want you and Sean to make sure of it tonight. Here's what we do . . ."

. . . Sergeant Burns stood rigidly to attention before the CO's desk, his leathery face set in an expressionless mask. Inwardly he groaned: "What did the silly little cow do that for? Bang go your stripes and increment, Burns. Christ knows what that'll do to your pension next year. Silly sod, why didn't you take your own advice? Never look back, you always said. Have your little bit of fun and move on. 'So Long, It's Been Good To Know You.' Serves you right, Burns my boy." But, even in his misery, the Sergeant noticed another officer sitting languidly by the window, sideways on, so that he could look out as well as in – but apparently barely interested in what was going on. And there had been no escort. He obviously wasn't on a charge . . . yet. He couldn't see the other officer properly, the winter afternoon sun was behind him. Made you blink to look that way. He slid his eyes back to the CO.

"Sit down, Sergeant. Colonel Parker from Intelligence . . ." the CO gestured and Sergeant Burns blinked into the sunlight again . . . "wanted to have a few words with you before we decided what to do about this." He pointed at the newspaper on his desk. Burns muffled another groan. It was worse than even he had thought. Intelligence. He tried not to look at the strange officer, who stirred suddenly and leant forward, quite obviously taking over.

"Grimy little bastards, aren't you, Burns, you and Slimey Sime?"

Burns blinked. It was an unusual approach to any sort of disciplinary hearing. Court-martial job, it sounded like.

"The British Army's version of James Bond, according to this. Not only that, but now the Number One Target for Mr Bloody Black Michael Sullivan. Christ, you must be half-witted."

Burns bristled and began to protest. "Shut up," said the Colonel. "You're in enough trouble and you *do* have to listen to this. Didn't you have the brains to spot a set-up when that pretty little Irish girl minced into your bar and practically invited the ugly pair of you to step outside with her? Don't answer. Your brains obviously work in reverse proportion to your cock. When one swells the other shrinks. Didn't you know that a number of other lads have been lured by girls and killed, lately? God knows how you've survived half the hot-spots of the world. Must be the luckiest fool alive – until now. Now you're top of Sullivan's hit-list, that's for sure."

He paused and there was an uncomfortable silence. Burns

noticed that the CO was also looking a bit red about the ears. He obviously didn't like hearing an outsider talk to one of his men like this. It didn't give the Sergeant much comfort. This man, though the same rank as the CO, obviously carried more authority and knew it.

"So we had to decide what to do about you..." The "we", Sergeant Burns was certain, did not include the CO. "The obvious thing to do was to ship you back to Britain p.d.q. But, I don't suppose you've noticed, this is as much a propaganda war as anything else. It's cheap for the other side and it does a great deal of harm to Britain, especially in the more stupid areas of the United States. So, if we shipped you back, it would be what the other side expects. And, though I can't really see what Linane's up to with this one, I have a decent reluctance to do anything he expects..."

By now Burns was lost, and it didn't seem to matter. It was as if the strange Colonel was talking to himself. "These Intelligence fellows, all plots and twists and turns," Burns thought. "It's obvious why the kid hanged herself. Her fellow had kicked her out. She'd been tarred-and-feathered, didn't have a place to go and there wasn't much future in sleeping around with rough old Army men like me. Obvious."

The Intelligence Colonel continued: "So, now to the useful disposition of the useless Sergeant Burns, who has caused us far too much bother. We can't let you continue to march about on patrol with your lads. That really would be setting you up as a target." He paused. "Now, I've looked at your record closely. There are some things you're quite good at — and fucking bar-flies is not what I mean, you grubby little man. Your rifle-shooting scores remain very high. You don't often miss and you're a good man to have around in a tight corner — as you're showing now. You don't panic. You wait and weigh things up. You have also, from time to time in the past, shown a nasty vengeful streak ... Like the warehouse massacre in Kuala Lumpur and the Arab-quarter raid in Aden. Oh, shut up. I know nothing was proved. But I know — and so do you — who was in there, obliterating the evidence."

He looked hard at Burns for the first time in the long

dissertation and leant forward so that the light no longer hurt the Sergeant's eyes.

"Right, Burns. Can I take it you don't want to go back to England in disgrace, face your court-martial for disobedience in the face of the enemy and be chucked out without your pension – which you've worked hard enough to lose over the years, God help you?

"Well?" he prompted, as Burns hesitated, not sure whether he should answer.

"Yes, sir," said Burns hoarsely, from a dry throat.

"Good. May I also take it that you don't want to spend the rest of your service shut up in an office here, pretending to do a non-existent job, just to deny the other lot a propaganda victory?"

"Yes, sir." Burns answered more clearly now, as the threat to his pension seemed to be lifting.

"Good. Well, there is a job you can volunteer for. It will help us all . . ." The CO cleared his throat and went very red, as Colonel Parker continued: "It's simple really. If they can do it, why can't we – very privately, of course. I want you to join *our* 'hit-squad'. And I impress on you that I didn't say that. There is no such thing. Do you understand?"

Sergeant Burns did. He chuckled slightly as he said so.

"Before I say any more: are you on?"

"You don't have to do it, you know. Purely voluntary," spluttered the CO.

Colonel Parker eyed him sardonically. "I think Burns understands the position, Colonel," he said.

"Quite. Quite so. But I just . . ."

"Well?" demanded Parker, ignoring the CO again.

"Yes, sir. I'll do it if it will help win this thing."

"Slimy little bastard – if it helps save your pension, you mean," thought Parker as he reached out his hand and said: "Good man. Let's shake on it." They liked that sort of thing among the proles.

When they moved back to their seats he nodded to the CO. "If you'll just leave us alone for a few minutes," he said. The CO went.

"You may be pleased to know, Burns, that by volunteering

you have increased your pay and your pension – even if we have to send it to your next-of-kin. Anyway, you'll get all the forms to fill in later. You might also like to know – and I'm telling you because it will please you particularly – that your first target is Michael Sullivan. He's too big. The Catholics here have built up a special hero/martyr thing about him. Gets in and out of the most ridiculous situations unscathed. I want his head. Here. This is your man . . ." He flung a sheaf of photographs on the CO's desk. "We've suddenly started to get some useful info' about him . . ."

Neither Sean nor Michael spoke that night, as they drove the stolen car onto the bridge overlooking the marshalling yard and stopped. They had been silent the whole way. It was unusual. Sean could seldom keep quiet, even if he was nervous. Michael didn't think he was still sulking about the punch, or the whole Tina incident. Sean looked ahead intently, his face set in unusual worry-lines.

"What is it, Sean?" Michael asked softly.

Sean shook his head. Michael noticed that he was wearing Maire's black cap. "I don't know. I wish I did. There's something wrong and I can't put my finger on what it is."

Michael slapped his arm with a heartiness he didn't feel. "Can't put that in the report to Linane, can we? We'd better get on. Got the stuff?"

Of course Sean had. But it was something to say. Another certainty was that the bombs would work. Sean had a way with bombs.

They hopped over the wall onto a narrow ledge. Sean hooked a rope over one of the buttresses and looped it round his waist. Then he passed another length of rope round Michael's waist and hooked one end to his own belt with a snap-clip. For some reason he did not completely understand, he eased his sharp knife in its scabbard before he began lowering his friend.

"OK," he whispered.

"OK," said Michael.

He dropped slowly into the darkness . . . five feet . . . ten . . . and every floodlight in the yard blazed into life. Searchlight beams picked out Michael, dangling fifteen feet above the tracks, and outlined the equally helpless Sean.

"Hold it right there, Sullivan. Don't try to move or fight your way out."

"Fucking comedian," breathed Michael, looking up at Sean. And his friend, with one economical gesture, slashed through the rope.

Michael heard the bullets whistling. But it was all right if you heard them. Sean had been too quick for them. Michael fell awkwardly but rolled immediately under a truck. Outside there was a commotion of shouting and whining bullets ... then a shrill scream from Sean, tied helplessly to the bridge. From where he lay, Michael saw the black cap drop to the tracks.

He had to get away, had to get his revenge. There had been no need to shoot Sean. He started to crawl forward under the line of trucks, which ran beneath the bridge to the safety of the darkness beyond. He groaned with the pain from his ankle. It was broken at least. There was blood on his sleeve too. He could hear the running feet behind him. They'd be up with him in seconds at this rate. It had been a set-up and it had probably cost Sean his life. He had to get away to find the informer. He pulled himself out from below the trucks as he reached the darkness, stood and hobbled on the smashed ankle. His anger eased the pain. "Got to get away," he sobbed to himself. "Got to get the bastard. Got to get away."

Sergeant Burns and his party of killers followed him, equally angry. They could hear the staggering, twisting steps of their quarry and sometimes even catch a groan. Burns had seen Michael fall – his rifle had been trained on his back when the rope was cut – and he knew he must be hurt badly. But he wasn't going to sprint and arrive for a shoot-out with his hands shaking. His lope was steady and determined – like that of a wolf on the trail of an injured moose. In Burns' mind a single refrain kept the twist of hatred on his leather face. "I missed. Christ. In my sights and I missed."

He was annoyed too that the others had taken out their anger on the red-haired boy on the bridge by pouring bullets into him. He would have been more useful as a captive.

Burns was fit and hard despite his drinking and "bits of fun", but he was panting after the first few weaving, dodging miles. Several times he thought "the smart little bugger" had slipped them, but then a stumbling footfall in a slightly different direction from the expected sent him on again.

Michael heard them clumping behind remorselessly. He could feel the blood trickling from his leg, imagined he could hear the bones crunching. But the pain was no longer a problem. It had turned him into a hunted animal, running to survive. Now he was in a street of bright lights and people. He could sense them gaping at him and beginning to react. But he was past before they could interfere. "Bloody Protestants. They would as well." He weaved from side to side, partly from instinct, partly because he couldn't keep straight. The street lights were a blur. The faces were a blur. His head went back and his arms began to flail.

"Steady, lads," cautioned Sergeant Burns behind. No need to hurry now. Occasionally, when the crowds parted, his long-sighted eyes focused on the staggering figure. Couldn't risk a shot here, too many people. Ricochets were nasty. "Steady, lads," he whispered. "We've got him."

Round a corner and even the "Got to get away" refrain had died in Michael's mind. His head lolled back once more and . . . a cross floated high in the sky like a strange mirage. "The cross of Our Lord, here to give us all shelter." He hobbled towards it. Now he couldn't see it. But he knew it was there. Here were the steps leading up to it. He could smell the incense, sense the hush. A figure swam towards him . . . a slight figure in clerical robes . . . the English Priest. He was reaching out and Michael spread his arms to fall to his knees before him. "Father, forgive me, for I have sinned . . ." But it was a buffet not a blessing that Michael received. He was hurled sideways into the narrow box of the confessional.

The nailed boots sounded on the steps outside. Father Hodgson looked quickly at the box. It was silent. He hoped Michael had either passed out or hit his head as he fell. He kicked a kneeler accurately into position over a tell-tale bloodstain, and then turned to face Sergeant Burns and his men, who clattered into the church and stopped in confusion.

He hurried towards them. "What is the meaning of this? Guns inside God's Holy Church. I have people making their confessions here."

Sergeant Burns was breathless from the long run and also, as a simple non-believer, in awe of all things clerical. His mind groped for the rules about church and sanctuary. "Hunt and destroy," Colonel Parker had said. But a gun-battle in church wouldn't be good for the British image. "Oh fuck," he breathed and then wished he hadn't.

"Not here, Sergeant," said the pale-faced priest who barred his way. He said it quietly, but the rebuke stung the more for it. "You haven't told me what you want?" He showed no sign of standing aside.

"We're after a killer," puffed Burns, his cheeks glowing as much from the rebuke as from the effort of the pursuit.

"The Holy Catholic Church is hardly the place to look for such people."

Burns began to recover his breath and his composure. "But Padre, we saw the man we want come in here."

Father Hodgson raised an eyebrow coldly . . . and hoped that this soldier had no knowledge of the layout of a Catholic church. "Did you actually see him enter? Can you see him in here now?" He gestured to the body of the church and could see Burns' puzzlement. He prayed that Michael would not start groaning in the confessional. And he had to offer the Sergeant something. "Are you sure he did not go off into an entrance close by – or along the alley beside the church?"

Sergeant Burns surveyed the still building again. "Well . . . if you say he's not here, Padre . . .?" The vicar was English, he told himself. Funny-looking cove. But there was no reason to doubt his assurance that Sullivan was not there. He shrugged. "Sorry to have bothered you, then." He looked once more round the church and then ordered: "Come on, men. He must have slipped away outside."

Father Hodgson followed them to the door. "Perhaps you'll return to this house of God again soon, more suitably dressed to join in our worship."

Burns whirled suspiciously. Was the vicar taking the piss? Father Hodgson contrived to smile benignly, while he cursed himself inwardly for being too clever.

But what could you do about a vicar anyway, thought Burns. You couldn't push him out of the way and do a thorough search. "This way, men," he said grimly.

Father Hodgson slammed the huge doors behind the soldiers as they stamped down the steps outside. He closed his eyes briefly to calm himself and just then, from the confessional with its remarkable penitent, came a high-pitched babble. "Father, forgive me, for I have sinned," screeched the barely recognisable voice.

"If I was younger, of a different creed, or in another age, I might believe this was a miracle conversion, my lad," said the priest as he stepped into the wooden box and began to prise the claw-like hands from the edge of the window where Michael was supporting himself. "Instead . . . puff . . . I know . . . puff . . . it's just loss of blood. Come on, damn you, I'd better get you out of here before that tough-looking soldier realises he's been tricked and comes back for you."

"Hail Mary, full of grace," wailed the slender black-haired young man as Father Hodgson hauled him aloft, and then staggered along the aisle with him doubled over his shoulder like a large sack. "Damn fine time for you to get religion, Michael," he grunted. "And will you shut up about Mary?" They had to cover a hundred yards or so in the close behind the church. So he grabbed the curtains from one of the side chapels with his free hand as he passed, ripping them down unceremoniously. He flung them over Michael. "Got to get them washed," he muttered, as if rehearsing the answer to any query from a police or Army patrol. "And I hope Mrs Mahoney forgives me, for spoiling the look of her lovely chapel."

CHAPTER XXVI

The sun shone pale and watery through the high windows. That was how Michael felt – pale and watery. He remembered a lot of the previous day's events but he didn't recall arriving in this room. It didn't seem to matter since this wasn't prison – unless they had suddenly improved conditions, introducing fresh linen sheets and soft feather mattresses. Equally, despite the cross that dangled on a hook beside the window, it didn't seem likely that he was dead and in heaven. It was warm in the winter sun, but it was not warm enough to be the other place. He struggled onto one elbow, the one that was not stiff with bandages and splints, to get a look at his surroundings. It was an austere room with heavy, old-fashioned furniture and a few religious paintings breaking the bleakness of the whitewashed walls. A priest's room, goddamn it, he thought, as his eyes fixed eventually on the figure sitting in the big leather armchair opposite him. The English Priest's room. It hadn't been a mirage he had seen just before he collapsed.

"What . . . ?" he began hoarsely.

"Good afternoon, Michael," said the priest. "I hope you slept well. I'm damned if I did. This chair is not really meant for anything as sensible as comfort . . . The Victorians obviously didn't believe in it."

"How . . . ?" began Michael again.

"Settle down and stop spluttering, my boy. You lost a lot of blood. And by the look in the eyes of those soldiers who followed you into the church you'd have lost a lot more if they'd found you. You're safe for the moment. For some utterly quixotic reason I tricked the British Army into going away and leaving you in my care. No, they didn't know I'd got you. And won't. I must have had some notion of talking some sense into you. After what happened to Tina, I don't know why I should bother."

Michael began to protest. But the little man was leaning over him now, pressing him back down onto the pillows, settling him.

"Just rest," he said. "I shouldn't have spoken of it . . . yet. Time enough when you're better."

That sounded ominous to Michael.

Father Hodgson checked the dressings on Michael's arm and ankle. "You're a bit of a mess," he said . . . "physically as well. We'd better start getting the simple things sorted out first."

Michael groaned inwardly – and some of the sound must have escaped his lips as well. The little man stood back from him, one eyebrow raised quizzically and familiarly.

"That's right, Michael. You can't trust a priest not to preach at you – especially when he has just saved your life and you are too weak to do anything about it. Perhaps you should have chosen somewhere else for sanctuary if you didn't want to be reminded of a few uncomfortable truths."

Even the way the little man spoke, part mocking, part serious, always paradoxical, hadn't changed. Michael smiled slightly – and caught himself switching off the smile in case of a reprimand. It was oddly reassuring. "And where do you suggest I should have gone?" He too could play the game.

"I can think of one place where I might wish you if I wasn't wearing my collar the wrong way round and wasn't charged with saving you from going there. Alternatively, you could have tried one of Cathal Linane's safe houses." Catching Michael's look of surprise he added: "Oh yes, I know who is your master. I hear a lot – in the confessional and outside it – *and* it doesn't go any further. I hear a lot and am not too excited by most of it."

Despite his weakness Michael was suddenly irritated by the priest's assumption of the right to censure.

"If my organisation has something to be ashamed of, what about yours?" he demanded. "What about your history of oppression of the people?"

Father Hodgson smiled thinly. "You sounded almost like a politician for a minute, there. So, I'll ask you some political questions. When in recent years, for instance, did my organisation, as you call it, lure people to their deaths by using women's bodies as bait? When did we employ snipers against our enemies, or blow up hotels and bars full of ordinary people?"

Michael strove to find an answer in his tired brain. But the priest was continuing. "You and your crowd have no sense of perspective, Michael. I can differentiate between the soldiers and their masters, as much as I can differentiate between you and your master. I doubt if you could say the same, or you couldn't kill soldiers indiscriminately."

He paused, eyed Michael's pale face and then added: "Anyway, since I can see the difference between you and Linane, I'm not going to nag you any more. I'm sorry – but only for the timing. You're ill and you'll be lucky if my unpractised medical treatment does you more good than harm."

Michael looked with alarm at his splints and bandages. "You mean you didn't . . ."

"Call a doctor," cut in the priest. "You must really be ill or you're just damn lucky to have survived this long. If I'd called a doctor he would have whisked you off to hospital straight away . . . and the Army would have taken it from there. I wonder how you'd react to the pail or the electrodes?"

The pail was a crudely effective method of interrogation the British used on their prisoners. They just dropped a metal pail over a man's head and then banged on the outside with a lump of metal or wood. The pain and noise made most men talk before their ear-drums burst. Or before their captors moved on to the electrodes, which were fitted to the tenderest part of the body and were then used to shoot painful charges through the victim. Used carelessly, they made a man permanently impotent. Again Michael was surprised by the priest's knowledge.

Father Hodgson continued: "Anyway, you don't have to worry. I trained to be a medical missionary. I know enough about simple wounds and fractures and the dangers from sepsis for you to be reasonably safe. If your wounds start going funny colours and your temperature breaks out of the thermometer I might have to yell for help. But by then it will probably be too late. You might have been right yesterday, when you clung to the confessional rail and kept on wailing, 'Father, forgive me, for I have sinned.' Perhaps your subconscious knew something."

While he had been talking – so fast that Michael's head began to spin and he had to stop listening – the priest had been fussing and tidying at the bed and its surrounds like a hospital nurse. Finally, he poured a glass of water and held out two small tablets. Michael looked at them questioningly.

The priest sighed: "Just take them, will you. You might have realised by now that I don't know much about killing – that's your department. But I do know something about curing and you don't."

He shook the tablets under his patient's nose. Michael took them obediently, swallowed them with a shudder and then gulped some of the water. He had remembered watching from the confessional as a delicate foot scored a goal with a kneeler over a tell-tale bloodstain. That was just seconds before he heard the unmistakable clatter of Army boots echoing around the church as if the angelic host had gone into military training. Perhaps Father Hodgson was not totally on the side of the angels, Michael thought, as he found himself drifting into sleep once more.

He slept a lot during the next few days. His weakness and Father Hodgson's pills made sure of that. But, when he woke on the evening of the fifth day, he felt clear-headed and fit. He had a few questions to ask the English Priest before he got up and left . . .

He didn't notice the grave expression on the priest's face as he walked into the room and began belligerently: "How did you get to know about Cathal Linane and the safe houses?"

Father Hodgson looked bewildered. "Can you be asking that seriously?" he began. "Yes, I see you can. Look, I'm a priest here, in one of the biggest talking-shops in the world. There's nothing like civil war to start people talking and spreading rumours and making heroes and monsters. Like you – Black Michael. Like Cathal Linane, too. You'd be surprised how many people are unsure which side he's on, apart from his own."

There was a pause while Michael framed in his mind the next question. But the priest cut him short, beating him to the point, anger mounting. "Look, let's not try working up to your real question by stealth. You've always been about as subtle as a bull elephant in must. You want to know if I'm some sort of spy for the British and if I've been tracking you like nemesis or, if you'd prefer it, like that Sergeant Burns – another mad bull elephant."

He saw the gleam of anger in Michael's eyes at the mention of Burns and he responded to it suddenly, unexpectedly, with tight-lipped fury of his own. "*You* can get angry with *me* over Tina's death? I ought to have turned you over to Burns, after all. I ought to have let him find you, drag you out of the cathedral and shoot you in the gutter."

For a moment he almost mastered his anger. "Look, Michael, I'll say this once – and then no more. If I had been a British spy, I could have turned you over to their Intelligence at any time in the last few days. They would have got all they wanted to know out of you quicker and better than I ever could with all the clever probing and questioning and assumed friendship you are accusing me of. Once you disappeared the other night you were outside any law, national or international. You could really have vanished and nobody would have needed to know that the gibbering idiot in some country asylum or the pentathol-filled corpse buried in the concrete supports of an English motorway bridge had been Black Michael Sullivan."

Michael felt the chill on his spine. The fate the priest described could still be awaiting him. He had to get away from here. He began plotting his escape, even while he asked the question the priest must have been expecting.

"Then who . . .?"

He only distantly heard the reply as he listened at the same time for the crunch of boots on the stairs, the sound of police cars. His inattention and its implications blasted away the last shreds of Father Hodgson's control.

"You want to know who set you up at the marshalling yard? Who made every one of your recent jobs go wrong? Who turned the disgusting trap Tina was setting for the soldiers, so that it caught her instead? Who arranged the tarring-and-feathering, so that Michael Sullivan appeared a lot less than the hero the people were beginning to make of him? You want me to join in this filthy game you are all playing, and point a finger at whoever I suspect, without having any evidence to support my beliefs? I won't do it."

Michael found himself analysing the tirade. Was it all acting? The white face, the gleaming eyes, the stabbing finger. Michael had seen sermons like that. "You can never trust a priest," they had taught him.

Father Hodgson was continuing. "I offered you friendship and help because the boy I knew, not so many years ago, had something good in him. I thought it might still be there, despite this filthy evil thing of using his own girl's body as bait in a trap for war-weary men. But, now, I see I was wrong. You can't even see or believe the truth any more. You're planning a way to escape before I kill you, or turn you over to the British, or some such sick and rotten thing you've dreamed up. There's no need. You don't have to plan your escape. Just go. And don't tell me where you're going. Don't tell me anything, damn you. I want no more of you. Get out of my house and live, if you can, with your own dirty conscience. And I wouldn't like to be you. I wouldn't like to know that Sergeant Burns and his squad of killers want me dead. That someone as cold as a snake, who claims to be on my side, also wants my head. And I wouldn't want to know that everyone who loved and trusted me had been killed or destroyed. And that I had contributed to each and every . . ."

The priest's voice faltered. He lowered his eyes and turned away. He crossed himself surreptitiously and then turned back, looking contrite. "I suppose it's no use saying I'm sorry? I went too far . . . ?" He answered his own questions with a shake of his head. "And I wanted to break the news so differently . . . Oh well . . . Michael, I came to tell you that your mother is dead. A couple of days ago. They tried to find you but couldn't. Someone thought to tell me because I knew her. That's all. Michael, I'm sorry . . ."

Michael looked at him blankly for a few moments. His mother. Dead. He had hardly thought of her for months now. It had been as if she had ceased to exist . . . Now she had. He felt nothing. A small frown puckered his brow. When had he last been moved by anything? Perhaps everything in him had died . . . Damn the little Englishman, he was getting through to him, eroding his determination. "Never trust a priest," they said, and then they quoted the saying of some priest to the effect: "Give us a child until it is nine and it will always return to the church." He turned back the bedclothes and started to get up.

"No, Michael. You can't go yet. I know I said too much but . . ." The priest hurried to prevent him getting any further. In his weakened condition Michael might not have been able to insist physically on getting his way. But he kept moving, his eyes set in a cold stare.

"You told me to go. So I'm going. Don't try to get in my way. Thank you for the help you've given me. But I'll not be indebted to you any more. If you'll let me know where my clothes are . . ."

Father Hodgson stood back with a shrug and pointed to the wardrobe. "In there."

"Thanks. I'll send money to pay for the food and bed."

"For goodness' sake. There's no need."

"Not for goodness' sake. For my sake and The Movement's sake, there is a need."

The priest rubbed his forehead with one hand in a despairing gesture. "Michael, I know what I said was unforgivable, but there's no need to be foolish about it."

Michael regarded him coldly and went on dressing.

"You're not fit to go out. And where will you go, anyway?"

It was a good question. But Michael didn't intend to let him see that. He shrugged. "There are places. I'm fit enough if I take it easy for a day or two." He walked unsteadily towards the door.

"Shall I make you a sandwich . . . ?"

As the priest asked the question he realised how idiotic it must have seemed and began to grin. Michael caught the flicker of amusement and the reason. Suddenly they were both chuckling.

"I sound like some old woman," said the priest.

"That you are," responded Michael and they both chuckled again. Michael continued: "Look, either now or in a day or so I have to go anyway. I can't stay out of touch and I wouldn't ask you to carry messages for me – even if my group would accept you as a messenger and not shoot you on sight. I really mean thank you. And, though I don't like being preached at, I'm not just going out of pride or temper. I'm not about to become the last of the Holy Martyrs."

The priest dropped his eyes. "I wish I could be certain of that. But God go with you."

They walked companionably to the door, where they stopped and faced each other in embarrassment.

The priest broke the silence: "You Irish were never any good at paradoxes. You can't see that a man who appears to be your enemy might be your friend, and a man who appears to be your friend could be your enemy."

Michael frowned. "I don't think I understand that paradox. But . . ." he paused, catching on at last. "You don't like Linane, do you?"

"No," confirmed the priest.

"I'm not so sure I do either. But at least he's a true Irishman, fighting our war the best way he knows . . ."

"What did you say?" demanded the priest sharply.

"I said he's a true Irishman f . . ." He got no further.

"But, Michael, he isn't," interrupted the priest, every line of his face indicating amazement.

"Isn't what?"

"He isn't an Irishman any more than Padraig Pearse or Arthur Griffiths were. I thought you must have known he was English."

Michael felt the world crumbling around him. It couldn't be true. It couldn't. But priests didn't lie . . . or did they? An Englishman. Another Englishman.

For some reason, at that moment he saw a vision of a face, Fallon's face, mouth open, crying to the night: "Why, Michael? Why?" He was surrounded by Englishmen. Even this priest standing before him was an Englishman. He staggered blindly along the alley leading from the house, into a back street.

The priest watched him go, unable to stop him or help him. He bowed his head, putting a hand up to smooth his forehead. He cursed his own stupidity. He shouldn't have told Michael like that. He shouldn't have driven him out of his house – into danger. He looked to where his former pupil hobbled painfully away from him – away from safety, away from God. And he began muttering a prayer. But there in the evening shadows a flicker of movement caught his eye. He strained to see. It seemed important . . . urgent even. A girl flitted from a doorway and fluttered along behind Michael. Flitted was the right word, thought the priest. She moved like a butterfly – no, it had to be a moth at this time of evening. Following Michael, her light. Slipped into doorways and out again, keeping well behind but following nonetheless. And somehow she – it? – seemed to need him to follow too. He wished he could see the girl better. He grabbed his cloak from the hall stand and put it on, feeling his normal prickle of irritation at it as he did so. "Damn theatrical piece of nonsense." Even though Michael had left him and his influence permanently, he could still try to help him. He tried to explain away what he was doing. He always had been a sucker for lost causes, he told himself as he locked the door of the presbytery behind him. If he hurried . . . Ah, there she was, and the limping figure was just a bit further ahead.

"Look. There goes the vicar. He's following him." One of Burns' men contributed the information in a harsh whisper to the Sergeant, who was already staring hard after the black-cloaked figure.

"Yeah. Wonder what he's up to? Lying bastard. I knew he'd hidden Sullivan. But why's he following him?"

"Don't ask me, Sarge," said his companion. "But we'd better get after them."

"Yeah, right," growled the Sergeant. "Call up the others. Tell them to catch up with us. This time the little sod won't get away – and no vicar's going to get in the way, neither."

He lifted his sniper's rifle lovingly and patted its stock. This time . . . He felt a certain amount of satisfaction already. He had realised the priest was lying almost as soon as he retreated from the church, five nights earlier, and saw that the alley-way beside it only led to a dead end, a high barred gate, over which his injured quarry couldn't possibly have scrambled. Since then, it had been uncomfortable and boring, mounting a round-the-clock stake-out at The Vicarage, as he insisted on calling it. But all the care and caution they had taken to make sure they were not spotted had paid off. This time . . . He could complete the job Colonel Parker had given him and settle down to some celebratory boozing – maybe a "bit of fun". He loped off after the black-cloaked figure, silent in boots wrapped in layers of bandages.

CHAPTER XXVII

Michael hurried blindly at first, unaware of anything but the puzzles in his head. His mother had cared for him over the years. Why wasn't he more moved by the news of her death? Had everything in him been burned by the flames of this awful war? Had he become so hardened to the suffering of others that he couldn't even feel anything about his own suffering? Was the priest right when he said . . . what was it . . . ? "Now everyone who loved and trusted you has been killed or destroyed." Yes, he was. Tina, Sean, Maire, his mother.

And Linane. Was he really an Englishman? Michael wondered for a second what his Christian name could have been. Charles . . . ? Colin . . . ? It certainly wouldn't have been so inspiring. The name was irrelevant anyway, in the face of the veiled accusations. Linane. He could almost see the man, smiling crookedly at him in the lamplight, mocking his struggle to grapple with the evidence, manipulating his mind even though he was nowhere near. Maire, Fallon, Tina, Sean . . . Michael Sullivan . . . all victims of the strange convoluted plots of Cathal Linane? Certainly the man was unmoved by casualty lists. Always he donned his mask of suffering for a few moments and then quickly replaced it with that crooked smile as he started on his next scheme. And you could hardly blame Linane for Maire's death, Michael argued with himself, before immediately providing the counter: "The gang was captured and Maire died to prove Fallon's guilt." Was Fallon really a traitor, an American plant, or was he just too powerful in The Movement for Linane to tolerate him?

Tina and Sean had died as a result of Linane's mistakes. But Linane didn't make mistakes. He worked it all out beforehand.

Then why? Michael could hear the priest's voice again, supplying the answer ". . . someone as cold as a snake who claims to be on my side and also wants my head . . ." The deaths of his friends had isolated him.

"Black Michael," chanted the crowds. "Black Michael," shouted the headlines. "A big new man in The Movement and rising fast," he'd read of himself in one of the innumerable assessments of the IRA in the learned London newspapers. Perhaps Linane had read the same assessment.

That last time, at the marshalling yard, the trap had so obviously been prepared down to the details. Only Sean's last act of love had made it fail. The raid had been planned by Linane. Linane had nominated him and Sean to carry it out. Only Linane, Sean and he could possibly have known enough about it in time to set the trap. He knew he hadn't told the Brits. Sean had proved his innocence.

Michael stopped short of completing the allegation in his mind. Instead he beat at his head with his uninjured arm. The priest. It was all to do with the priest. He had raised the doubts. He had planted the seeds of the Sargasso weed that was growing so fast and choking the old certainties. Once it had all been simple. The Brits were the enemies, as they had always been. The Prods were their quislings, carrying out their bidding. Linane was the man to lead them all to the victory, completing the task Michael Collins had begun. Five days with the priest, and he wasn't certain any more who was friend or foe, what was truth and what lies.

Linane, English. What a thing to suggest. And yet . . . the joke accent, so carefully contrived . . . the sneers about all things Irish.

He tried to convince himself that being English didn't necessarily make the little man any less an Irish patriot. Pearse had proved that. But somehow it didn't seem to work. Linane was no romantic.

A slight sound behind brought Michael sharply back to the reality of here and now. He cursed himself for a fool, running blind when, if the priest were right, every hand was against him. And he had also been heading towards the safe house where he expected to find Willy and Shirley. Leading the enemy to a safe house! He began the routine of the hunted – remembering one other occasion when he had been the hunter, with a big smiling man as the quarry. He found a dozen reasons for glancing over his shoulder. There was someone there. A figure in black. He increased his speed, almost running through a well-lit patch and then risking a look back. A scarecrow figure flew behind him like a black crow tossed raggedly on a spring gale. The priest. He frowned. Only the priest? Better to be safe. He recognised the area vaguely. Railings above a slope down to another low fence and another street. Even with his injuries it wasn't a big thing to vault over and roll into the inky blackness. It hurt briefly, but he shut out the pain with his concentration on what was happening above. He saw the priest scurry past – "On lissome, clerical, printless toe," as Rupert Brooke had put it. He sat up, congratulating himself. But there was something else. Someone. The big Sergeant, rifle in one hand, eyes intent, loped past, followed by two other soldiers.

The priest had been leading them after him. Michael managed a painful smile. Now he was leading them away. They followed the priest, hoping he would keep on my trail, thought Michael scornfully. Amateurs . . . except for those rifles.

He hauled himself more painfully over the next set of railings and set off to find Willy and Shirley. It wasn't that he was desperate to see them. But they would know where he could find Linane. That was vital. Linane would clear up the mess in his head – one way or the other. And he would know what to do if the little man gave the wrong answers to the questions he had to put . . .

"Damn it. I've lost Michael and I've lost the butterfly girl," thought the priest miserably, as he peered into the gloom. "He heard me when my rosary rattled against that gate back there." He turned to retrace his steps. It had been absolute carelessness. But how could he think things out properly when he wasn't even sure why he was following Michael? He gasped as big hands reached suddenly out of the darkness and whirled him round by the front of his cassock.

"Going somewhere, Padre?" demanded Sergeant Burns,

thrusting his nose to within an eighth of an inch of the priest's face.

Father Hodgson felt the same sort of panic that had seized recruits and rebels under interrogation in many corners of Britain's dwindling Empire. He couldn't speak.

Burns, anger overcoming his superstitious reticence about religious figures, lifted Father Hodgson from the ground by the front of his robe and shook him until his teeth rattled. "I asked you a question. I want an answer. And don't try lying this time. I might forget you're a priest," he growled.

"I think I'm going home," said Father Hodgson weakly.

"But that wasn't where you were going, was it, chum?" said Burns, letting the cassock go and bringing his big fist up towards the priest's face.

Father Hodgson was frightened. Physical violence always made him feel slightly sick. He coughed. There was nothing to be lost in telling the truth. "You're quite right. It wasn't where I was going." Even to himself he didn't sound convincingly defiant. The quavering rise of his voice on the last two words made sure of that. The fist pushed menacingly closer. "You know where I was going," he added querulously.

"Yeah," conceded Burns, lowering the fist. "You were following Sullivan, who didn't run into your church five nights ago and who you didn't hide in The Vicarage."

Father Hodgson smiled fractionally, not because of the quality of the wit but from relief. He daren't let the smile persist, though. "I was following the girl who was following Sullivan," he corrected. "And I lost them."

His honesty didn't get the expected reward of, at least, acceptance. "Are you trying to pull something else, Padre?" demanded Burns threateningly, advancing his nose into Father Hodgson's face again.

"No. No. That was what I was doing."

"But there wasn't no girl." Burns was puzzled now. And when he was puzzled he became even more belligerent and intimidating.

"But I saw her. I was following her."

The two men repeated the exchange a couple more times, while the two other soldiers looked on curiously from close range.

"Must have been at the communion wine," joked one of them, when it seemed that the same catechism and reply might be repeated yet again.

Burns shrugged, cooling down at last. No point in stirring up too much trouble by thumping a priest in public. "Anyway, girl or not, he gave you the slip. Sod's got more tricks than a monkey. But he's on the run somewhere out there," he waved a hand expansively to take in the whole of the city, "and when they're running they're a good target." He patted his rifle fondly. "All I need is half a sight of him with this . . . then all your doctoring will have been wasted."

Father Hodgson nodded numbly. This man had the look of a carnivore which knew its prey was injured and could not run much further. He wore a wide self-satisfied smile. The priest half expected him to start grooming himself like a big cat. Instead he gestured with his head. "You'd better go home now, Padre. We've got work to do."

The priest looked at the big man speculatively for a moment. Should he defy him? Burns shook his head, as if reading his thoughts. Father Hodgson believed in signs. He also believed in keeping his body in one piece. He hurried off as he had been told, with a muttered goodbye. After a few dozen paces he stopped and listened. They weren't following. They were busy. But he meant to find Michael before they did.

He walked slowly, pausing often to look about him. And he came to a length of low railing with a grass slope running down and away into the darkness. As he stared into the deep shadows he shivered. This could be the place where Michael had got away. He stared again. Wasn't that a movement down there? Wasn't that . . . a flicker of skirts? The girl, the strange flitting girl the soldiers claimed they had not seen, was there. And where she was, Michael had been. He tested the railing for height, gathered up his cassock with one hand and vaulted over lightly. He walked down the grassy slope, watching for that movement in the shadows.

Michael was tired when he left the safe house. Shirley was alone there, since Willy had disappeared the day before. She told him where he would find Linane. She was also full of questions about where he had been and what he was going to do. Then she left before he could ask where she was going. Odd girl. Ever since the jail raid she had been strange with all of them.

He pondered her oddness as he walked. He knew the way blindfold and he walked as if he were. It must have been fatigue switching off his senses. Once or twice he became aware of it and tried to bring his concentration back to the immediate. He had been followed once. A lot of people were out there looking for him. You never knew when a stray British Army patrol might appear. The priest was out there – Michael was sure he would not have given up yet. That terrible Sergeant Burns was out there, still loping on padded feet with his rifle ready. He would have called his headquarters to warn them that Michael Sullivan was on the loose. They'd start turning over the Catholic estates, looking for him. Shirley Connolly was out there, but he didn't know her purpose and he had made too many guesses already for one night.

He drifted again. He was weary. It wasn't his wounds but the whole weight of knowledge he had acquired in the last few days, some from the priest, some from his own thinking. He was tired too of all the fighting and killing. The weight lay heavy on him. He felt himself stagger and resisted the temptation to sit and rest – or just turn back and make up a bed in the safe house. He had to see Linane and ask the vital questions.

Father Hodgson was puffing to catch up and wondering how long Michael could keep on walking. He was also worried about Burns and the sounds of police cars, distant yet, but still ominous. That odd flittering girl had led him to Michael and now she had vanished. "There was no girl," Burns had said. He was fairly sure Burns was right. But there was . . . something. And sometimes it reminded him of Tina. He hurried on, as oblivious as Michael to the need for caution and cover. Though he wasn't sure what he would do when he caught up with the boy, he knew he had to keep going.

It was the distinctive, cloaked shape of the priest that first caught the eye of one of Burns' men. "Look over there, Sarge," he hissed. "The little priest. In a tearing hurry, he is." Burns saw and, like the hunter he was, read the message. He let his eyes traverse the broken-down street ahead of the priest. And, through a gap where there had been a house, he saw what he was looking for. He dropped to one knee, rifle sliding up his shoulder in the same smooth movement. The others didn't protest or ask questions, they followed his rifle tip and saw the target. They crouched beside their leader. It was a long shot — even with the special sights they had fitted.

Burns picked out a wider than usual gap and sighted on the start of it, waiting for that small bent figure to stagger into view. From this distance, with Michael hurrying in a peculiar swooping, hesitating, lurching run, it had to be a great shot. "Like shooting woodcock," Burns thought, recalling a sporting outing he'd enjoyed back home. Here he came, stagger, swoop, hesitate . . . "Now." Three guns roared almost simultaneously and the figure below disappeared. Burns swore. He wasn't certain. He looked at the other two. They shrugged and shook their heads. "Close in," he ordered grimly. He was sure he hadn't missed altogether. He was also sure it hadn't been the killer shot.

Michael felt the blast, the agonising pain, as one bullet thudded into his thigh, slamming him to the ground. A second plucked at the back of his jacket, tearing the material and letting him feel the cruel heat of it, but not ploughing into him. The third ricocheted off the lamp-post beside him, wailing its disappointment at missing its target.

He crawled into the cover of a wall and pulled himself up by it. He had to go on. He wanted to give up, collapse where he was and watch the blood form in a pool round him . . . He felt the big gun in his pocket. It was heavy. He tottered around a corner in the grim street and stumbled against the wall of one of the ugly brick houses. The windows were all boarded up or blocked with corrugated iron. It was all so familiar . . . like a film seen for the second time. Like a . . . like a . . . dream. Only more painful. Just like that boyhood dream. He could hear his own heart pounding, feel his pulse racing, feel the blood rushing through his veins to get to the hole in his thigh and escape. Just like the dream. But this time there was to be no awakening to the peace of a comfortable bed – or was there? He found himself praying that it was his dream . . . that he didn't have to go on to that house, up those steps, crawling now. But there was one thing. He grinned triumphantly as he hauled himself up the steps and the door flew open. There would be no Tina. But there was, though she wasn't there and he knew she could not be. He felt her presence more powerfully than he felt that of the real occupants. And a thin familiar voice cut through his longing to grasp the will-o'-the-wisp.

"Michael. Why did you come here? You were always a fool and now it sounds as if you've got the whole of Ulster half a pace behind you."

Michael tried to focus on the slim figure before him. The Englishman, Linane. He gasped as he realised that with him was Shirley Connolly, another traitor. He tried to raise the heavy gun to point it at Linane, the man who had killed Tina and Sean . . . and himself. But he couldn't lift it. He was too weary. He blinked helplessly into the barrel of Linane's automatic.

"You always were a bloody fool, Michael. Now you've become a menace," said his real enemy. "You're too big for The Movement. You're too big for me. I'll just have to do Burns' job for him . . ."

The world was full of a bright orange and blue light and a noise more thunderous than anything he had ever heard before . . . And there was Tina . . .

Father Hodgson heard the crashing reports of the pistol and broke into a despairing run. He reached the steps of the house seconds before Burns, half a minute before an Army Land Rover screeched to a halt close by. Burns sprang past him on the steps, hurling him aside, gun ready as he stormed into the house. He glanced quickly at the body on the floor and ran on through the hallway. The curtains were still swaying on the kitchen door. But there was no sign of anyone out there.

"Wait, Burns," rapped the voice of Colonel Parker, who had walked from the Land Rover. "We've got one target for tonight. The other one will do later. It's Linane. You won't catch him now. There's another day tomorrow. And he's your next quarry."

Parker stood, hands on hips, over the body—like a white hunter posing for his photograph with the kill, thought Father Hodgson, fighting back tears, swallowing to stop himself being sick. He must not show his weakness before these men.

Burns knelt over the body, examining the wounds, gloating over his marksmanship. "He couldn't have got far, sir," he said. "We'd have got him anyway."

"Well done, Burns," said the Colonel. "That last shot of yours must really have been something."

Father Hodgson closed his eyes and gritted his teeth again. There was his duty. He stepped forward, clutching his Bible like the gun he wished it was. He eased the Colonel aside. "If you'll excuse me," he said. "There are things to be done here." He couldn't trust himself to say more to them.

He concentrated hard on the form of words of the general absolution and he heard the soldiers say their hypocritical amens at the end. He looked hard at the lad who lay dead on the floor. One of the shots he had heard in this house had torn away most of his face. Michael was unrecognisable—maimed and torn by these and the other hunters in the jungle he had never really understood. But Father Hodgson could remember. He created a picture of a head, slightly smaller than this one, under the shade of the same mop of black hair, the jaw jutting pugnaciously, the fists clenched slightly, lips pouting as he stood before the blackboard, in trouble again. "Michael," he muttered to himself, "you were the best of them all." Then he turned, blinded by his tears, and staggered towards the covering darkness.

"Don't go away, Father," said Parker. It sounded conversational. But it was an order. So he waited. The ambulance had arrived and the men were picking up what was left of Michael on a stretcher.

Parker was speaking to him again. "You've know Sullivan since he was a child, I believe?"

"Yes. Yes." He was able to speak at last. But he didn't want to answer their silly questions now. Had they no hearts?

"Well, perhaps you can identify him for us . . ."

And suddenly Father Hodgson's overburdened heart gave a soaring leap. Here was something he could do for Michael after all. Michael, with his dream of the Black Irishman. How was it the legend went . . . ? "And when he finds that all around him have false hearts and evil thoughts, he will just disappear to renew his search in another era."

"Michael, Michael, this is for you." He crossed himself surreptitiously. Surely he could be forgiven one more lie to save a young man's dream.

"I'm sorry. I don't understand." He acted for all he was worth. "What do you mean?" He knew that Michael had been carrying nothing but the pistol when he left the presbytery. No identifying papers or labels. Nothing.

"I mean," grated Parker, impatient now with this strange priest, "will you please identify this body for us."

"But I can't," said Father Hodgson softly. "I've never seen this man before in my life . . ." He paused, as if suddenly catching on. "You mean . . . you thought this was Michael Sullivan?"

"But it is, you little bastard," Burns lifted him off his feet yet again, fury in his voice. "You know it is."

"Burns," rapped Parker. "That's enough." He looked at the priest with a wry smile on his lips. "Yeeees," he drew out the word. "Yes. I think I see what you're up to." He gave a little snort and a shrug. "There's nothing I can do about that. You're the only one who could have identified him, I suppose." He nodded. "Yes. You would have thought of that. Clever little bastard, aren't you? You've just made bloody Michael Sullivan immortal and above the battle." He turned away in disgust. Then he whirled back: "One thing, Mister. One thing you've forgotten in your cleverness. If Sullivan isn't dead, they can't have a martyr's funeral for him, can they?"

Father Hodgson didn't reply. He smiled gently to himself and walked away.